Consenting Adults OR
The Duchess Will Be Furious

Consenting Adults OR
The Duchess Will Be Furious

A Novel by

Peter DeVries

Little, Brown and Company   Boston / Toronto

Second Printing

Library of Congress Cataloging in Publication Data

De Vries, Peter.
  Consenting adults.

  I. Title.
PZ3.D4998Cp [PS3507.E8673] 813'.52 80–14054
ISBN 0–316–18184–6

Lines on 197–198 adapted from "The Tryst" by Walter de la
Mare as follows: "Flee into some forgotten night and be / Of
all dark long my moon-bright company: / Beyond the rumour
even of Paradise come, / There, out of all remembrance, make
our home: / Seek we some close hid shadow for our lair, / Hol-
lowed by Noah's mouse beneath the chair / Wherein the Omnipotent, in slumber bound, / Nods till the piteous Trump of
Judgment sound." Quoted with permission of the Literary Trus-
tees of Walter de la Mare and The Society of Authors as their
representative.
Lines on 39 from "The Worms at Heaven's Gates" by Wallace
Stevens, copyright 1923 and renewed 1951 by Wallace Stevens.
Reprinted from *Collected Poems of Wallace Stevens* by Wallace
Stevens, by permission of Alfred A. Knopf, Inc.

BP

*Published simultaneously in Canada
by Little, Brown & Company (Canada) Limited*

PRINTED IN THE UNITED STATES OF AMERICA

Consenting Adults OR
The Duchess Will Be Furious

One

For as long as I can remember, my father hibernated. Come late November or early December, the familiar signs would be evident, the familiar preparations begin. Already some days unshaven, the hair seeming to mat his chest a bit more thickly than usual, whether illusorily or otherwise, he would stuff himself on lots of good greasy food, like potato pancakes and pork butts, give us all a bear hug, and shuffle off to bed for the winter. Of course he didn't sleep straight through till spring, any more than any hibernating creature does — or any more than any of us sleeps uninterruptedly through till morning on a conventional night. He would stir every few days, eat a meal or two, perhaps a stack of pancakes soaked with honey, or some blueberry muffins similarly sweetened, drowsily read the paper or one of his comic books for an hour, yawn, scratch himself, and climb back under the covers. Christmas morning would find him rooting under the tree with the rest of us. But he would not emerge permanently until he could hear the ice breaking up on the river, so to speak, in February or March. Something in his metabolism seemed to need that yearly rhythm.

This and comparable facets of home life had their effect on me, hurrying the natural tendency of youth to rise above its origins. I took piccolo lessons, and learned the meaning of words like putative and adumbrate and simulacrum. To say nothing of whilom, terraqueous, consuetude and puggaree. I have by now forgotten the meanings of most of them, and though actual occasions for their use were all but inconceivable, they gave me a sense of security, like a gun kept loaded just in case. "That kid's going far," my father would say, scratching his tattoos, one of which was a tribute to Motherhood showing a woman being borne heavenward amid clouds of indigo and magenta, a titular streamer covering her pudenda. Years later, I was to meet a young woman who said she married to get away from the furniture at home. I was destined to see its borax horrors close up with my own eyes and could well believe her; but she hadn't the propellants I had. Many of the word meanings I have retained, of course; for example, all this is propaedeutic, which means providing introductory instruction. "That kid'll go very far." Yes, and as soon as he can get out of here, I would think to myself. Not that I disliked my father, harsh disciplinarian though he was (being ordered into long woolen underwear was sometimes a mid-July punishment), or that I resisted the conversation he disbursed with his own big words, such as remarking after dinner that his epizootic was sagatiating, or his personal style of whimsy, like wringing my nose in his index and middle finger, then displaying a thumb-end protruding from between them, as though he had pulled my nose off. For a while I would feel my face in feigned panic, but then all participation in the dido abruptly ceased. I must find my own idiom.

The plan was vague and amorphous at first, but sustained by a scenario filled with scenes of a charged specificity. The society of people who did not ask for ketchup in public restaurants would be cultivated on a broad front. Eating ice cream directly out of the carton, especially with a shoehorn, would be nothing more than a burning memory, as would buttering a slice of bread in toto and then eating it folded over. I would not say "Keep the change," simply telegraph as much to the waiter with the simpering nod of the elect. I would know when a wine was supple and when it was parochial, and say so. Sought after by hostesses rather east of our Pocock, Illinois, I would be seen disposed on hassocks dispensing obiter dicta progressively more silken as the years went by. "But really, Tanya, what is self-disparagement after all but a subtle inversion of conceit?"

These simmering multitudinous figments, phantasmal enough in themselves, yet somehow clustered about the image of the White Rabbit in *Alice*, muttering to himself as he patters along consulting his watch about how late he is, and what a rage the Duchess will be in if he keeps her waiting, "The Duchess will be furious," was how it somehow crystallized itself in my mind, though those weren't his exact words, as I realized when rereading the passages long years after. But that was how even in relative childhood I cast myself in the role of one ardently sought after on the highest social levels, contributing to the felicities of summer-garden afternoons, or the evening's *délicatesses*. There would be champagne with the strawberries, rose petals floating in finger bowls known to exist . . .

Meanwhile there was the formative milieu of home, where my earliest recollection was that of my mother picking ticks off my father and dropping them into a coffee can filled with gasoline. From the bathroom came the sound of my grandmother brushing her tooth. My father was a barber *manqué*, who after drubbing many a neighborhood noggin found his true calling as a furniture mover. Psychological explanation must now be available for an obsession with furniture as something to envelop you till you all but disappeared within it, as he nearly did in the van and in the loving congestion

of the den where he hibernated. He was well beyond the
reach of the fiction writers' cliché about "comfortably clut-
tered" rooms. The placental snugness of Barney Peachum's
retreat was well augmented by the masses of comic books he
had always read in and out of bed. He had bought them regularly since the first issue of *Action Comics* hit the streets
in — when, 1938? — and I don't think he ever threw any of
them out. *Terry and the Pirates, Superman, Blondie, Mutt
and Jeff,* there they accumulated year after year, systemati-
cally stacked for rereading. When in an early burst of erudition I told him he was anal-retentive the answer was inevitable. "Anal my ass, but keep talking like that. It'll get you
into Harvard or Yale."

Why shouldn't he hibernate? What the hell is it to you?
Or you or you? You with that grandfather who spoons bourbon out of a soup plate to fool his wife into thinking he's
drinking consommé. And that cousin we've seen wiping his
spectacles on a shirttail end after wetting the lenses with his
tongue. Well? All right then. The hibernating was small
inconvenience to others, even contributed something to
the hearthside peace, and as for running the office around
the corner, my mother was not only capable of it, she took the
kind of pride the feminists do today in administering the
whole shebang somewhere. That was by now a three-van
business. She got on with the crewmen, all of whom liked
her and at least one of whom, Pinky Montmorency, took more
than a casual interest in her. Probably a bit of a canoodle
now and then in the room behind the office. She could back
a truck into a parking spot herself with emasculating skill,
though I wished there weren't so often a Camel cigarette
hanging from her lip as she leaned out of the cab to do so.
Also a sensitive son could have done with rather less of
tweed caps worn with pencils stuck into them over one ear,
the visors bent nearly double. I was not permanently scarred,
but such histories can be traumatic to chaps of a texture,

chaps of a grain. A youth named Fabian was to tell me years later, "When I saw my mother sawing a plank in two, I knew I should never marry."

But we were companionable enough, the three of us, as family bosoms go (and they *are* going), often taking summer vacations together when Pinky could mind the store. I remember how we spent two weeks peeling postcards off the birch trees around Escanaba, and once we went to New York and watched the smoothies come out of the Harvard Club.

But the hibernating thing.

I sometimes overreacted to a degree bordering on the hallucinative. I had noted an alarming rise of berries in my father's diet. He often ate an apple core-and-all, spitting out the stem or not, as might betide. Then once in the dusk of late October I saw him moving on all fours across the floor of his bedroom, and thought, "Jesus, this is it." The atavism was complete, in its own way paralleling that of the werewolf. A case of lycanthropy could hardly have been worse. The apparitional hulk moved dimly toward the door: heading for the woods? A chill ran up my spine. Here we were, then, a family locked in a Kafka metamorphosis — mother, son, and quadruped father. Come spring I would see him scratching his back against the bark of a tree, or scooping fish out of the river with one paw. Christ on tossing Galilee, what would become of us? But soft. He was only gathering up some loose change that had spilled out of his overturned pants as he clamped the lined-up cuffs under his chin, preparatory to draping them over a hanger. Still, the scare sharpened the need to escape, plans for which were secretly stepped up. I learned the meaning of crepuscular, plangent, anfractuous. At twelve I knew the difference between glaucous and glabrous, though, again, their respective meanings, once cathartic, totally escape me now. The scenario steadily unreeled. Headwaiters would signal me to my table with the wand of a forefinger. Evanston girls with convertibles would hear woodwinds when I kissed them, and I would compensate with streams of wit the North Shore families from whose bosoms I had plucked their daughters for my pleasure, as ancients poured honey into the earth when picking vervain, to reimburse it for the loss of so great a treasure.

"What is the format of this hibernation?" a media person up from nearby Chicago asked. She was a reporter working on a metropolitan daily whose editor had heard of my father's life-style and sent her with a photographer to do a feature story for the Sunday supplement. My father was dressed in a red flannel shirt buttoned snugly around bulging muscles of which he was justly proud, and a pair of maroon corduroy slacks that whistled like a teakettle when he walked, though at the moment he sat in his favorite armchair, like a man granting an interview. "You don't sleep straight through I imagine?"

"No, no more than anybody does. And I keep changing positions a lot, like we all do. I tossed and turned all last January, vexed with baleful dreams." The phrase was one of several he had picked up from an eighth-grade class poem I had written, and which he worked arbitrarily into his conversation, not always with equal success. "The sleep clinic of a well-known university ast me up for the winter semester, but we couldn't come to terms."

"You get up every few days to eat something you say. Can you tell us about your diet?"

"Just like everybody else. I'm . . ." My father glanced over at me for assistance.

"Omnivorous," I supplied.

"Yes. I eat everything. I may get up and have a stack of flapjacks, or a thick steak. Or I may inhale a couple skeins of spaghetti. Of course I get up to go to the bathroom."

"What do you like on your pancakes? Are you fond of — honey?" the young woman asked gingerly, hesitant about a question that might strike a sensitive nerve.

"Oh, sure. Honey's good for you. It's been predigested, by the bees."

The reporter reviewed what she'd scribbled on a spiral notepad propped on a crossed leg, whose swelling thigh I traced in fancy under the plaid skirt half concealing it from my pubescent gaze. I remember burning with the desire to impress her.

"Mr. Peachum, you can only hibernate because it's economically feasible for you. You have no qualms about turning over all the responsibility for the business to your wife while you winter?"

"Zilch. I believe in the freedom of women. Let them work. Establish their what's-this."

"Independent identity," I said, responding like a shot to another inquiring glance from my father. "If I may interject a word here, my mother enjoys running the business. She's your New Woman. She'd rather be confined to an office than incarcerated in the kitchen."

"Just listen to that kid talk," my father said, beaming. "They'll see him come out of the Harvard Club, with the rest of the smoothies. You watch."

"There's no penis envy in this house," I continued.

"Get Motor Mouth over there. Is he Ivory League material or is he Ivory League material?"

The woman having finished her interview, the photographer sprang into action, likewise walking on eggs when it came to some conceivably touchy point.

"I want to get some shots of your — lair, of course," he said, "but first I'd like a front and then a rear view of you kind of . . . you know . . . sort of lumbering, or shambling, off into it? For the winter?"

"Fine, but I'm sorry the young lady is troo wit me. Maybe she'll come see me again about half past April."

"Why, Mr. Peachum. He does have a beautiful physique, though, doesn't he?"

"You're aces wit me too, lady." For such flirtatious occasions my father had a smile lupine rather than ursine, a kind of engagingly slimy grin, at the moment enriched by a missing bicuspid, a grin which crept slowly up one cheek. "The art of growing old disgracefully is one I intend to hone to a fine edge," he said. God alone knows where he got that line. Probably from some brittle television comedy. But he was adroitly shunted out of this horseplay by the photographer, who, after getting the shots he wanted of the subject lumbering off to retirement, snapped him in bed "asleep" in flannel pajamas, then propped upon a mound of pillows reading a comic book.

"My kid claims this is returning to the womb," he said. "You put any stock in that?"

"Oh, sure, sort of," the photographer said, snapping away. "Why not? We all do it. Curled up in the prenatal position, one thing and another. Now could I get a shot of you at the kitchen table, eating some honey? Do you ever eat it straight out of the jar with a spoon?"

Of course the story dismayed me, with its implication of something Neanderthal in the family, but my embarrassment redoubled when it went out on the Associated Press wire, and hardly eased when follow-up journalism turned up a number of hibernators in other cities. An eventual spread in *Life*, again featuring my father, pictured or listed a score, nearly all men, living in various parts of the country where the winter months are cold enough to encourage this rhythm, principally hairy mesomorphs of diminishing gentility who sacked out with the first snow and slept till spring. Again the circumstances were "economically feasible," most accredited instances involving seasonal employment or cyclical businesses that themselves fall somnolent when the first leaves fly, like roadside ice cream stands and restaurants in summer resort areas. One case was a Carvel concessionaire who cleaned up eight or nine months of the year. There were two estivators — creatures that sleep through the hot months, like turtles and lungfish — both owners of motels in upper New England where handsome enough livings were made from skiers and tourists motoring up for the autumn foliage.

These were only attested cases. In addition there may be closet hibernators, though I feel a little foolish putting it that way. But there wasn't enough company out there to take the edge off of living in its shadow, or lessen my resolve to flee the family hearth at the earliest possible moment and cultivate some people with less of a charisma problem than the old folks at home. It is in this light that my being taken up by the d'Amboises is to be seen as a quantum leap.

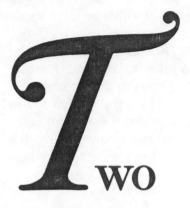

Two

Mrs. d'Amboise, who like all women of quality chewed her gum with her front teeth and rarely popped it within earshot of people with known academic degrees or season subscription boxes to the Opera, was a sculptress who had seen me play a lounge lizard in a high-school dramatic production and decided, from some of the supine postures I affected on parlor sofas throughout the course of the action, that I was ideally suited to pose for a major work on which she was about to embark: a piece depicting the drowned Shelley as found washed up on the shore of the Gulf of Spezia. She could see me clearly in her concept, which was to differ from the famous marble in University College at Oxford. So it was that I found myself stretched out on the floor of her basement studio, dressed in blue tank tights, my hair matted into ringlets on my brow, one arm outflung and my head averted in immortal repose. We had experimented with a number of facial expressions, and after a succession of mugging contortions on my part she had decided on a sort of torn-pocket mouth which I must now maintain for the twenty-minute stretches alternating with ten of rest, for three hours, at four dollars an hour.

"Your mother is a dear," she said as she set to work on a lump of clay standing on a table some ten feet away, "but we just couldn't make any of the parties she asked us to."

That was just as well. Paralleling my mother's belief that people must try to put themselves in the other fellow's shoes was a companion doctrine that newcomers to a neighborhood should be officially welcomed, usually with a Sunday-night get-together featuring a large ceramic porcupine bristling with toothpicks on which were impaled squares of cheddar, olives and Vienna franks, followed by a ham or casserole dish after which Mrs. Thrallkill would sing "Where My Caravan Has Rested" or "Santa Lucia," my father calling for some sort of encore like the nightgown song, "Love Lifted Me." Directly after the d'Amboises had moved in down the block my mother called to invite them to such a soirée, but Mrs. d. had had to regret, owing to a prior engagement. Two other dates were proposed, with something just penciled in for both of those evenings as well. "I don't understand it," my mother said, shaking her head. "How do they expect to meet people if they're busy all the time?" Before the d'Amboises could be got socially afloat it was I who drummed up an acquaintance with them, thanks to the play they'd gone to see because they had a daughter in it, a young girl named Columbine, recruited from grade school for the bit part of a kid sister.

"We're not really from out of town, you know, just moved from the north side of Pocock here to the south," Mrs. d'Amboise went on, worrying her gum about as she concentrated on her work. Exemption from response — in fact an order not to talk for fear of disturbing the death rictus settled on for the duration of this job of work — freed me for independent trains of thought, in this case worry about an upcoming French history exam. In which leg was Talleyrand lame? Did

Voltaire really reply, when asked whether he ever laughed, "No, I have never made ha-ha"? Which king was it who sought to cure his hemorrhoids by rubbing them with the crown of France?

Something Mrs. d'Amboise was prattling about snapped my wandering attention back to her monologue. "When we run up to By a Dam Site for a weekend we see absolutely nobody."

"Where?" I mumbled carefully, like someone with a face frozen by novocaine. I simply had to ask, to be certain I'd heard what I thought I did.

"Sh. By a Dam Site. It's a little summer resort cottage we have in Indiana, just below the Michigan border."

I smiled to myself — mentally, that is, without disturbing the death grimace. The more so as Mrs. d'Amboise superfluously explained what I had already perfectly grasped as something I had "on" the d'Amboises, something strictly from hunger that seriously qualified their right to look down on the Peachums.

"It's located on a stream with a dam, you see, on the site of an old flour mill, now long abandoned."

"Uh-huh."

I began to feel drowsy, having had a strenuous workout with the basketball squad before reporting here, and I guess I fell asleep, to daydreams of slam-dunking rebounds to the delight of screaming girls. Because the next thing I knew Mrs. d'Amboise was waking me up to tell me it was time for my rest period. I usually took the intermission sitting in an armchair while she critically inspected what she had done so far, shaving something here or gouging something to rights with a thumb there.

"I understand your father hibernates."

"Yes. And the renown that has fallen to us in consequence seems to have gone to his head. We hope we can all survive the resultant celebrity. Why, this resort place of yours with the cunning name. Who thought of that?"

"Oh, that wasn't our idea," said Mrs. d'Amboise, slipping out of my grasp like a wet fish. "It came with the place. The previous owner, a person in the copper tubing game as he called it, gave it that name. We just saw no point in prying off the shingle, cutesy though it be. Now then, once more into the breach?"

Wasn't it "unto the breach"?

Trudging back to the Gulf of Spezia, I began to wonder whether meeting up with the d'Amboises had been such a quantum jump after all. There were small signs other than the By a Dam Site that seriously prejudiced their claims to being absolutely top drawer — or at least my ebullient early assumption that they were. "Doctor" d'Amboise turned out to be a chiropractor still looking for a neighborhood more abounding than the last in people who fancied having their bones manipulated, and there was a grandmother seen in vacant lots picking dandelions to make wine with, and who carried her harvests home in a satchel secured with a length of twine. At the same time, I was glad to learn of all these things, including the cottage with the corny name, for the reason already stated: that it made my family seem less culturally underdog. Now though Mrs. d'Amboise had in principle eluded my clutches on the By a Dam Site business, at the same time their ratifying the name by not prying off the shingle proclaiming it made them accomplices with a man of supposedly even denser sensibilities, a low-down high-up in the copper tubing game who probably snapped his galluses as he watched the sun go down behind his property. "I must tell my father about By a Dam Site," I chuckled as I lay down on the fabled sands once more. "It's the sort of thing he gets a bang out of. He has a driver working for him with a resort place called Dew Drop Inn."

All of this typified the kind of divided sense I had about loved ones who must be put behind me as fast and far as possible, but for whom I yet felt a protective flare of resentment every time I sensed the least patronizing air in others. After

all it wasn't as though one's father sat in a tire eating ba-
nanas — if that's what you think, you — you what, out there?
You New York–Dutch–descended, probably wrong-Strauss-
loving officer of some music society or civic uplift group. I'd
like a peek at some of your Rorschachs, you old sofa-crack
feeler, you. Slipping a palm furtively under cushions and into
crevices as you fish for coins in other people's chairs in a
fashion whose psychological symbolism is all too readily apparent, you cranny rummager, you wrong-Scarlatti admirer.
You — secretary-treasurer!

I'm sorry. I shouldn't have said that. You must forgive my
occasional outbursts. I have so much more in my craw than
you, in all likelihood. I take exception to being upstaged.
Loading a furniture van is a fine art, and my father was re-
nowned for the jigsaw-puzzle precision with which he locked
a load together with the pieces called for, maestro-like, from
the tailgate. "Me that armchair. Now me them two suitcases." And he would kneel the one over a chiffonier with a
carton of books on top of it without an inch of space either
between the carton and the armchair, or the armchair and
the roof of the van, and then stack the suitcases as snugly on
top of a trunk to seal up a tier precalculated to a gnat's eye-
brow. So I wouldn't preen myself on. seeing to it that the
ladyfingers and coffee arrive on time for the Palestrina Society meeting, you toothpaste-tube–tightening, envelope-
instead-of-stamp–licking, sofa-crotch–feeling secretary-treasurer you. I'm sorry.

Mrs. d'Amboise's passion for classic themes had me next
posing as the Discobolus, wearing again the tank tights and
clutching a Frisbee, "for verisimilitude." By now there had
been a most disquieting development. Mrs. d'Amboise had
somehow got it into her head that I was going to "wait" for
her daughter Columbine, then ten or so as against my sixteen. The notion had even got circulated along Pocock Street

(cradle also of the rumor that my mother was a Turk). Mrs. d'Amboise, one given to talking about "brilliant matches," in the manner of women who chew with their front teeth and so on, clearly had her heart set on an ultimate union of her "quivering fawn" and this "thewy lad" who broadjumped and hammer-threw for Pocock High yet at the same time won prizes for orations ablaze with words like eleemosynary and symbiosis and propinquity, to say nothing of starring in comedy dramas like the one in which I had been discovered. Dr. d'Amboise, who read popular works on psychology, said that boys didn't marry the girl next door at all, that was a myth, but rather the girl across the street whom they could see in the round and in full stride as she came and went. Columbine met that requirement, albeit a little diagonally, but at ten and still two-dimensional, her downsitting and her uprising wouldn't normally cut much ice for a good six or seven years, by which time I would be a blood of twenty-two or three, with words like stacked and jugs also looming large in his glossary, along with such cautionary concepts as jail-bait and San Quentin quail. I wondered, as Mrs. d. toiled at the likeness of her son-in-law-elect hurling a Frisbee forever into Olympic space, whether she dreamed her steamy speculations were making me take premature notice of a treasure I might otherwise have decently ignored, at least until the age of consent. If in an adolescence lubricious enough I got pimples from impure thoughts, let it be on her head. Was she familiar with the term short eyes, or must that await my trial and subsequent warehousing? She would send me brownies and gum, visit me, learn that I was being rehabilitated, taught a trade ...

"You're good stock, you Peachums," she said, kneading something or other in my simulacrum.

I could hardly keep a straight face. Besides my father (typifying for Mrs. d. the "earthy" strain with which rarefied lineages like her own were wise to crossbreed for the con-

tinued enrichment of the race), besides him there was, let's
see, an Uncle Blanket on my mother's side, an exterminator
manqué who after a vivid bankruptcy in that line of en-
deavor was now employed in a soap plant in Duluth. There
was an older cousin who had left his wife and was rumored
to be living in Detroit with a woman who owned a cleaning
business acquired in a divorce settlement. I had the standard
quota of eccentric aunts, one a notorious returner of unused
portions, canceler of subscriptions, and stopper of payments
on checks. Our nearest thing to a bon vivant was a grandfather who had climaxed his career by contracting a venereal
disease during a brief stay in a health spa near Baden-Baden.

I touched on none of this to Mrs. d'Amboise then. Later I
might pay out the dismal details little by little, as a way of
dampening their enthusiasm for Puck Peachum as a catch, if
I found it necessary to extricate myself from any uncom-
fortably tightening assumption that I was encouraging little
Colly's expectations. Perhaps more embarrassing than all,
yes, how could I have forgotten our prize Neanderthal, was
a Valparaiso uncle on the paternal side who according to clan
legend once asked for a doggie bag at a hundred-dollar-a-
plate Republican fund-raising dinner. His defenders sometimes said the story was apocryphal — oh, I hope not! —
then that he had done it as a gag — if that made him any less
an oaf. I might in passing mention a shirttail, but also thewy,
cousin by marriage who wound up on the All-American foot-
ball team as halfback, and still holds the national record for
field goals missed in one game.

"I understand that as a child you cried with only one eye,"
Mrs. d'Amboise said, gouging me briskly in the whereabouts.
I seemed to have sympathetic twinges in the bag of jewels.

"That's right," I said, speaking rather woodenly in the fear
of shifting my position as I readjusted my grip on the Frisbee; any disturbance of my pose brought an admonitory
cluck from Mrs. d'Amboise. "The other was plugged up."

"With what?"

"I don't know."

"You haven't shifted your right arm just a weeny bit, have you? There, that's better. Couldn't something have been done to correct the condition?"

"It wasn't anything important. And now it's academic."

"How do you mean?"

"I don't plan to cry anymore."

I suddenly wanted to let fly the Frisbee and go out and enjoy myself. I'd much rather have been squatting behind a billboard watching pedestrians try to pick up a half-dollar that I had soldered to a sewer grating, or lounging disdainfully against a corner mailbox drawling to my disciples, "Let me live in my house by the side of the road, and hurl the cynic's ban."

"I bless the day we moved in across the street from the Peachums."

"My mother thanks you, my father thanks you, and as for me, that goes without saying."

"Ah, the goat cry of a boy." The reference was to the surviving croak of my changed voice — and another of Mrs. d'Amboise's typical literary thefts, or at least allusions without credit. The phrase was stolen from *Look Homeward, Angel,* as I knew from having been force-fed it in high-school English. "You're on the threshold of manhood, and so pretty soon it will really be waiting and not just talking about it."

"Waiting?"

"For my bijou."

This must be nipped in the bud, provided it wasn't already in full flower. My own attitude in point of actual fact had been to wait and *see.* Who knew what this prepubescent reed would be five or seven years hence? Possibly the same unrounded stalk as now, since the mother she took after in terms of bone structure and pigmentation was herself very sparingly upholstered; or possibly billowing where desired. Colly was pretty enough, with Mrs. d.'s pale oval face and great dark liquid deer's eyes, but she occupied a category her own brother Ambrose called "nervous girls," to be shunned at all costs as a sure investment in ruinous psychiatry bills: future hysteriasts, alcoholics at thirty-three (so ran Ambrose's baleful prospectus), conducting daylight infidelities in the Babylonian boredom of the suburbs. Suddenly snapping in the supermarket aisle as the soothing strains of "My Blue Heaven" or "Sweet Sue" from the Muzak louvers finally get to them; found, then, bowling grapefruit or heads of lettuce up the fresh-produce alley; or taken at the meat freezer declaiming the role of Rosalind as played in a Wellesley production of *As You Like It*.

"Of course girls are different from boys. They're more — nervous."

Aha! Another heist. Mrs. d. might have been reading my mind as she pilfered now, if memory served, from *Our Town*, even to the long pause before "nervous" in most productions. She strove at a stroke to exonerate Columbine from special stricture as to the feminine temperament. The girl's being more than normally high-strung was a marketing liability Mrs. d. hurriedly skirted by pressing comparison with Katharine Hepburn. "Don't they quiver like tuning forks, those two!" But lyric vibrancy wasn't the whole story. Our bijou as the delicate one was prey to colds both summer and winter, flu, migraine, vertigo, nausea, allergies, asthma, and, as I was about to learn, cosmic monstrosity.

I had been given a telescope for my sixteenth birthday, and Columbine asked to be let look through it. She flitted into our back lawn a little after ten one Sunday night, huddled into two or three coats against the mid-October chill, having been prefortified with a cup of hot Ovaltine. I set the telescope on its tripod and invited her to have a look.

"The distances between some of those stars is astronomical, my dear."

I had prepared a surprise. A shower of meteors, the Orionids, was visible tonight, and there was a gasp from Colly as our sweep of the heavens reached the point where the pyrotechnics were in progress. I was deep in a term paper on meteorites, and so was able to lecture on the phenomenon as Colly watched, strewing my dissertation with a crackle of information also prepared for a speech I would shortly have to give in science class.

"The fall of a meteorite is often preceded by the flight of a fireball through the sky, and by one or more loud detonations. It was inferred by Chladni in 1794, that the fireball and the detonations result from the fierce passage of the meteorite through the earth's atmosphere. Solid bodies (chiefly stone or iron) enter the atmosphere at a velocity of about twenty-six miles per second, while the earth's orbital velocity is about eighteen and a quarter miles per second, at which combined insane speeds heat is generated, the meteor becomes incandescent, and the phenomenon of the streak is produced. The friction usually exhausts the falling body, but occasionally fragments of the original mass fall upon the earth."

Columbine gave another small cry, and I could hear her teeth chattering and her knees banging together. Tuning fork was good! Hepburn indeed! I continued, rolling my tongue around names even more luscious than Chladni.

"As many as three hundred and fifty are estimated to have fallen on Toulouse; at Knyahinya, over a thousand; while no fewer than a hundred thousand rained on Pultusk and Mocs. Where are you going?"

"Home."

And home she streaked like a meteor. We were being more than usually tuning-forkish these days as the result of having recently seen a revival of *The Phantom of the Opera* on television. She had screamed when the Phantom's mask was snatched off, and now she probably saw the meteorite showers not, like me, as goldfish darting about in a sea of ink, but as a chandelier crashing down out of the sky and threatening to bury her alive. So that I should perhaps not have dilated further on meteorites and other astral pyrotechnics when by chance I fell in beside her as we walked home from school a few days later, I fresh from a successful lecture on the subject, Colly from the fifth grade at Longfellow. Out there, I assured her, were galaxies of galaxies whirling in a mad Void, exploding supernovas, masses of boiling gas ranging upward in size to the supergiant Alpha Herculis, two billion miles across, so big that our sun together with the earth and the ninety-three million miles between could be laid end to end twenty-five times across the middle of it.

"Gosh," she said. "And where did it all come from? The mind of God?"

"There isn't any. And of course it'll all come to an end. The sun you can't look at now will be a clinker, like the moon; the moon, a mote in the Eye of Nothing . . ."

Posing for Mrs. d. the following day, clutching now a cook-pot lid in lieu of the Frisbee lost in the bushes somewhere by one of the numerous d'Amboise young, I sensed constraint on her part. Wearing clamdiggers and sneakers under the perennial blue smock, she was silent as she worked, rather than her talkative self. Something was on her mind. At last it came out.

"Did you tell Colly the universe was running down?"

"I may have mentioned it. Why?"

"You oughtn't have. She's very upset. She's not taking it at all well. Entropy and the laws of thermodynamics, and absolute zero and all the winding down and what not. Time enough to learn about the World Ash when you take her to Wagner later. Now you've got her reading Millay's 'Epitaph for the Race of Man.' "

"But I was only reciting that to you the other day during rest period when you asked me!"

"Well, she overheard it through the cellar door. Probably crouching up there listening right now," said Mrs. d'Amboise, lowering her voice. "Shivering. And Swinburne. 'Only a sleep eternal, in an eternal night.' She *can't* sleep, and neither can I with the poor thing slipping into bed with me every night, twisting my hair in her fist so I won't go away. This is untenable. The signs are not good."

"What are some others?"

"She wants to eat dinner at five o'clock, like people in institutions, then doesn't touch her food."

"I'm truly sorry about all that. But on the universe thing, there's also the countertheory of eternal renewal. That it may go on expanding indefinitely or until it collapses back on itself and starts all over again, this in cadences of eighty billion years. We might tell her that. Anything to settle her nerves. Not that inexorable perpetuity isn't in its own way as chilling a thought as obliteration. In any case, I've never seen any harm in the bottom line."

"Not to a masculine intellect such as yours, no. But to an ethereal creature like Columbine the existential abyss is not what the doctor ordered. Your likening her to a tuning fork was most observant. But Katharine Hepburn is older, and you can tell her anything you want."

"I don't think that I — "

"She sets up vibrations in you, then?"

"Katharine Hepburn?"

"No, no, Colly."

"Well, if by vibrations you mean — "

"She returns your feelings." Out of the tail of my eye I could see Mama gouge at something with her thumb in a way that gave me another sympathetic twinge amidships, then stand back and view what she had done to the clay thus far. "In addition to this ethereal sensitivity of hers, she's going through a special preadolescent turmoil over the boy across the street who brings out sexual awareness perhaps a lee-tle too — "

"Oh, now Mrs. d'Amboise!"

"That's why I don't want her in the studio watching you pose, sitting there mooning on the cellar steps. And advanced ideas such as black philosophy add to the bogeys already plaguing a young girl. You should know that. We're going to like you in the family, none more refreshing in your way, but not as a bête noire frightening the d'Amboises half out of their wits. Especially Colly. The specter of ghoulish galaxies banging about in an ungoverned universe destined to pile up on the cosmic scrapheap she doesn't need!"

"How is that allergy of hers?" I asked, eager to change the subject without rudely dropping that of the bijou herself.

"We're not sure now it's an allergy. It's something respiratory very possibly not unrelated to premature sexual awakening."

"Is she taking anything for it?"

"She inhales with Primatene Mist, and that seems to relieve it. Not all patent medicines are hokum."

"Whenever I see the name advertised or see it on television I always think of it as meaning something like primordial, you know? Something about prehistoric ages."

"A schoolmate of hers died recently, and so she's had that first shock we all get at one time or another, that drives home the fact of mortality. That for most of us is not the time for Bertrand Russell and God is dead. That's the time for" — here Mrs. d'Amboise spread her arms wide, exposing an inch or two of midriff under the smock — " 'I know not where his islands lift their fronded palms in air, I only know I cannot drift beyond his loving care.' I think you've earned a rest."

"Like, 'Our brute ancestors stalking the earth in the primatene mists.' "

"I understand." She lit up her inevitable cigarette for our

intermission chat as we sat on facing armchairs, or rather not quite facing, hers set a bit to one side in deference to the fact that I was in tank tights, so that a frontal view of me would not have been quite ladylike. "The will-o'-the-wisp of philosophy is something most of us stop pursuing at last, you know. That's for youth, and males at that. That's another difference between the sexes. Men flog their brains about these questions, but has there ever been a woman philosopher? We're the custodians of life, who dislike its being questioned. We don't like to bring it into the world only to have it doubted."

"Yes," I said from the herniated armchair in which I took my breaks, a familiar wayward spring twanging against one haunch. "You breed, we brood."

"Precisely. And so we don't like this Absurd thing, because it discredits everything we bring into the world. So you, even with your free thought, can understand this hankering for belief, for faith. What I'd call the nostalgia for the absolute."

Mrs. d. had in this case burgled Camus, but since I hadn't read him then yet, the theft would have to wait a few years to be detected. For the moment I gave a mental whistle of admiration for her phrase, though probably secretly suspecting it had been purloined like all the rest. But the nostalgia for the absolute was keenest in me precisely when I did come to read *The Myth of Sisyphus*, because by coincidence I was weathering a crisis of just the kind Mrs. d. represented as overwhelming the bijou, who was being a mess that year for reasons I was actually beginning to think were partly my fault. I felt as though I had my foot caught in a clump of barbed wire from which it was going to take all the skill and diplomacy I could summon to extricate myself.

Three

In early youth we wear our nihilism with a certain bravado. It's part of our panache. Then suddenly we're brought up short with the realization that everything we've been so glibly spouting may very well be true. "My God! Can I have been right all along? Surely not that." The death in a sailboat accident of a college classmate wrung me with my first apprehension of mortality — as piercing as Columbine's to her. The handwriting on the wall is then at last decipherable as "This means you." A cold wind from Aldebaran sent a shiver through my blood. The MacLeish I'd been airily quoting was fact, then? The top of the circus tent blows off and there above is the pall of nothing — nothing, nothing at all. Christ, one had been babbling the truth, one had hardly banked on that! One was a stick of bone and a strand of gut riding for a piteous splinter of eternity on a speck of astral soot. A fresh gust from Aldebaran at my heels, I ran upstairs two at a time and pulled the covers over my head. Thus began my nervous breakdown.

Varying the hallucination of interstellar drafts chasing me into a corner, I sometimes had the sensation of having fallen into one of the black holes said to infest a universe monstrous enough in all conscience without them, voids of such gravitational density that light can be sucked into them, light the speed of which was once held to be at least a constant left us by Relativity — now no more. And what the hell happened to gravitation that the mad galaxies are all flying away from one another at velocities that boggle the mind, their whirling components accelerating at rates that in some time warp could have us seeing the backs of our necks?

When they brought the news to me that another bunch at Oxford had scrapped Causality, I stretched out with an icebag on my head. Then it was all random. Certainty was a gone goose, and the soul with it. The soul was a clinker, cold as the meteorites that fell on Toulouse, Knyahinya and, if memory served, Pultusk and Mocs. Man has no purpose. There is no Why, only a What and a How in a universe morally vacant. And so forth and so on. And only yesterday you and Ambrose d'Amboise, when he could get his father's car, would gesticulate wildly at the rear wheels of some motorist as you shot past him, at the same time shouting unintelligibly, then make a U-turn and, coming back, find the driver stopped beside the curb, anxiously peering at his underside or bewilderedly circling from tire to tire. Then you would slow to a pause yourself and from the other side of the street resume the jabberwocky. "Your kleeks were sort of woppling against your grops, fella!" "My *what?*" with an inquiring squint that was something to behold, cupping an ear. "Kleeks, kleeks! They're mastaquorf!" you called as you shot off again. But that was before God was dead, and morning was at seven, and Pippa passed saying all was right with the world. Now one could but repeat "Pultusk and Mocs, Pultusk and Mocs," through the insomniac blanks.

A mound of flapjacks will remind me of a bosom, and the endless consumption of them as almost my sole daily nourishment was perhaps one outward symptom of my crackup. I must have eaten the height equivalent of Pisa in the three months or so of my spook-out. My mother, to whom the obsession was not as strange as it might have been had she not had a cleaning woman with a bread-eating compulsion, fixed them willingly to "build me up." And of course my father had established another precedent. Each plumply perfect golden heap, like Grishkin's friendly bust uncorseted, gave promise of pneumatic bliss, momentarily enabling us to forget how intrinsically unstable free neutrons are and how they break up spontaneously into protons and electrons within thirteen minutes of being kicked out of the nuclei convulsively formed in the primatene mists. But after gratefully devouring the buckwheat cakes and licking up the last of the maple syrup with which they had been drenched, I would shuffle off to bed again, there to turn my face to the wall with an epistemological groan, hardly consoled by the assurance that under pressures and temperatures for which there is certainly no excuse, these free neutrons (free, who's free?) can coexist with protons and electrons in quite heinous numbers, so that, in fact, a kind of dynamic balance will be established in the general hellbroth. I would fling over onto my back again, wiping the beaded terror from my brow. What was in it for me? Precious little, to tell the truth, and a fat lot of good any of it would do me. When I ventured outside it was rarely at night, and when I did I gave the Pleiades as wide a berth as possible, lowering my head as I hurried past Orion. I sank my head into my overcoat. It was late October, the first few snowflakes had fallen, and one longed to bed down under it all until spring. . . . Supernovas burst all about one, worlds were born and died in the galactic nightmare. I floated, a dead man, in the illimitable Void, and my mother made weekly deposits in her Christmas Club fund while down the disreputable aeons ever-new configurations belched and burned. Dear little Columbine had been right. It was rather a delirium.

What had been long adumbrated, or at least thought possible, happened. Some of our light got sucked into one of those black holes, and over a period of seven or eight days we watched it slow down from the supposedly immutable speed of 186,000 miles per second, to 100,000, then a mere 1,000, as that gravitational quagmire did the dirty work of which nattering scientists had long thought it capable. Soon light was doing only 65 or 70, easily passed by motorists who derived some inexplicable glee from racing it on the thruways. Light had become pathetic. In time one would be able to fulfill the drugstore wag's boast about turning it off and jumping into bed before it went out. Ebbing strength left me with little stomach for the attempt, indeed I hesitated to switch it off at all for fear of disappearing in the obsidian black, sliding down a bottomless rathole in the space-time continuum, vanishing at last in the uterine underground along whose passages one would wander forever, wondering what the Duchess must think. Wheatcakes lost their appeal, and my coffee cup cackled on its saucer when I reached for it. I had outdone the character in Graham Greene's *Potting Shed* whose ex-wife complained that he went everywhere looking for Nothing. I had found it — or it me. The search was over. There was no God and Jesus Christ was his son, and there was a good quarter inch of rich green pond scum on one's tongue. Antimatter ran out of one's ear, for which one's mother brought paregoric.

So ran my nightmares, sleeping or waking.

Why had one read so much? Yet one was driven again to open Bertrand Russell and reread "A Free Man's Worship," the rock-bottom, bottom-line, undeclinable platter of Nothing. That the whole schmeer was headed for the cosmic junkyard is declared in that paragraph at which one again gingerly peeked, in hopes of finding some least grain of qualification. ". . . all the labors of the ages . . . the whole of man's achievement must inevitably be buried beneath the debris of

a universe in ruins ... only on a firm foundation of unyield-
ing despair can the soul's habitation henceforth be safely
built." Still one scavenged for the crumb of hope. Ah, here's
something. "All these things, if not quite beyond dispute ..."
Yes, clutch at that straw and swim for shore. The shore of
what — faith? No, no, that is forever gone. Of *doubt.* As believing man once feared it, wised-up man now scrounges for
it, some faint chink of light in the black inane. Not a Yes,
only a tremor of Maybe to challenge the tyrannical sover-
eignty of No.

"Uncle Punk?"

It is Columbine, standing beside my bed with a nutritive
goodie, a bowl of custard no less, let in by my mother who
then retires deferentially, closing the door soundlessly behind
her as she slips away like an Oriental servant, or pretending
to have slipped away, because she is listening outside with
her head cocked for every word, like an Oriental servant. She
is herself shaken by continuing rumors that she is a Turk.
Could they be not entirely unfounded ... ?

Colly is now four years older than when first frightened
by cosmic monstrosity, perceptibly rounding, not quite so
tuning-forkish yet vibrant to wind and wave. Some of her
verses attest it. The oval face tapers delicately to a firm chin,
one that a good bone structure tells the speculating youth
that at forty it will be unwattled. The eyes are chocolate
pastilles. This is good. But why does she part her auburn hair
from the middle outward and downward, like those New
England spinsters who in portrait oils come down to us so
resembling spaniels?

"What's the matter with you, Uncle Punk?"

One had played Puck in a high-school production of *A
Midsummer Night's Dream,* well enough for the nickname to
have stuck for a while. Its corruption by louts and dolts made
one grit one's teeth. With the courtesy "uncle" of Colum-

bine's, hung over from the days when the difference in our ages might have accommodated a note of sportive respect, the combination was something dismal to a degree.

"What's psyching you out?"

What could I tell her that she didn't already know? The sun would burn out in A.D. 47,000,000,000, by which time the rest of the solar system and we with it would be uncountable millennia down the Dispose-All. Such things no longer bothered Colly, who was through her crisis and in the bloom of happiness that would, according to Russell, in some version again be mine as well, once I had crawled on my epistemological belly through this hideous cave each of us must traverse before gaining the garden of chastened acceptance awaiting us on the other side. Each of us, unless totally bovine, has got to eat some despair. It is written. We must sooner or later be trundled into surgery for what her brother and my good friend Ambrose called an illusionectomy. It's either that or the lobotomy performed by some religion or other. So ran Ambrose's remorseless options.

"You really look like hell. I mean what's got you spooked out?"

Why, the inexcusable distance from Betelgeuse to Potlatch, Idaho. What else?

She was absorbing the slang of the day with great speed, with whatever that might imply in the way of burgeoning suitability for oneself; so that like Proust's narrator reaching out from *his* bed to gather Albertine in on the strength of the same evidence — the use of a few reassuring expressions in rapid succession — I impulsively put my hand out to take hers when, bending over me, she murmured, "Hang tough, Unc Punk." There were to be literary echoes of quite another kind as well.

Twitching back from my touch, she went to the door and jerked it open with an abruptness that sent my possibly Ottoman mother scuttling, fetched a spoon from the kitchen

downstairs, returned, then sat sidesaddle on the bed and
force-fed me the custard, like Leonard Woolf getting a little
something into Virginia, once again prostrated by the approaching publication date of a new book, with its attendant
terror of what reviewers would say of it, and of her. It made
her literally ill. Later our sweetling fixed me some hot tea,
the cup again cackling when I lifted it from the saucer. I
could smell the soap in which she had just bathed. "You're
twenty and she's fourteen, for God's sake," I said to myself,
closing my eyes as again I inhaled her fragrance. "Do you
want to go to prison?" Made librarian, liked by the warden,
up for parole . . .

"Remember the night you showed me the — what were
those meteorites again?"

"The Orionids."

"How scared I was? It might be fun to look for some more
of those fireworks through your telescope." I groaned something in the negative. Colly pinched my great toe through
the covers. "Ambrose thinks he can help you. He had the
schmerks himself once. Got unbalanced reading too much
philosophy. I didn't realize, you know, men, um, can go
through a mental crisis like that. I thought it had to be loss
of *religious* faith sent you bonkers."

"Then you do know what this is all about."

"I wanted to hear it from you. Anyway, remember what
Shakespeare said."

"What was that?"

"I dunno." She laughed. "Isn't there something in Shakespeare for every occasion? Well, you read too much. You and
Ambrose both."

"You're very sweet, Colly," I said, ashamed of the foxfire
in my loins again. Parole denied, demoted to punch press
operator, shunned by the other prisoners . . .

"Thanks. Well, hang in there, Punk. I know you can get
yourself nailed together."

A milestone in our personal relations almost slipped by un-
noticed. She had dropped the Uncle foolishness. I didn't
realize it until she was gone — among other acts of ministration, to prod Ambrose into paying the promised visit.

Like me, Ambrose had an environmental problem, only his
was quantitative, not qualitative like mine. One of nine children, none of whom save Columbine could have been conceived of as bluebirds fluttering down out of Maeterlinck's
heaven, Ambrose knew from earliest days an oppression as
great in its way as a cosmos wobbling along under entropy:
dethronement by one sibling after another. He had always
been minuscule, so that being cast as a grain of dust in the
cosmological *cauchemar* was not especially calculated to bug
him; the reverse of the fact that being an only child had ill
prepared me for the discovery that that was what I was. I
could not say with Margaret Fuller, "I accept the universe,"
even to hear Carlyle respond on learning it, "Gad! He'd
better!"

By the time Ambrose came along, as number four, Mrs. d.
had begun to resent the obstetrical grind that seemed to be
her portion, and legend has it that on getting the report on
the rabbit test she exclaimed in the doctor's office, "Not another d'Amboise! Deliver me!" And so in due course they did.
She went into labor on Labor Day, making that Ambrose's
birthday, a fitting enough irony for someone who was never
to do an honest day's work in his life. He was twenty-one at
this time and I was twenty, a college junior taking my non-
resident term in the form of this crackup. From that stand-
point it was probably for the best that I didn't get into Harvard, where, even if they had NRT's, it was doubtful that
they would give credit for a nervous breakdown. They agreed
to give me the credit at Burwash, provided I wrote the experience up to the satisfaction of both the Psychology and

English departments of this highly advanced college in upper Minnesota.

This was Ambrose d'Amboise's plan for pulling me through.

He was going to use what is known in medicine as the homeopathic method. It consists, as you know, of fighting like with like, of administering to the patient regulated doses of the disease to be treated — in this case cosmic monstrosity. As in *The Magic Mountain* Hans Castorp's tuberculosis is muddled out into the open by the very Alpine air that must further its cure, so my heebie-jeebies would be muddled until they became the screaming meemies — but only for a time. In the end the criminal mileage between Rigel and Punxsutawney would not leave one wiped out.

Before commencing the regimen, Ambrose threw out an alternate metaphor to the disease-muddle parallel, namely, of breaking the sound barrier. Pioneer test pilots experimenting with attempts to crash through it found that as they approached sonic boom the plane shuddered as though it must surely fly into smithereens if they "pushed the stick" one inch farther forward. So they timorously retreated, drawing it back — until someone intrepid enough acted on the hunch that pushing the stick all the way would, after one last convulsion, heave the plane onward past the barrier into calm sailing once again. On that example one suffering through a crisis of despair must act. There must be no failure of nerve here. One boggled at the abandonment of hope. But one must abandon all hope, enter head-high the pit of disillusion, slog on through the slough of despond and so forth and so on, and come out the other side into that Santayanan calm expressed in the principle that there is nothing to do about birth and death but enjoy as much as possible the interval between.

"Where would you place yourself, philosophically?" Ambrose asked. "What school? What would you call yourself?"

"A self-pitying stoic. I founded the school myself."

"All right. But you're not being true to it. And what we've
got to do is get rid of the adjective and keep the noun." Brisk
rubbing of hands here, as though we are about to pitch into
some job of work like washing a window or fixing a car, not
reassemble a disintegrating psyche — much less quench a
soul on fire! "You're no doubt familiar with the three great
narcissistic shocks endured by modern man," he resumed as
he paced back and forth, sentinel-like, across the foot of my
bed, wearing tan chino slacks and a pullover shirt of an unforgiving green, his modest stature further shortened by the
Harvard slouch cultivated since the day he too was rejected
by that rather off-putting school. He had a curious tic, or not
tic exactly, but a facial habit of periodically wrinkling his
nose with a twitch that made his glasses jump. And no birds
sang. "Galileo dethroning the earth as center of the solar system, let alone universe, ha!; then Darwin demoting man from
crown of creation to just another species; and lastly Freud,
showing that he's not even master of himself, so far a cry
from the rational creature he fancied himself as to be nothing but a can of neuroses bred in good old home sweet home.
A jumble of instincts."

"Of which the quest for meaning is one," I reminded him,
finger aloft.

"It's a hunt for a unicorn," he retorted somewhat crypti-
cally, and seeing that I had hauled myself about with the
covers wrapped around my head, and had stuck my fingers
into my ears through the bedsheet, as a sign that I wanted
to hear no more on the despair thing, he bustled round and,
kneeling on the bed, pried my hands away. "Whatever ships
you take, they will sink," he said into my ear. "Whatever path
you follow, it will peter into wilderness. Whether there be
prophecies, they will fail — "

"I notice you quote Scripture when it suits your purpose."

"Never to cozen and beguile myself or others with illusions

insupportable to the intellect or repugnant to honesty. I
know that in contentment you still feel the need of some
imperishable bliss, but pull down that vanity. Nothing
awaits you in the end but the selfsame oblivion out of which
you came, a black blank less than that first primordial
muck — "

"I know, I know! Here we go with the primordial slime
and the primatene mists again. Knock it off about the primatene mists, and our first ancestors shambling through it in
the hope of heaven and the fear of hell."

"I want to see you face the facts," Ambrose said, stripping
away the cocoon of bedclothes in which I had wound myself,
"not mummify yourself in craven fictions. Meaning, out
there? Zilch. Purpose? Zilch. Any awareness in the cosmos of
the fortuitous concatenation of atoms called man? Zilch." He
rumbled on in this lugubrious vein for some time, piling zilch
upon zilch. I must get a grip on myself other than clutching
my head in both hands, must stop quivering at the abyss that
yawned, and rather pluck the flowers with which its preci-
pice is strewn, and one thing and another. I thought he might
be going to spread my arms and, pinning me down by the
wrists, straddle my chest while he crucified me to the Truth.
The homeopathic symbolisms rained in a downpour I must
say I found amazing in its range and variety. I must eat the
very Absurd by which I feared to be eaten. I must turn and
pursue that which I had been fleeing, must crush in my own
embrace the horror I had sensed enveloping me. I must, like
Joseph Conrad's exemplary swimmer, to the destructive element give myself, and let the deep, deep sea bear me up. I
must — one final metaphor now seen in tranquil retrospect
as among the best — I must behave like those desert reptiles
that to escape the noonday heat bury themselves deeper in
the sands whose surfaces they find intolerable. Only thus
would I find the Santayanan calm awaiting me beyond the
Beckettian mangle through which I was being currently ex-
truded.

I suddenly yawned. "So sleepy. I could sleep for ... ever ... in the ... Latmian cave," I mumbled, a little ashamed at giving him back Millay for Stevens and Pound.

"Let's reverse your nightmare." Ambrose readjusted the grip with which he had in fact pinned my arms to the bed, straddling me in order to do so. "Think of the unutterable Vast as actually minuscule," he said, ignoring the first ominous signs that I wanted to drop off for three or four months, an inclination not without precedent around here. "Take just our earth. Think of the hideous gastrointestinal gases boiling in its unspeakable bowels. Nothing. A child's balloon pricked with a pin. Think of the continental land masses breaking up beneath the sea through inconceivable aeons. Nothing. A piece halvah crumbled in an old man's fingers. Unchartable wastes of water in which the melting Polar Cap even now seals our ultimate death by drowning. Nothing, in a Milky Way itself Nothing to the mad galactic bouillabaisse bubbling in all directions. The mind boggles until — until terror is itself thus anesthetized. See? But if unattended Cessation is horrible, what of our beginning? Do you know how it all got started?"

I shook my head drowsily in the negative. Let him eff the ineffable. My path was vague in distant spheres. The first snow was a white shuttle weaving a long winter's refuge ...

"I mean the apparent origin of the universe."

"Uh-uh."

"This universe, whose scheduled reduction to clinkers you take personally, had a genesis which — Punk, for Christ's sake, wake up!"

"Yeah, O.K."

Seeing he had shaken me back to attention, from the kind of stupor into which shock sometimes sends us, he resumed pacing.

"The universe — this is the final homeopathic dose of cosmic monstrosity that either kills or cures. It won't be a piece of cake."

"Shoot."

"The universe was all created in — *one hour of nuclear cooking.*"

"Oh, Christ. You woke me up to tell me that?" I bleated, stuffing the bedsheet into my mouth.

"That and more. This is what happened."

His account of the thermal stew occurring billions of years ago had the earmarks of something boned up on for a past college final, now remembered in possibly doubtful detail. It seems there was this nuclear chain reaction involving a mass of neutrons, protons and electrons all boiling in some lunatic All-kettle that can be only dimly apprehended, and the thought of which made my own head feel like a pressure cooker about to blow its lid. Suspicions that he was regurgitating bygone term papers were reinforced by the authorities he quoted, such as George Gamow's *The Creation of the Universe.*

"We see that, in order to cook the atomic species properly, and in percentages corresponding to those actually found in nature, we must make a delicate adjustment of Ylem density — Ylem being the primatene, Christ, now you've got me doing it, I mean the primordial stuff out of which the elements were supposedly formed. Too much pressure would overcook hydrogen and undercook uranium, whereas too little would produce the opposite result."

"Of course. Couldn't have that, could we now?"

"When did this occur, you ask."

"Who's asking?"

"It occurred when the universe had been involved in a gigantic Collapse. That era could have lasted from minus infinity of time to about three billion years ago."

I ate some more of the bedsheet, as though by miming estoppage I could get Ambrose to shut up. He paced the room some more, his hands in his pockets, the shirt of an unforgiving green hanging with the tails out.

"After that eventful sixty minutes of atomic bouillabaisse, nothing much happened for the next thirty million years."

"Oh, good. Time for a breather, what? All need it. Some pizza with the works and a half gallon of beer. Send out for it."

"No hurry in any case. It was all there, in that caldron, including the not yet molecularly tidied but nonetheless inherently existent components that would one day in due course launch Punk Peachum on his brief parabola into obliteration."

"That oblivion which was but the echo and simulacrum of the Stygian Nothing whence he came. But does he care? Not a fig."

"Way to go, stout fellow, good show and all that. Not that you mean it, *now*. Just whistling in the dark as you hurry past the boneyard in which you as good as already lie, with Housman and his 'primal flaw,' with Hardy and his 'mudball earth that God forgot.' To say nothing of that Badroulbadour whose eyelashes no worms will ever cunningly deliver to the gates of heaven. But as a dress rehearsal for when you *do* mean it, let's by all means encourage that line of talk."

"Hold it. What's this with the Badroulbadour bit? Who is he and what does he want?"

"Subject of a little perversity by Wallace Stevens. 'The Worms at Heaven's Gates,' in which he pokes fun at the notion of immortality. 'Out of the tomb we bring Badroulbadour,' the worms say. Something something 'we her chariot. Here is an eye, and here are, one by one, the lashes of that eye.' So there is nothing, no answer from the eternal Void, only the *ou-boom* in the Marabar Caves, echoing mindlessly forever, the undying worm itself. But you're no worm, you're a man. So up, lad, when the journey's over there'll be time enough for sleep! Eat and drink, for tomorrow you die — hell, even the Bible you can't seem to let go of tells you that."

I threw back the covers and put my feet over the side of

the bed. He was right. I must shake off this drowsiness with its ominous temptation to seasonal oblivion.

"Bring me meat and raiment, that I may refresh and gird myself," I said. "Bring me sustenance and drink, yea wine to gladden the heart. Let there be maidens with flowers bedecked, and those that pluck upon stringed instruments, that we may dance the night away, yea till the sun rise."

"Way to go."

"He who once said with the Psalmist, 'My soul waiteth for the Lord more than they that watch for morning. I say more than they that watch for morning,' he sayeth that no more. No way. For there shall no Lord come, neither the feet of him upon the mountain proclaiming good tidings, but only the morning itself. Suffice the morning, then, for him. But the day is now far spent, time hath been wasted in vain repining."

"And how!"

"Therefore shall I tarry no longer, nor languish upon my couch."

"Go, go, go!"

"Bring me a ewer of water that I may wash myself, yea also a razor to take unto my head, that the damsels when they look upon my countenance not barf their cookies and say, 'Behold what the cat hath dragged in.' And another reply, 'He hath been pulled through a hedge backwards. Let us go hence from here, and seek one who does not make us upchuck.'"

"Go, go, go!"

I wobbled unsteadily toward the bureau and looked into the mirror. I blanched, or must have under the stubble. My tongue looked like a slice of bad cheese, and my eyes were so bloodshot they resembled cherry pits. While I reflected on my reflection, Ambrose got in a few booster shots for the Absurd, the despair which must be drunk to the dregs before the healing fountains could start, etc.

"Remember the note some philosopher or other left on his desk the night he died. 'There are no answers. Farewell.' What's the matter?"

I had tried a little more of the meat and raiment bit, but was feeling as flaky as Columbine said I looked, and so I wobbled woozily back under the covers. I ate some more bed linen while Ambrose got in a few more licks of black philosophy, or *pensées noires,* a term admittedly coined to singe a few of Pascal's tail feathers. He wrapped up this session with a sort of *Götterdämmerung* coda emphasizing that thanks to entropy the galaxies, stupefying enough in their prime, would indeed one day pile up in the megacosmic garbage alley, as richly deserved for being so devoid of meaning. And you could wait till it all dry-rotted for Godot.

I awoke to find my mother shaking me by the shoulder.

"Wake up, for God's sake. You've slept for forty-eight hours. Around the clock twice. Ambrose is here."

I'd been roused from a dream of having my identity simmered away in the primal *pot-au-feu,* that hour of nuclear cooking reconstructed by physicists to their apparent satisfaction, and now as I stared into space I had the unmistakable conviction that I did not exist. I had reached that point — a state not, of course, unknown to psychiatrists. Ambrose was again wearing the shirt of merciless green, with brown corduroy trousers that gave off a steady rhythmic hum when he paced across the foot of the bed. He wore an earring on one ear, in keeping with current style. I was surprised by my mother's tolerance of it. "As long as he don't wear two," she said.

Ambrose was apologetic about this turn of events, and slightly worried; he had wanted merely to muddle the ailment, not me.

"If you think you don't exist, you are thinker as well as

thinkee," he said. "That puts you safely under the Cartesian umbrella. I think, therefore I am."

"Sartre proved the fallacy of that in *Being and Nothingness.* I'm sure you read it. There are two I's in the proposition. The second is not the first, being on another level. Ergo the reasoning is fallacious and ineffectual as proof of existence."

"But if you have discredited Descartes's proposition, you must have existed in order to do so. If you don't, then the fallacy has not been noted, and the proposition stands. And if it stands, so does the proof of your existence."

"Nothing can be proved for the simple reason that the senses themselves must do the reporting on what the senses take in, and are therefore not trustworthy in the face of the argument that everything is an illusion."

"That's that Oriental crud."

"No, it's perfectly scientific. That shirt of yours, what color is it?"

"Green."

"No. Green is the one color of the spectrum that it reflects back. Ergo it's anything but green. Green is the one thing it ain't. Like grass. Like asparagus, like — "

"Look, why don't you see a shrink? Or even have good old Doctor Dee come see you. A doctor of the old school. He still makes house calls."

"He not only makes house calls, he uses leeches. Oh, not to have learned the human cry for meaning, to be always asking Why? Better an aborigine carving an idol in the paleolithic dawn, or an eagle soaring over the Alps in the primatene mists."

"What's this with the primatene mists all the time? What the hell is that?"

"I don't know. It seems only yesterday we were soldering quarters to sewer gratings, and sending out invitations to open houses so that, squatting behind neighborhood hedges,

we could watch guests stream up the driveway to people
sitting on the porch swing eating watermelon in their shirt
sleeves. Where has it all gone?"

"Look, why don't you gird up your loins, anoint your head
with oil, and all that, and sup with me? We'll have a couple
of hamburgers at the Burger Baron's. Or one of those foot-
long hot dogs with sauerkraut and the works."

"Hamburgers and hot dogs are the pornography of food."

"Think quail."

"I tell you I can't be sure I exist. There's no firm evidence."

"There will be in the back seat with Judy Jowett."

"She says 'tasty' and 'hopefully.'"

"All right, I'll take her. What about Snooky von Sickle?"

"She's built like a Clydesdale. One of the brewer's horses."

"Then it's settled for Saturday night. I think I can get the
station wagon. Burgers with the works after the works with
the girls on the beach, in all likelihood. If it warms up a
little."

That was how the stage was set for a crisis worse than anything brewed in the zodiac vats.

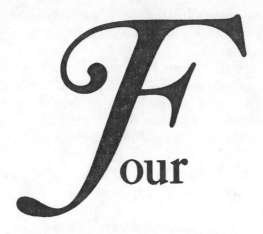

our

What both Camus and Mrs. d'Amboise have called the nostalgia for the absolute makes us often empathize with adherents of faiths we wistfully look back on as outgrown, or otherwise hopelessly untenable to ourselves, but my fascination with the Prophet, as he was known around town, arose rather out of a secret fondness for cranks and crackpots, especially religious nuts. I was in any case glad to see him holding forth on the beach when our foursome wandered onto it, trailing our coats on an unexpectedly balmy Saturday night in the late Indian Summer that suddenly enveloped us after that first fall of snow had melted off. Gone with those early flakes, too, was the temptation to doze off into a winter's refuge from inclement truths, a danger ever lurking in the genetic blueprint of the Peachums, as we know. I would make an effort not to look back at the absolute; nostalgia would not have me refusing to face up to the insoluble riddle of life, or hurling the human "Why?" at the unanswering welkin. After all, one should not take eternal Vacuity personally. So here were Ambrose and Judy Jowett strolling hand in hand, and Snooky von Sickle and I behind them. What was Snooky like?

The adjective "horsey" has never been necessarily pejorative in my book. How many young mares provoking it wouldn't a man like to mount! Snooky had everything Schopenhauer deplored in his famous lampoon of women: wide hips, short legs, and I don't remember exactly what all he pinned on "the unaesthetic sex." She was even slightly bowlegged, what the hell, with strong, solid hams completing a gestalt that, however collectively off-putting to the author of *The World as Will and Idea,* might make another's head spin with visions of quadruped pleasures. She had a rolling gait that made you think of a tolling bell, or made me think of it at any rate. The conceit struck me as we made our way across the sand. A blood-orange moon was just rising over Lake Michigan, and at a curve in the shoreline we could see the Prophet silhouetted against it, his staff raised aloft as he harangued a party of boisterous young people dancing to radio rock around a roaring bonfire.

"Ye wicked and blind," he was saying as we hurried up, led by me as one always eager to catch his stuff, which I thought rather good of its kind, though of course derivative. "For if the works which are done in thee had been done in Evanston and Westport and Sausalito, they would long ago have repented in sackcloth and ashes. And if the word which is proclaimed in thy midst had been uttered in Scarsdale and Grosse Pointe, a suburb of Detroit, they would long ago have bended their knee to the Lord in whose name it cometh."

"Way to go, man!" one of the young people shouted, with echoing cries of "You tell 'em!" and "Amen."

"Zip your lip! saith the Lord!" the Prophet shot back, brandishing his staff higher, a bough roughly in the shape of a shepherd's crook. He had misunderstood. There were several Jesus freaks in the crowd, and they were cheering him on, not heckling him. But he let them all have both barrels. "For the day of his vengeance is at hand. 'Ye are no longer my people, ye fancy schmancy,' saith the Lord. 'Wastrels and spoiled, ye eat the tender tips of asparagus and throw the rest away, yea that which is still edible. Lo the lean years will come when ye shall learn your lesson. Yea the entire stalk will ye eat, and glad to get it.' Gluttons and pot smokers and fornicators, the Lord will smite such, for they are an abomination unto him, a stench in his nostrils. He shall bring a sore affliction to this people, so that the fillings will fall out their teeth, then their teeth out of their heads, the hubcaps off their cars in the general disintegration which shall consume all things, their bones will rot. A new virus he's working on will kill them all off like flies," the Prophet ranted on with excruciating relish, "worse than the Legionnaires' disease any day. Then shall he that is smitten, knowing his days are numbered, say, 'Let me put my house in order. Give us yet a little time to see to our investments, even our portfolios. Let us weed out the dogs and the weak sisters, that our widows and children may be reasonably well fixed, and not beg bread in the streets, yea even a crust of Pepperidge Farm.' But the Lord will say, 'Screw your portfolios, what are these things to me in which ye have put your trust, yea the fly-by-night growth stocks someone let you in on the ground floor of, the electronic shares that skyrocketed from 8½ to 2¼, that you gambled on so your wives and children might have meat and raiment." The oddly echoing coincidence with my own meat-and-raiment bit of a few days before gave me a shiver of surprise, and I strained to hear what the Prophet would say next, as did most of the beach party, where they had turned the portable radio down to listen. He pulled out all the stops and minced no words as he sailed on into what you sensed to be a peroration.

"The Lord shall hold them in derision. He shall say, 'Ha! Don't make me laugh. Ye have worshipped the almighty dollar, forgetting that I alone am almighty. Slipped your mind, did it? Well, slip this on for size: the day is not far off, verily is at hand, when the dollar won't be worth a plugged nickel.

It's on the skids right now in Zurich, Paris and Tokyo. So get your ass in gear,' saith the Lord, 'and hurry down to my house, fall on your knees and there ask forgiveness. Maybe we can work something out, but I can't promise a thing for sure, so great are your transgressions, so noxious the odor of your abominations.' Thus saith the Lord through the mouth of this his servant."

And with that the Prophet gave his homemade toga an imperial flourish and marched off, to harangue others elsewhere in town, digging his stick into the sand with every other step. He walked right by our foursome, with a nodding glance at me as one probably recognized as a fan. Shaggy brown hair hung to his shoulders, the toga consisted of odds and ends of old burlap and muslin, and he smelled like Finnegan's goat. All in all, quite a figure as he vanished in the firelight, muttering apocalyptic threats of tribulation. "This administration . . ."

We had arranged to take turns in the family station wagon Ambrose had been able to get, and which was parked in a dark and secluded corner of the beach park. He and Judy availed themselves of the back seat first, while Snooky and I got lost for an hour. We strolled along with our shoes in our hands, arms around one another's waist. Snooky's conversation could be disjointed, but inevitably she would throw off an arresting thought, or dish out a colorful scrap of gossip, or ask an interesting question.

"Why is the guilt complex so widespread just when man no longer has any sense of sin?"

"Maybe for that very reason. Something rushes into every vacuum. My guess is that the less religious people are, the more superstitious they can be. Neurotic compulsions are called rituals, you know — "

"Like washing rituals and so on. I see what you mean. Go on, Punk."

"So these neurotic sequences, and we all have them in one

way or another, counting, ticking off our fingers in a series,
I think are because we don't engage in *religious* rituals any
more. I have a hunch Catholics have fewest neurotic compulsions. Freethinkers the most. I mean somebody who
crosses himself all the time probably never throws salt over
his shoulder."

"The two are the same in your estimation?"

"Mmm, yeah . . . I guess."

"Then you're not a *Göttesglauber,* as my grandfather says."

"God . . . ?"

"Godbeliever. But — now what was I going to say? Oh. Of
course you could reverse what you just said, and say ancient
tribal rituals are all neurotic compulsions."

"I suppose."

Silence, save for the scuff-scuff of our feet in the sand.

"What's your sign?"

"I don't know," I said, perversely, for the question always
bores me. Then he repented him, and his heart melted in
pity for the damsel the Lord had sent him, in order that he
might rejoice in his youth, even the fair maiden called
Snooky the Shulamite. "Pisces, I believe. February."

"Do you believe in astrology?"

"I don't even believe in astronomy. Do you take it seriously?"

"It's just a sort of game. We got sick of the Freudian
key to personality so we started another. So you're poetic,
kind of lazy, go by intuitions. Like good food and wine. I'm
Pisces too, though it's March. By the way, did you read about
that kooky astrologer on our block?"

I hadn't, and so she launched into the story as I glanced
covertly off toward where the station wagon stood, a dark
shape with no heads discernible in it.

A woman in her neighborhood, named Beerwagon, had
fallen through an attic floor, then through the floor below
into a ground-level living room, where she became embedded

in a wall. She was finally rescued by the landlady, who said she heard noises, mumbling, muffled sounds just faintly audible in her own semi-attached apartment. Medical measurements of body-water loss indicated she had been encased in the wall for a minimum of three days, but the woman said she was only in there three-quarters of an hour.

"What was she doing in the attic?"

"She said she went up there to read some of Edgar Allan Poe's stories, the better to savor their gothic quality? She read in a rocking chair, tipped over backwards too far, and fell through the rotted floorboards, then through some more rotted floorboards a floor below, finally fetching up on the ground floor where she remained fixed in the plaster and lath work of the living-room wall until the landlady heard her mumbling. I suppose you don't believe that."

"Ralph Richardson fell out of Laurence Olivier's attic into a guest room below, where he landed on a bed which collapsed under his weight. Luckily it broke his fall. Olivier had been showing him some frescoes painted on the beams by monks or something, in what was a remodeled abbot's lodge. This after Richardson had lit a rocket in the garden of a previous house of the Oliviers' on Guy Fawkes Day and sent it straight into a dining room, where it set fire to the curtains and destroyed a lot of antique crockery."

"The strangest things in the paper lately. An Arkansas farmer is accused of having eaten his hired man. By the way, do you know what part of the human body cannibals consider the greatest delicacy?"

No, it's not, as you no doubt think, you filthy beggar, the labia major or the underside of a breast, but the fat part of the hand just above the thumb. So you guessed wrong, you lubricious person, you sofa-crevice fondler, you secretary-treasurer. Forgive me. I get carried away, and it's all in fun, or at least partly.

And he gently drew the damsel across the sand toward the

station wagon, which out of the corner of his eye he had seen their companions vacating. And it was thinking in this wise that he reflected within him on the delicacies of her flesh, musing on the tender portions of Snooky the Shulamite as he opened the back door and aided her along. And he went in unto her, that he might know her, and he gat no heat. And she whispered unto him, "I feel the same way. I find this off-putting too. You're prolly getting my negative vibes. Do you believe that, that you can get somebody else's negative vibes?"

And he answered that it was even so, not that he hadn't some of his own to spare. He was thinking of Mrs. Beer-wagon falling two floors to Ralph Richardson's one, in the house of Olivier.

"Punk, my folks will be away next week. I'll have the house to myself. We'll go to bed together, darling."

Then gat he heat, and she said unto him, "No. Put that away. I don't want it here, not in the back seat of a car. Honey, *in my bed?*"

"Right."

And it was to be even so, as she promised. For tonight, the four of us finished it off with hamburgers at the Burger Baron's, where an incident occurred I'd rather have done without, ridiculously insignificant though it was.

We were in the drive-in section, eating hamburgers the size of sofa cushions, when I suddenly slumped down in the back seat I was occupying with Snooky, so fast the reflex seemed to have preceded the sight prompting it: that of Mr. and Mrs. d'Amboise getting out of the other family car and walking toward the restaurant, with Columbine between them. She seemed older than when last seen, a week or so earlier, but they floated in a borscht of red neon light that distorted everyone's features. She also struck me as being a mite more tuning-forkish again, giving off the 144 cycles per second in standard international use, because of the tense manner in which she gestured as she spoke now to her mother, then her father, himself a lean, nervous man, completing the double measure of vibrancy guaranteed in all the d'Amboises. How strong was my need to please, with its corollary wish never to give offense, was driven home to me by what I now did.

Wearing the hamburger as a disguise for the lower half of my face, I shoved the bill of the baseball cap I was wearing over my brow to cover the upper half and slouched down until I was sitting on my spine. This program left just enough visibility to be sure that Mrs. d'Amboise caught a fleeting glimpse of me as I sank from view. The three went on into the restaurant. I don't think Ambrose noticed them, but in any case he would not have called my attention to them, as he himself was opposed to his mother's campaign to have me wait for Columbine. Strongly so. He firmly stated that when full grown she would never be a girl to be made free with. "You know those warning signs on the crockery in china shops: BREAK IT AND YOU'VE BOUGHT IT." Roughly translated, this meant, "Keep your cotton-pickin', chicken-pluckin', oyster-shuckin' hands off my sister."

"Punk, you're awfully quiet tonight," Judy Jowett said from the front seat as I surfaced. "What are you thinking?"

"I was thinking that anybody who sticks a feather in his cap and calls it macaroni has problems."

"I couldn't agree more. Now we'll have no more offbeat dialogue. Who wants some music?" And she switched the dashboard radio on.

The word quotidian sits on the printed page and stares at you with those big awful frog's eyes, defying you to stare back. All right. Now. Apprehension about running into Mrs. d'Amboise was quotidian, such a pall did the memory of having seen her, or her having seen me, cast over my daily life. Why? Whatever for? The answer must lie in the truth, not that I'm a twirp, but that there are some people whose disapproval is an abrasive not to be gainsaid, any more than understood. I could still feel those dark eyes boring holes into mine as I sank from view in her own station wagon, and it was worse when, returning some library books a few days later, I saw her come out the door and head straight down the stairs toward me. She had been to an exhibit there of works by another local artist, an Albanian who utilized the grain of the wood on which he painted, thus redefining the random, etc., etc. We stopped to chat.

"Well, well, Teddy," she said, smiling rather tautly as she tapped my nose with a catalogue rolled into a truncheon expressly for the purpose. "I see you like the Baron's burgers too."

I grinned engagingly back. "The good that I would I do not, and the evil that I would not that I do, and there is no health in my bones by reason of mine iniquities."

"What?"

"I ain't nuttin' but a hound dog."

"I'm sorry to hear that." She looked thoughtfully off toward the blue Pacific two thousand miles away, tapping now her own teeth with the catalogue. "I like to think the potential is still there."

"Let's hope so."

"I'm thinking of starting a new piece. Saint Sebastian."

"He's the martyr."

"Yes."

"All the arrows."

"I want to do him on his knees."

"Eyes rolling heavenward."

"In his death throes, or what he thinks are. Because of course he wasn't actually killed by Diocletian's archers, only left there for dead, to be clubbed to death later. All that you know."

The word quondam squats on a lily pad too, daring you to try to stare it out of countenance. It meant former, if memory served. Well, I was a quondam model, and was going to stay quondam.

"We'll use rubber tips."

"Aha."

"And I think kind of slumped against a tree trunk. Has your father retired yet?"

"No, he's still up. It's a little early. Colly seems fine."

"She made that custard herself she brought you."

"It was marvelous. I appreciated it."

"I'm glad you're up and around again, Ted, after your sinking spell. We were worried about you. I hope you can get back to school for the next semester."

I did, got a B+ on my nervous breakdown, that being how the A— the psychology teacher marked my paper and the English Department B averaged out, and, come graduation, couldn't get home fast enough to see Snooky von Sickle. I had dated her several times since the first night on the beach. One night about a week after returning home for the summer, I was to pick her up at seven-thirty to take her to an eight o'clock concert at our outdoor bandshell on the Pocock Mall. She didn't come downstairs till about a quarter to eight, causing me an uneasy fifteen minutes under the green gaze of Mr. von Sickle, who bore an unnerving resemblance to Bismarck. He was fiddling about in the parlor with his stamp collection.

"Do you haf any hoppies?"

Hoppies, hoppies. Little Tolkien-encouraged creatures that wipe their noses on rhododendron leaves and — Oh, hobbies, of course. Well, let's see. I liked bobbing up and down on his daughter, like a gull on a wave, endlessly, dreamily, that was nice, but other than that, let's see. I enjoyed underlining passages in books aimed at baffling those who would come after. We've all penciled sentences or passages that struck us as worth having attention called to them for our own future reference, or for the edification of successive

readers, because of their pungency or incisiveness or epi-
grammatic worth, and we have all encountered such under-
scorings by others. I took pleasure in singling out bits that,
thus isolated for special attention, made no sense whatever.
On a page of *Bleak House* I underlined "Joe Pouch's widder
in North America? Then he wouldn't have got himself," and
in James's *The Ambassadors,* "about such things, on the other
hand, in the Boulevard Malesherbes." Most of this editing
was done in library books, guaranteeing no end of people
scratching their heads in bewilderment over specifications
not to be made head or tail of. But this was hardly a hobby,
and certainly not to be mentioned if it was.

"I collect old grain receipts."

"Are you sure?"

"Positive. There are still lots to be found, if you know
where to look. The attics of families whose ancestors helped
settle this part of the Middle West, when there were a lot of
hay, grain and feed stores. Old stores that were once general
stores, with records in the back room in boxes and chests.
Two bushels of wheat, fifteen cents, or whatever. Seeing the
faded ink on those slips gives you such a feeling about those
people, such solid worth . . ."

At last Snooky came down, in a cotton print of blue and
pink flowers I'd had the pleasure of slipping her out of before. We got into my car and I sped toward the Mall.

"I'm afraid I'm late," she said.

"That's all right. I'm sure we're in plenty of time. And if
we can't get seats we'll lie on the grass. I've got blankets in
back. I understand the pianist who's doing the Chopin concerto plays in his stocking feet. Helps with the pedal work I
imagine."

"I don't mean that kind of late."

There are moments when a single word can like pluck a
violent pizzicato of fear from every nerve in your body. I
could feel a jangle of horror from my head to my feet. For a

second my tongue literally "clove to the roof of my mouth."
When I did finally manage a sound, it was a muffled, glottal
noise, very like the late Bert Lahr's celebrated "Nngaa,
nngaa."

"Haven't you been taking the pill for God's sake?" I
brought out at last, as though through a mouthful of epoxy.
An image of the Duchess flying into a rage on hearing of this
entrapment of her young protégé, the sudden foreclosure of
his future, came actually to mind. "He's thrown it all away
on some silly chit," she would say, her earrings trembling
with her indignation. Then in a flash of revelation the picture
became even more chimerically awful, as a slight shift in
focus froze me with the terrible realization. The Duchess was
none other than Mrs. d'Amboise.

"There has been so much bad publicity about the pill
lately that a lot of us are going off it, but I thought it would
still be safe. I mean that I, that we had protection from the
last time I took it. But it's only a couple of days. I've been
overdue before. Don't worry about it, Punk. I wouldn't have
mentioned it if I'd know it would upset you so. You look pale.
Have you got a cigarette?"

"In my coat pocket. Light one for me while you're nngaa."

Five

We stretched out on the grass listening to the Franck D minor. The first movement is marked Lento, calling for the slow, suitably solemn elucidation of thoughts on the part of a Pocock, Illinois, youth contemplating suicide because he has a girl in trouble; then Allegro non troppo for a quickening tempo as wedding arrangements are hastily launched by the girl's family — invitations, catering, and the like; and finally Allegro without the modifying non troppo, to depict a further acceleration, this time on the part of the hero as he trots around town looking for a job. The second movement is marked Allegretto, for the fantasies he weaves about his forfeited smart life while he discharges his boring duties as teller in a bank, where, in the third and final movement, again marked Allegro non troppo, he drafts a scheme for an electronic check swindle enabling him to take it on the lam to Tristan da Cunha, a remote island in the South Atlantic supplying the title of his favorite Roy Campbell poem, which begins: "Snore in the foam: the night is vast and blind." What a line! What a mess!

The pianist turned out to be a fur-bearing animal named

Boris Borealis who came on stage not in stocking feet, as rumored, but barefoot, no doubt to achieve an even richer intimacy with the instrument. A suspicion that his toes were prehensile could not be explored from this distance. The opening movement of the Chopin F minor concerto, marked Maestoso, develops its thematic materials in a stately manner appropriately depicting the hero's measured march toward self-destruction. The flight to Omaha with three raggedly dressed children, all mouth breathers, and a wife with irreversible eczema is set forth in an introductory passage presently gathering both orchestra and soloist in a sweeping amalgamation of tonal resources dramatizing his selling burial plots door to door while simultaneously going through bankruptcy as a haberdasher *manqué* . . .

I did little more than kiss Snooky good night in her hallway, where overhead the creak of bedroom floorboards prophetic of domestic stupefaction could be heard by way of an alternate theme subtly intertwined with the principal motif, that of erotic anguish. I stumbled down the stairs with my eyes blurred and my head swimming, while everything went quondam and quotidian.

I scarcely knew, during the next few days, whether I wanted to see Snooky or not, both longing and fearing to learn what was what. But the following week I spotted her entering a supermarket, scuttled surreptitiously inside myself, and watched her wind her way up and down the aisles while ducking from cover to cover myself. One such vantage point was a huge "Today's Special" display, in this case boxes of breakfast cereal arranged in a construction with holes in it, like a Henry Moore sculpture. Peering through one such cavity, I could appraise her from a distance of ten feet or so. Wildly I consulted her appearance for signs of the "maternal glow" said to be discernible in the newly kindled. And sure enough, oh, my God, wasn't there a certain stately fullness about her (recalling the opening measures of the Maestoso)?

But hadn't there always been? Hadn't she always had that
... Junoesque quality? As well as that ripe-peach complexion? Only now she seemed lit from within, oh, my God, lit
from within, all her being aglow with the incandescence of
her Secret, the still privately cherished joy with which she
trundled the shopping cart round and around the store, pre-
figure of the day soon to come when she would be trundling
something else. I passed a hand across my brow as everything went quondam again, and as the brasses belched out a
final invitation to despair, mockingly interlaced with the
reeds and strings singing, "That's it, Mac, no delinquent
hours in Mozambique, or running barefoot together into the
amethystine seas, just the selling burial plots door to door for
the three mouth breathers in Omaha," I threatened to pitch
forward into the dry-cereal construction, burying myself under a mountain of Cheerios. Instead, an awareness of someone close behind me caused me to dart a glance over my
shoulder. A store functionary wearing an identification label
on his lapel reading "Albert Henley. Call me Al," was watching me quizzically. "I was just looking for — can you tell me
where the — oh, I see they're over nngaa." I skittered out
sideways through an empty checkout lane, drawing odd
gazes as I slithered balletically through the electronic
doors.

I contrived to be in the parking lot when Snooky at last
came out. Hiding in this instance behind a bread truck
stopped there for deliveries, I could note the sense of immemorial grace with which she carried her sack of purchases;
there seemed a thousand years of accumulated ease in it, so
that one should not have been surprised to see her transfer
the bag to the top of her head, like a woman of Judea carrying an urn to the village well. And Snooky the Shulamite said
unto him, "Why hidest thou from me? Have I not found
favor in thy sight, as thou with me, and am I not carrying thy
child? Why then hurriest thou from my gaze? Whithersoever

thou scrammest, shall not my kinsmen find thee, yea those with the broad shoulders and the muscles like unto rippling serpents?"

I banked almost mystically on the name's being simply inconsonant with calamity. Surely no one named Snooky could get you into trouble. Not that it wasn't a nickname for Sandra, or that von Sickle itself hadn't baleful enough overtones. The rhythm of the strong loins under the long skirt again struck me like those of a swaying bell, now tolling my doom. Those hips were beautiful peasant's hips, commodious for a held infant to straddle comfortably while the mother with a free hand churned something, and the father tilled the soil in a nearby — no! Not yet, Lord, I am too young. There is still Innsbruck and Marrakesh and the old Moulmein Pagoda.

As she pulled out of the parking lot I rushed over. Catching sight of me, she waved, slowing, and cranked the window down.

"Anything new?"

She shook her head with a smile. "And how are you?"

I did my Bert Lahr.

"Ted? You probably know the von Sickle tribe have this big family reunion every Fourth of July. They come from all over the country for a picnic, making mit der beer und der wurst. This year it's here, over in Gomer's Grove. It's the day after tomorrow. Want to to come?"

"Nngaa."

"Swell. See you then. Any time after noon."

I slept poorly, dreamed voluminously. Once, that I was lowered down over a Lover's Leap by block and tackle, to relative safety below. Indistinct figures stood nearby, deriding it as a craven form of descent. The act of a poltroon. Another time I caught my foot in a tangle of barbed wire, driving up the price of eggs.

Then there were the dreams I now saw as cruelly snuffed

out, what I had come to think of as my Journey Dreams, those fancied *Wanderjahre* I had never doubted would be the first and vagrant portion of my manhood. I had seen myself as rambling the round earth over, each day improvised, every night an adventure, and of course women everywhere. Women the continental suns have burned the color of tiger lilies. Heiresses purring like the motorcars you handed them into, divorcées smelling of sandalwood, ravishing and ravished under the palpitating stars of Spain, vacationing schoolgirls tearing with you down the Grande Corniche in rented convertibles, or frolicking on beaches gold by day and silver by night. The moon hanging like a gong over the Mediterranean and roses pouring over every wall. Opera! Chocolates! Themes repeated by the oboes! Raptures on the wing and then regretless farewells, blown kisses as the *rapide* pulls out of Bordeaux bound for Paris. Europe eaten and divided and drunk among whispers, it's on to Afric and to Ind. A scented letter awaits you in your Cairo hotel, and then dinner and the caught felicities of fresh encounters there, camel rides to the Pyramids and being joined for Turkish coffee later, and dawn coming up like thunder surely somewhere, though you're going to bed to it, not getting up. Moondawns in Singapore, the starlit silver of equatorial seas — and all the steaming virgins of the East. As you drift southward down a chuckling river God knows where, or fly north over reeling mountaintops, your mind is a voluptuous jumble of memories and anticipations. This one had breasts like quicksilver under silk, that one a voice like tinkling bells. Caramels sent round! Berlioz stumbled on in heathen Zanzibar! Elbow-length gloves peeled off to take your gambled touch! An exchange of sighs instinct with promises of bliss to come as the maestro flails the air like a madman . . . Oh, bleating bassoons! Oh, pining violins! Oh, Christ, what have I done!

Was my snared foot now doomed never to take even the first step of that fabled journey? Must I, lumpenfool, settle

for a two-week honeymoon taken tourist class, with the bride
dispatching me for pickles as night descends on Kansas City?

The word wanderlust is German in origin, I thought as I
slunk through Gomer's Grove toward the von Sickle annual
family reunion. I watched from behind a tree on the edge of
a clearing where the picnic was in full swing. Ten thousand
Germans were pitching horseshoes and blowing horns and
giving suck and eating ham and potato salad and drinking
beer. Anybody's ballpark figure would have been as valid as
the next. Any number of pregnancies promised an increase
among the subjects before the census could be completed.
These, then, were the Hun hordes into which I was to sink
without a trace. I had the same sense of woozy engulfment
as when the size of the universe was borne in on me, and the
same sensation of personal obliteration, so that the delusion
that I didn't exist threatened to return in flood force. The
sheer galactic multiplication of brothers and sisters and aunts
and uncles and children and grandchildren and great-grand-
children inspired the identical sense of nonentity. When
would I awaken from this dream? Meanwhile, how would I
conduct myself with these Heinies? Why, as a local exquisite
who didn't take no garbage from nobody no time.

The concept of the family reunion, I mused as I watched,
is fine theoretically, having sentimental overtones that uni-
versally touch us, but few things can be more drenched in
the general human pathos than the reality; and nothing can
more abundantly communicate this than Germans assembled
in the quantities with which the sensitive youth was now
confronted. Clucking and shrieking *Hausfrauen* overflowing
dresses tighter than last year appear to outweigh in collective
tonnage their husbands, half of whom seem to have passed
that dark day when a man decides he must wear his belt under instead of over his cascading paunch. The thought of
how they were all once what their sons and daughters are

now is exceeded in melancholy only by the reverse, namely
the apprehension of what their children will one day be —
and here your correspondent was pierced to the quick.

This must be the most physical of races. One inevitably
recalled Katherine Mansfield's little lampoon entitled "Germans at Meat," and had Oscar Wilde not called their poetry
attenuated beer belching? They are blowing horns on every
street corner or gorging themselves on sausages and strudel
when they are not trying to stuff the rest of us with their
starchy metaphysics. *Weltanschauung* and *Zeitgeist* and
Ding an sich and Humperdinck and pumpernickel and
Schwanda der Dudelsackpfeifer. *Schwanda der Dudelsackpfeifer* for Christ's sake! Every word sounds like a trunk falling downstairs. Do you know how they test new beer in
Munich, we are told? It's poured over the benches the
burghers are going to sit on to drink it. If when they stand
up again the beer-soaked bench sticks to their lederhosen,
the beer is deemed O.K. A good year. If the bench sticks to
their seats all the way to the door, it's considered a truly
great year. Can you believe it?

A thrown horseshoe narrowly missed conking somebody
and there was hearty laughter, with slapping of thighs and
calling out, "Hans, you Dummkopf, you want to dent dot
horseshoe?" A softball game was started, with apparently
twenty-five or thirty players to a team, judging from the
length of time they were choosing up sides. Someone told a
story of how at a previous *Vereinigung* they had played ball
in a cow pasture, and how one runner had slid into what he
thought was third base. The slapping of thighs could have
been heard a mile away, and the sensitive youth wondered if
he must come to it, once their ranks had closed round him
like quicksand. O, Glockenspiel!

The fifty or so men who were to make up the two nines
traipsed off to a nearby pasture similar enough to its predecessor to guarantee plenty more robust humor, and shifting

my position behind the tree, I next turned my attention to another corner of the jollification where some fifteen or twenty picnic tables were arranged in two squares. Each table (to my still-fevered, not to say delirious, imagination) could be conceived of as a galaxy merged in and contributing to a supergalaxy. And Milky Way would not have been an inapt term for one at which no less than three *Muttervolke* were nursing kids. Every time I see a Valkyrie like one of these haul up an udder I want to climb aboard and make a litter, but that is neither here nor there, not part of this poor chronicle. The burning issue at stake was: would Snooky have joined the dairy by next year, with me out there in a cow pasture trying to stretch a triple by sliding into what I thought was home plate — to enter Teutonic legend forever? I might even get into the repertory today.

Snooky was hurrying over, having spotted me lurking in the underbrush.

"Come and meet everyone," she said, taking my hand and towing me into the clearing. "This is my grandfather," she whispered, of a hirsute party in a suit of impenitent blue who was bearing down on us, smoking an alto saxophone. Or no, hold it, on closer view it might be a meerschaum. "Sort of head of the clan. Owner of the brewery and all. I'm his favorite because I'm the only issue of *his* only issue, namely, my father. Make a good impression on him or he may cut me out of his will."

"Will?"

"He's set up a trust fund for me for when I'm either married or twenty-one, whichever comes first."

"You mean he's nngaa . . .?"

"Don't be afraid of the word. Yes, loaded. Milwaukee beer. So you're mad about Wienerwald, remember."

"This . . . trust — what is the exact — the nature — ?"

"Half a million."

Is there a sight more heartwarming than a family reunion,

or a people who more beautifully exemplify it than the Germans? What a splendid folk they are! How solid and substantial, and with what unabashed *Lebenslust* they throw themselves into their enjoyment of food and drink — in both areas of which they have contributed so much to the enrichment of our own lives as well. What a delight it is to see them gathering in great masses to celebrate and reaffirm that sense of kinship that is our one bulwark against mortality. So *gemütlich,* in the word that captures its own meaning with the phonetic felicity of their entire language. Roll some others on your tongue, do. *Weltanschauung, Ding an sich, Sehnsucht, Abendschein.* And the names! Wolfgang, Gretchen, Irmgarde, Bruno, and Schwanda der Dudelsackpfeifer, mustn't forget him. Or their music as such, and that only one facet of a creative genius that embraces all the arts, and which must forever absolve them of the charge of physicality. So far from their poetry being attenuated beer belching, their beer is contrariwise liquid poetry — and as for those vintage Rhines and Moselles fluting on the palate! How they love life, and each other, keeping their feast days with recipes handed down through the generations, cherishing their heirlooms and bequeathing their patrimonies in that dedication to the sanctity of lineage of which this convocation, in a grove rendered thereby sacred, is but another exhilarating example. I have heard the charge "starchy" brought against their formidable metaphysics. Well, what about Leibniz's "windowless monads." Would even the wittily imaginative French like to try to beat that for fancy? And if you find the categorical imperative too much for you, then stay out of the kitchen. Legend has it that when a new beer is tried out in Munich it is poured over the benches the burghers sit on. If when they stand up again the benches stick to their bottoms all the way to the door the beer is termed great. Love it.

My own opinion of Wienerwald would have run, "If you

love beer you'll like Wienerwald," but I slurped away at a
stein of it with many a hearty "Ah!" between mouthfuls, at
the same time careful not to make too Bacchic an impression
on someone who, knowing I was mingling here as his grand-
daughter's boyfriend, might wonder how sound might be my
stewardship of half a million clams. I was inevitably open to
suspicion as a fortune hunter, as well as censure for what
would soon be recognized as a shotgun wedding, no big deal
today, but still so to a tribe of entrenched Lutherans. Such
a trust fund could supposedly be dismantled by a donor still
alive — which *Grossvater* was very much at eighty-six. He
had inherited the brewery from his father, who'd founded it
soon after emigrating from Düsseldorf. Collateral branches
of the family had been proliferating, rather than forebears in
Snooky's direct line of descent, a condition that kept the
great-grandfather's wealth from being dissipated in all directions, rather than coming down straight to oneself.

"What is it you want to do now that you're out of school?"
the grandfather asked, speaking with an accent relatively
thick, as he had emigrated when still a growing boy. A thick
reddish beard gave me the feeling of being carefully watched
from within a thicket, and my own gaze kept spilling down
the front of his bulging vest, spanned by a gold chain with a
watch that could have served as a blunt instrument.

"Own an art gallery," I said, somewhat to my surprise, as
that had been rather far down a list of several possibilities
that kept revolving in my head in shifting orders of prefer-
ence. The theatre and motion pictures had a higher priority,
but to mention either of those might have given him visions
of enormous sums poured into risky projects by an irrespon-
sible bounder. Too, I had learned that he collected paintings.

"Ah, coot. Ja, a fine pisness, und ingreasingly important
dese days when so many peeble gollect."

"But..." I shrugged sadly. "It takes capital, so I'll probably have to work hard for several years, sir, in order to save

up enough to launch myself toward the realization of my
dream." The impression of industry combined with a cherubic ignorance of any money whatsoever in the family into
whose ranks I was pitching was a good blend in the circumstances, considering the mess I was in. But again I felt the
gimlet eyes directing a laser beam into my skull, and to keep
from being stared out of countenance I took another hearty
swig of the Wienerwald which was rapidly nauseating me,
and said "Ah!" again, wiping foam from my lips in tribute to
departed brewmeisters. My attention was recalled to what I
had in my left hand. I was trying to gnaw my way through a
pfeffernuss you could have pitched three innings of hardball
with. I swirled some dregs around in my stein and said pluck-
ily, "Maybe I can get a job *in* an art gallery first. That way
get to learn the ropes, sir. Work from the ground up."

"Ja, dot would be good. You had a general edugation in
college? Liberal arts?"

"Ja, yeah, but I don't consider myself 'educated' in the true
sense. That takes a lifetime. Well, so! You're interested spe-
cifically in der Cherman, German Expressionists? A powerful
school."

"I also haf a fondness for George Grosz, despite his draw-
ings are terrible garrigatures of der Cherman peeble."

"Aw, no, hey, they're not ethnic so much as social, I mean
his lampoons. It's the bourgeoisie he's after, not the Germans
qua Germans."

"Well, I'm afraid I'm poorgeois too, so I got a double dose,"
von Sickle said, laughing heartily. "I own three Groszes, so I
guess I'm a mazochist. Tell me, what's your religion?"

I don't know why Martin Luther's obsession with his bowels came to my mind at that, and also the fact that he was a
fiendishly anti-Semitic bastard who wanted to drive out the
Jews four hundred years before the Nazis got around to it.
I suppose there was a flash of resentment with a known Lu-
theran churchgoer and probably philanthropist conducting

this third degree, behind which was ultimate anger at myself for this mealy-mouthed submission to it. Also I may have felt like a jerk in the face of this Buddenbrooks solidity. Was I a jerk? What do you think? You know me by now. Well, so I had got into a jam as old as male mankind. Let him take his money and put it where the sun didn't shine, which would probably have pleased the founder of his faith no end.

"We've always been regular Presbyterians," I said, longing to add that Luther probably wouldn't have minded our being Presbyterian after learning that we were regular. Dot was a goot one. Slapping of *Ubermensch* thighs, etc. Does any of us ever know what anybody else is thinking? Probably no, and a damn good thing it is. My regular attendance in church meant turning up faithfully every third or fourth Christmas. Still, I'm generally regarded as a nice chap mit no glaring vaults und only a few shingles missing. Und only vunce in a vile a little sofa-crack feeling around in mit der fingers, mit all dot dot implies, ja? Ve got all dot from Freud, *nicht wahr?*

Von Sickle painfully tweaked my nose, signifying that the interview was over, that is, in a formal sense. But his society was not to be sloughed off. Slinging an arm through mine, he dragged me back to the beer barrel and there challenged me to a game of horseshoes. It's a sport I find a trifle esoteric, and by dint of making no ringers and pitching a few into a birch grove I managed to let him beat me 21–9.

After a third or maybe fourth stein of shampoo my head began to spin. I had been through too much — the birth and death of the sun, the arrogance of Space in a universe devoid of meaning, and now this. Finding an opportunity to escape, I slipped away into the Black Forest and there dozed under a tree, knowing that before nightfall kindly woodcutters would discover me and, after sharing with me their supper of black bread and cheese, set me on the road to the Algonquin. Forty winks did refresh me, but I snapped awake with the distinct certainty that I had been had on toast. I loitered a moment on all fours, shaking my head to revive my senses, like a boxer taking nine, then climbed to my feet and shuffled back to the picnic.

I saw Snooky in grave conversation with Otto von Bismarck — her father, remember? I preferred not to be subpoenaed by him just yet and quizzed about my little tarradiddle concerning the old grain receipts, so I waited till they separated before going over to lead her out for a walk. The hordes were still playing ball, and as we skirted the meadow three of seven outfielders collided under a high fly.

"Grandpa likes you a lot."

"And I him. I also like the way you put me on a while ago. About his salting away half a million for — heh heh — away for you?"

"Well, it's nothing like that anymore. That was when I was born."

"I see. Like your father was able to get his hands on it, and then some Uncle Brunos — "

"What with smart lawyers, people at the bank administering the trust."

I might have known. All a pipe dream. Whittled down to enough for a honeymoon that would be a week's camp-out at the Wisconsin Dells, if even that could be swung. Maybe a quick spin by car around the Midwest before the child was born. Staying with cousins along the way to effect economies. Waffle breakfasts in Holiday Inns. A TV in every room, reruns of Lawrence Welk and *Gilligan's Island*. Some nice folks met in Grand Rapids. Hunting for pickles after midnight. Souvenir belt buckles and Sheboygan, Wisconsin, teaspoons . . .

"Everybody seemed to have a say about investing it while little Snooky grew up."

"Too many cooks." Lethargically stripping a twig from a tree. "Snow on the desert's dusty face." The image lugubriously conjured for irretrievably melted funds.

"I mean with a lot of people pooling their savvy about the

market, after nineteen and a half years it's probably nearly doubled. I'll ask Daddy."

Unter den Linden! Strolls hand in hand along Anything-strasse, feeding the pigeons in Anywhereplatz! Champagne and frosted cakes beside the unbelieved Danube! Moon-dawns over the Baltic! Evenings lapped in myth, dawn burn-ing the ice on Alpine mountaintops! Gliding on buckled feet across the ballroom floor! Then again the heaving bosom of the Mediterranean, clothes strewn along the shore, running naked into the sea while wind-exported Andalusian odors spice the insatiate night!

Dusk falling in Pocock, Illinois. The sound of family cars starting up. Soon the last would be rolling homeward, or heading for the local motels. Silence would descend on the meadow, except for the distant rumble of fireworks on the beach, and lying down together on the sweet grass we could catch glimpses of far-off rocket sparks, dying in dreamy co-rollas among the steadfast and benedictive stars.

"Everything is all right, Ted. No need to worry any longer."
"But it's still the same between us? I feel we have such a rich relation going."

We were on the prowl in Ambrose d'Amboise's family sta-tion wagon, one afternoon shortly afterward. He was driving, I sat beside him, and there were two of my disciples riding in the back seat.

"What's your present philosophical position, Punk?" one of the disciples asked.

"A self-pitying stoicism. Pull over," I said to Ambrose.

"I see," the disciple persisted. "Combine the solipsistic with the objective in a kind of narcissistic heroism. What happened to your neo-Manichaean dualism?"

"Nothing. No, over here, the guy with the dogs," I continued to Ambrose.

He drew to the curb where a man in a white turtleneck and a porkpie hat was walking a pair of matched Afghans along the sidewalk. I cranked my window down and leaned out.

"Do you know where Hepplewhite Street is?" I asked the man.

"No," he said, shaking his head. "I don't."

"It's the first right after the next light, and then a diagonal left up the hill runs you right into it. You can't miss it."

And Ambrose shot away as I raised my window.

I was quite myself again. Life once more had a sense of purpose. The Absurd had been staved off. Reason was restored, meaning reenthroned.

ix

Columbine never slept on her back. She was afraid a chunk of plaster might fall out of the ceiling and land on the bed. That had once actually happened in her nursery when she was a little girl, not exactly where she'd been playing, but close enough for the resulting shambles to leave her with a fear of ceilings, and perhaps, Chicken Little–like, of the sky's falling, as it had on Knyahinya, Pultusk and Mocs.

The bijou and I were exchanging intimacies of this nature one evening some weeks after the von Sickle reunion, while sipping punch at the opening of a show of her mother's works in a new civic arts center. I figured as model in two of the pieces (the Saint Sebastian project had apparently been scrubbed, or postponed). Six of the d'Amboise offspring were on hand, including the oldest, Luke, a bricklayer *manqué* who, or so I fancied, seemed to grind his jaws and clench his fists every time he looked in my direction. I was either waiting for his sister or I wasn't any such thing, and he was going to clean my clock as soon as he found out which of the two the punitive measure was for. What if on this visit from Chicago, where he worked as a bartender and bouncer, he learned about Snooky, and that I was churning her butter while "encouraging Colly's expectations"? He would rearrange my features some. Then he would hand me my head.

Truth to tell, I could see his point. At fifteen (Colly insisted she was fifteen and a half!), at fifteen and a half, then, her steadily emerging topography foreshadowed that day when I might feel more than the vague, half-ashamed arousals experienced tonight, scandalous echoes of what I had felt for the moppet sitting on my bed at the time of my malaise. I think I'd have been equally suspicious of a matured blade said to be hanging around waiting for my sister to reach the age of consent — to put at its worst the ridiculous trap into which I had let myself be drawn. I must as soon as gracefully possible vacate the chair to which Mrs. d'Amboise had led me, before fluttering on to other guests.

"I have a fear of heights *from the ground*," I said. Why do we use up so much cocktail-blather time certifying ourselves as complex? "I mean I can go to the top of the Empire State Building and look down and it won't bother me. But looking up at it from the sidewalk, I have this vertigo."

"I can't look up into a dome, like in a cathedral or courthouse? It reminds me of that crater in the nursery ceiling. I imagine few people sleep on their backs. It's mostly flip-flopping from side to side. Daddy says, um, imperial types sleep on their backs. Maybe it's imperious. And if it's with their arms folded, look out. They're conquerors scanning the horizon for new worlds."

I was familiar with d'Amboise's spiels about the psychological significance of the positions in sleep. Most hopelessly infantile were those who lay spraddled on their stomachs, the pillow locked in both arms — alas, one's own favorite tableau.

"You might try a canopy bed," I suggested. "You know, one of those tester tops."

"Yes, I might. I think I'd like one when I get married. Have you met Luke?"

The bruiser in his more than audible jacket had strolled over after refilling his cup at the punch bowl. Drinking anything pink somehow didn't suit him, I mused as he planted himself squarely in front of us.

"Yes, we've met," I said, rising.

"What are you two talking about?"

"Beds. Ted likes the canopy kind."

"He does, does he?"

"Well, actually I was recommending one for Colly. So she can lie on her back?"

"I see." Big Brother studied me for a moment. "On the bus coming over I read a book called *Lolita*. Ever see it?"

"Yes, a masterpiece, don't you think? Not just of storytelling but of exposition as well. Breathlessly exciting from beginning to end, indeed impaling — and texturally so rich. All that Pantagruelian nuance. Indubitably and beyond all cavil one of the gems of our time."

"It's a pot of filth."

"Perhaps you're right."

Not since a primate in a North Side bar offered to distribute me evenly along Slocum Street if I cared to step outside had I so strongly wished to remain in general agreement with an interlocutor. What a broad intellectual spectrum was represented in the nine d'Amboise offspring! But then it's such a rich country, isn't it, such sprawling vitality. As I had been telling my disciples only the other day, if America can be thought of as polarized between two sets of James brothers, Jesse and Frank at one end and you know who at the other, why, we dramatize to ourselves in this one configuration its infinite cultural variety. Something of the same breathtaking sweep could be remarked as existing between Luke occupying one extreme and Ambrose the other, graded on a scale of one to ten. But I was glad Luke didn't live here, happier to learn he had to get back to Chi in the A.M. Till then, here he was, keeping an eye peeled for the tuft hunters. Such was the

absurdity of my position, who wouldn't have harmed Colly
for all the tea in China.

That was one thing. But now my involvement with the
d'Amboises took on an additional dimension: the attempts of
still another brother, Vernon, to matchmake me with his
wife. Vim, as we called him, hadn't been married to Kathy
Arpeggio long before the two found that it was not a good
glue-up. The chemistry wasn't right, as we say today, I hope
not for much longer. Vim owned the main street bookstore,
and had tough sledding owing to the reluctance of publishers
to extend credit to establishments spelling their names totally
in lowercase. It was nervous-making, seeing it on letterhead
and plate glass, all the more so when done with the inverted
chic of "main street." Kathy, after exploring a number of
avenues for the expression of her feminine independence,
had become a policewoman on the Pocock force. Vim had
offered no very strong objections, except to the danger to
which the life of a cop might expose her — indeed, he had
known she'd been toying with the idea when he married her.
She was a very pretty Italian girl of twenty-five or -six, of
the blondish persuasion hailing, I think, from the north, and
the sight of her directing traffic with her arms gyrating and
her ponytail swinging was something not to be missed. Never
openly protesting this choice of career, Vim may nevertheless
have secretly chafed under his surface compliance, and that
may have started the worm of incompatibility burrowing
through the fabric of the marriage. Who ever knows what
gives, even with couples of whom we consider ourselves intimates? Anyway, they amicably aired the problem of their
discovered unsuitability as mates, and agreed that they should
divorce. But Kathy kept postponing action, for reasons vague
at first, but gradually defining themselves as based on her
fear of being cut adrift. For all her pursuit of female self-
determination, she confessed to a basic need of a man —
even dependence on one. Vim sensed that if she were assured

a safe anchorage with another somewhere, she might be more amenable to splitting up; if she were not, it might be no soap. That was behind his playing Cupid, with a few other eligibles as well, including Phooey Haverstick, one of my disciples. But Kathy you had to like, as an illustration of the precariously balanced contrarieties that make up all our gelatinous psyches. I mean a pistol-packing clinging vine, ready to move you along with her nightstick as well, is something we wouldn't want to miss, now, would we, all you Jaspers out there?

So I had now this triangular entanglement with the d'Amboises. There was Mrs. d. wanting me to wait for Columbine, with Luke standing by ready to feed me some knuckle pie if I didn't do right by the bijou. There was Ambrose fixing me up with Snooky von Sickle as a way of siphoning my attentions *off* his sister. And now there was Vim throwing his wife at me for reasons having nothing to do with Columbine at all, about whom he was perfectly neutral vis-à-vis Ted Peachum. What an embarrassment of riches!

Vim and Kathy elbowed their way over as Luke shoved off, scratching himself in the basement. Vim's hair and teeth are both parted in the middle, and he gave his Terry-Thomas smile as he extended his hands with "Well, here I am with the fuzz." The fuzz had never looked prettier, and seeing her, and smelling her, I knew the winch of indecision was going to be given another cruel quarter turn. She had lustrous gray-green eyes, a clear skin, and (in common with Snooky) one of those wide, rubbery mouths that make you think of the word orifice. Pulpily erotic in its intimation of labial pleasures, both major and minor, don't you know, with a pinkness provoking all too shameless supplementary associations in the mind of the wrung chap. Christ, it's a tough course, isn't it, all you Jaspers out there? Poor devils simultaneously kindled and squelched, stirred and denied. I understand the toll it takes, and those unsavory little releases of yours, fidgets

and habits of which you're secretly ashamed, I quite understand. We'll say no more about it, you secretary-treasurer
you.

"The fuzz arrested my attention clear across the room," I
said, bending to kiss Officer Kathy's hand, and Colly squealed
with delight at the continentality into which she would soon
marry. Rising to take my cup, she wriggled away to refill it
and her own at the punch table, and, watching her go, I remembered a line from a novel whose title and author escape
me, a description of just such a filly worded something like,
"She had that awkwardness for which grace is a poor sub-
stitute." I was about to ask Vim if he could identify the
source, some British woman novelist I seem to recall, when
Kathy said, "She's one smitten kitten."

"Oh, now for God's sake let's stop this nonsense, shall we?"
I said, anxiously turning to make sure Luke was still out of
earshot.

"Yes. We've got to put an end to this folderol of Mother's,"
Vim chimed in, as I wondered whether any woman could be
happy with a man who says "folderol," though of course such
a marriage might just have an outside chance if it were the
other way around. "Ted's not waiting for anyone but Godot.
How are things now, Ted? Ambrose told me something of
your tailspin. Knocked galley-west. Pretty well over it?"

"Oh, sure."

"I'm glad to see somebody with the old-fashioned kind of
nervous breakdown, where people stewed over losing their
faith and the meaning of life and all," Kathy said, indicating
that one had been gabbled about on a broad front, "and not
because their mother didn't nurse them or some such. But
you don't think Colly is gaga over you, Ted?"

"Rubbish. And what girl would want a truck driver anyway?" This in reference to my supposedly temporary employment in the family firm.

The fuzz laughed, that mouth like a blossom bursting into

glorious flower. "Better a truck driver than a bookstore owner who spends all his time at home pounding a typewriter."

"Yes, Vim, how's the novel — ?"

"That's a certainty," Vim agreed. "Look at the magnificent shoulders on him now. Not that he's really a furniture mover, he's a fledgling middle-class businessman working at what he's going to inherit no matter what else he eventually does." He never stopped recommending me.

"I'd a damn sight rather work on the truck than in the office."

This was honest enough. I enjoyed the sheer physical exertion of humping a trunk or a barrel of dishes, your body lashed to your burden with the burlap sling encircling you both, and twisted in your grip at chest level. I liked the very smell of burlap, so pleasurably coarse, smothering, not unlike the musk of sex itself. I took pride in being able to carry an empty dresser on my back, or rassle my end of a loaded one with Pinky Montmorency or Buster Bailey. But even these satisfactions could not compare with the utter physical exultation of managing my share with those aristocrats of furniture movers, a piano crew. There were even sexual rewards in knowing an admiring housewife was watching from above or below as you wrangled a Steinway up a sonofabitch of a stairway. You felt like a young Hercules then. I felt a prickle of pleasure now as Kathy took in my physique.

"Let's feel your muscle."

There was nothing to do but flex an arm so she could grasp my biceps with an admiring murmur. "It's like the trademark on that baking-soda box."

"Ted's gangbusters, all right," Vim agreed, with a commending nod to Kathy.

"Of course the greatest reward of my profession is that entourage of motorists I collect everywhere I go, watching to see where I stop for coffee. Well, sir, once I drew a string of devotees clear into — "

"Bet you're a truck driver's truck driver," Kathy said. "*They* watch where you go. So do I, in fact."

"Oh? Where do I go?"

"You like Mama Mia's diner, just off Main. I've seen you go in there two or three times. It's on my parking-check beat. I'm the Cossack who puts a blue chalk mark on your tire and who's dying to tag you, but you never overstay your fifteen minutes."

"It would be a pleasure to fall into your hands. Better yet, stop in with me for a midmorning coffee-and sometime."

"Or lunch," Vim put in. "I understand Mama Mia's ham and eggs and hash-browns are out of this world."

"I often have them for breakfast there, and Vim's right. A plate of those, with a fat wedge of her cornbread, and you're ready to face the world."

"I'd love to," Kathy said.

"Done and done," said Vim, giving his cloven smile. Things were going well from his point of view, humming right along. And with Phooey Haverstick and a handful of other eligibles still in reserve.

Columbine returned, having by now wormed her way back through the crowd, and as she handed me my replenished punch cup Kathy said: "How's your allergy, Colly?"

"Which one? I have eighteen."

"I thought it was only sixteen," I said. "I hadn't realized there were eighteen."

"One other turned up, and maybe two. It seems I'm allergic to — You won't laugh?"

"We'll just have to see," Kathy said.

"Double Gloucester."

"What in the hell is that?"

"It's a cheese. One of Mother's discoveries. It's an English cheddar — "

"Beloved of T. S. Eliot," Vim interjected with another solemn nod. He had this way of bobbing his head to stress a point that might otherwise have slipped by his hearers un-appreciated. "One of his favorites." With this prestige con-ferred on her affliction, Colly went on in her rapid gliding whisper:

"Well, I had some crackers with it last week, and, um, after a few minutes my throat started to swell up, O.K.? To sort of tighten up, O.K.?" She enacted a pantomime of strangling herself. "I mean, I could hardly swallow. Even water. I think, this is it. I have seconds to live, all right?"

"Holy smoke," I said, feeling some comment should be made, however banal. But the silence had only been in-tended as a pregnant pause. Colly continued:

"Well, I wasn't sure it was the double Gloucester, all right? So the next day I ate another piece, just to see, O.K.? Well, the same thing happened. So I called Doctor Twerp, that's my allergist, and he said to take a piece of it along next time I'm due for a shot, which is tomorrow. I'm to eat it there, so he can treat me if there's a reaction. But Mother has to go to a meeting and can't take me. Nobody can, so it seems I haven't got a ride."

"I can't get away either," Vim said. "Maybe Ted's got a minute? It's not very far, and there's no bus going that way."

Vim was playing a shrewd game here. Ostensibly arrang-ing an hour with someone he theoretically wanted to steer me clear of, as competition for his wife, he was in fact plot-ting an episode calculated to drive home once and for all the trouble she was likely to be to anyone marrying her, even when no longer O.K.ing you to kingdom come, and make me see that his wife was much the wiser choice. This despite the difference in our ages, roughly the same as that between Colly and me, in reverse. In any case, it wasn't a favor I could graciously deny. So I said, "Sure I'll drive you over," words I was to rue before another sun set.

So things were taking shape, for better or worse. We had — at last! — a novelist *manqué* trying to pair me off with a

wife who was by chance the daughter of my garbage man
and now a cop in her own right, while I supposedly encour-
aged the expectations of a just-nubile girl with eighteen allergies, including a favorite cheese of T. S. Eliot's. This
seemed a solid base from which to mount an assault on the
fashionable world as conceptualized in a Duchess impatiently
awaiting one's arrival at her ancestral country seat, or fuming
across the parquet in a Belgravia town house. Or maybe you
don't think so, you secretary-treasurer. Developing some
more creepy habits, are we? Drawing sofa-cushion tassels
furtively through our fist during the Palestrina? That kind
of thing?

Eleven-thirty the following morning. I have loaded a job
with Pinky and Buster, six rooms going to Wilmette, but they
can unload it between them because, though there's a piano,
it's a small spinet two can handle easily. My father is with
another crew moving four rooms across town. My mother is
minding the office. Unfortunately the family Buick is in the
shop for radiator work, so the only thing left for me to take
Columbine to the allergist in is the third van. Heading for
her house behind the wheel of this rock-solid utterly satisfy-
ing Mack behemoth I pass within a block of Snooky's place,
and wonder why she hasn't returned two calls of mine. I
haven't been able to date her since the *Vereinigung* in the
woods, for some reason. Worries about it are driven out of
my head by the sight of the Prophet near the d'Amboise
house. He's not "on" at the moment, only on his way somewhere, and he comes over to watch me back the van into a
parking space small enough to test even Mom's mettle. He
tries to guide me, wagging his hand this way and that, as I
inch in backward. I have to flank meticulously in beside a
brand-new Mercury station wagon.

"Graze not the fender on the left, neither cut in so steeply
as to roll thy right wheel over the curb and thus into the
grass."

"Check."

"No, it doth not serve. Come thou out and try again. No, too close. Thou wilt bruise his left rear with thy right."

He was now out in the middle of the street directing as well the traffic that had piled up behind me there — and we were also picking up spectators among pedestrians pausing to watch the show. I pulled out wide into the street and tried again, this time successfully maneuvering into the space available, though not without bumping over the curb and gouging a trough out of somebody's lawn before bumping back onto the asphalt again.

"Thanks," I said, alighting. His name, I had found out, was Skimpole, though I hesitated to address him by it.

"I have a warning for thee. The Lord has laid it on me."

"Oh? What might that be?"

"Beware of those who go down to the sea in ships, yea the yachting and sailing set who by reason of sitting about on the waves drinking martinis on the Lord's Day have become such a stench in his nostrils." Since he was to the windward of me I could have said something about that. I couldn't take this portent seriously, since if there was one set I didn't mingle with it was the nautical — either those with stinkpots, as the sailboaters called motor launches, or the stringpullers, as the stinkpotters called the yawl and ketch crowd.

I said as much, but thanked him anyway for his solicitude. Then I asked him something about which I had been long itching with curiosity. "How do you get these warnings and messages?"

"From the Lord."

"You mean you hear voices?"

"I hear a voice. But I have a vision of thee in peril of those who will yet hear the noise of his waterspouts. Knowest the hullaballoo about the proposed marina, which the Lord despiseth?"

"Yes, and a lot of us agree. I happen to be acquainted with Kopple, who's pressing for it. I spake unto him, saying ...

I mean I distinctly told him this would be a bad thing for
the town, spoiling all that fishing area and bringing some
more pollution. But — you know the nautical set."

"Verily, and beware of them. I see a shipwreck."

"Yes, well, I'm a landlubber, and I guess I'll stick to that.
Thanks again anyway."

"You're welcome," he said, and marched off, clutching his
staff.

Colly was delighted at the prospect of riding in the truck,
and hauled herself up onto the seat beside me with exclama-
tions of pleasure. But we had no more than started for the
doctor's than she looked into a paper bag she was carrying
and said, "Oh, God, I've brought the wrong cheese. This is
the other — the Cheshire. They're so much alike. I'm sorry."

"What's the difference? Isn't cheese cheese? Or at least
cheddar cheddar?"

"Fish is fish, but there are people who break out in hives
with one kind who aren't affected in the least with all the
rest. I'm sorry, O.K.?"

We went back for the double Gloucester, and were barely
in time for an eleven-thirty appointment. A sense of constraint had developed between us, which I felt the need to
thaw out, somehow, by striking a lighter note.

"The Prophet says I'm going to be in a shipwreck."

"Fly."

"He did predict that fire originating in the smoke-alarm
unit."

"That's just the kind of thing he would rant about, and it's
just a coincidence that it happened. Like drivers having accidents fastening on their safety belts."

Two slots luckily side by side were open in the doctor's
angle-parking lot, both of which were required to accommodate the van. There was nobody ahead of us in the waiting
room. "Doctor Twerp wants you to eat your cheese now, so
there'll be time for a reaction before he sees you," the nurse-

receptionist told Colly, who sat down and opened her bag
and began to nibble on the slab of double Gloucester. She
looked quite prim. She broke a piece off the other end and
offered it to me. "Try some? It's good. Mother says it has,
what was it again, a dry, grainy quality like nothing else she's
ever tasted."

I found it quite lived up to its billing, transatlantic and
cisatlantic, and felt that I would have no trouble polishing
off all of the rather large chunk that had broken off in Colly's
hand. We sat side by side, munching contentedly away for
several minutes. Then a patient left the consulting room, and
the nurse presently said, "Dr. Twerp will see you now. He'll
see that you wait over long enough for a reaction."

I was eating my gobbet of the d.G. when the nurse looked
up from her desk and called over, "What's your name?" I
told her. I assumed she might be trying to place me from
somewhere, perhaps having seen me in a high-school dramatic
production, or heard me in an oratorical contest. But then
she asked for my address, and next inquired as to who had
referred me to Doctor Twerp. At which point the confusion
was apparent.

"I'm not here to see Doctor Twerp. I only drove Miss
d'Am — "

That was as far as the clarification got. I had been talking
with a rather largish wad of the d.G. in my mouth, and in
hastily trying to get rid of it had got it lodged in my throat.
I tried to swallow it down but it stuck fast, an immovable
lump. Dry grainy quality indeed. I drew a paper-cupful of
water from a nearby cooler, but couldn't swallow that either.
Most of it ran down my shirt front. My throat was completely
plugged up. In what rapidly became panic, then terror, I realized that I could neither speak *nor* breathe. The quid of
d.G. was stuck fast in my larynx. Mumbling inarticulately, I
pointed frantically to my throat, at the same time heading
instinctively for the doctor's quarters. Equally instinctively,

the nurse rushed to open the door for me, yelling out, "Doctor Twerp! The Heimlich! The Heimlich! Hurry!"

Instantly another inner door opened, and out flew a shock of kumquat-colored hair and a white coat which spun me around, thumped me four times on the back and, that proving ineffectual, clasped me in a bear hug from behind. He dug both hands in directly under my diaphragm, and heaved up. Nothing happened. The thrust was repeated, then again, and on the fourth heave, which must have sent fifty pounds of air pressure up my lungs and into my throat, the obstruction shot across the room like a cork out of a champagne bottle. The graphic details laid on you might serve as a course of instruction enabling you to save somebody's life in a restaurant or at a dinner party, one day.

I thanked the doctor for his ministrations and returned to the waiting room, and another stop at the water cooler. Colly had no reaction to the d.G. this time, and we left. Homeward bound, she bent her head toward me and pressed my arm in both her hands. "You might have . . . You know. If the doctor hadn't been there to know what to do. It's called the Heimlich maneuver."

"Good thing to know. You seem more and more to read about people choking to death."

That was far from the end of the morning's interest.

We were tooling along Pocock at a point where it was a sort of highway leading into the city. It intersected Main Street in a busy crossing whose traffic light was for some reason temporarily reduced to a blinker, always a nuisance where there is any flow of cars at all. I slowed down and then edged or darted forward again, like everyone else in the general uncertainty. Coming up Main and crossing Pocock in front of me on my left, or port side as I may as well start putting things if I'm to describe what happened, was a green station wagon drawing on a trailer a twenty-five-foot ketch with the name *Lolly May* blazoned on her forward gunnel.

Everything seemed clear sailing. But just as the driver of the station wagon finished crossing my bow, the ketch still dead ahead on Pocock Street, a car parked at the curb on the block of Main Street which he was now entering, and which was thus not far off my starboard, suddenly pulled out ahead of him with no warning. To avoid hitting it he instinctively slammed on his brakes, causing me, with not enough time to stop, to collide with the ketch. I rammed her amidships, driving her stern hard around as in the last instant I brought my own craft hard to port in the attempt to pass behind her. The *Lolly May* almost capsized, trailer and all, but righted just in time.

In an instant the intersection was a bedlam. Cars clotted it from every direction. Horns honked, motorists and pedestrians alike swarmed forward, gesticulating wildly and jabbering unintelligibly. And at the center of the nightmare stood the other principal in the scene, a seaman in somewhat rumpled nautical attire, clutching a pipe and yelling at me at the top of his voice — the driver of the station wagon. How can I describe him? Think Popeye, O.K.? Perhaps the pipe ignited the association in my mind, but there was some facial resemblance as well, such as a jutting jaw and a mouth like a blowout in an inner tube. The general maritime hallucination was quite vivid, and still is in memory. Until I climbed down out of the cab I thought he must be shouting things like "Shiver my timbers" and "You crazy son of a sea cook." Closer up they turned out to be "You dumb sonofabitch you," and "Why don'tcha watch where the hell you're going?"

"Listen, mister," I said, looking straight at the scrambled eggs on his cap, "it's nobody's fault but that guy who pulled out in front of you, and he's gone scot-free. Didn't anybody see what happened? Somebody must have seen it, for Christ's sake."

A young man clutching a briefcase stepped forward out of

the crowd to which I had appealed. "That's right," he said. "I'm in a rush, but here's my card if you want me for a witness." After handing it to me he gave another to the owner of the sailboat. "He's right. It's not your fault or his. It's that other klutz. Did anybody get his license number? No. So he's on his merry way. I happen to be an insurance man myself, and this is really a no-fault situation. I advise you to exchange names and be on your own way. There's not much damage to the boat. More to the front of this man's truck. Ah, here's the police."

Kathy d'Amboise picked her way through the mob and took efficient charge. She whipped out a notebook and jotted details. She paced off distances to fix the positions of the motorists on the street, and in relation to one another's vehicle. She even helped simmer the agitated sailor down, and after hearing my witness's testimony convinced him that it was one of those accidents where "everybody takes his damage and goes home." We shook hands on it. She tidied everything beautifully. She even managed to scare up a broom from a corner shopkeeper, and the last thing I saw as I drove off was Kathy in the middle of the crossing, sweeping up the glass from my broken headlights. What a fine housewife she would make for the right man, I thought.

Three o'clock of a Wednesday afternoon a week later. The sun has nudged an inch closer to the autumn equinox, has cooled a fraction of a degree Fahrenheit toward the clinker it will one day be. The weevil will not delay. There is still *keine Antwort,* no answer on Dial-a-Question. The Most High's phone is off the hook. We still do not know whether space is concave, curving forever outward and downward like a blanket on a horse, or saddle-shaped, curving forever upward and outward. Try as I will, walking along Pocock, I cannot capture the feeling of the woman in Proust who thought of the earth as a balloon under her feet. Rather I feel like a lumberjack trying to keep his balance on a spinning log in a contest on a river banked with multitudes of spectators: Descartes, Kant, Spinoza, Hegel, they are all there. I have not slept too well lately, and last night I crept out of bed and stood in the backyard for a bit. And from the cool sweet cisterns of the midnight air did my spirit drink repose? No, since you ask, just another belt of the old *keine Antwort*. Taking a deep breath, I felt I could smell the brass of the stars, and the rumored sun. With a deeper inhalation still, I fancied I had caught a whiff of infinity itself. I sucked a long, ammoniacal whang of it into my bursting lungs till my head reeled and my temples throbbed. Now here I am shuffling down Pocock Street again under entropy, feeling the faint, steady phosphorescent flicker of that rot in my toes. The problem is soon put to rout. I see a familiar figure coming toward me. It does an odd sort of pirouette into and out of a storefront doorway, like someone caught in a reflex of flight who knows in the same flash of instinct that the reflex must be checked, for he too has been seen. The figure that had wanted to duck me continues forward. It is Ambrose d'Amboise, looking a bit tempest-tossed himself.

"I'm going to marry Snooky von Sickle," he says, and, clutching the lapels of my coat in both hands, his lips begin to twitch. This sounds as though his lips are doing the clutching at my lapels, and that is precisely the surrealist effect I want to convey for this terrible moment in human relations, so let the dangler stand. "I know you and she," he stammers. "That there ... the ... between two ... Nngaa."

"Nngaa," I bleat, and fall on his neck and wish him all the best.

"It happened all of a sudden, the way those things things ... Combustion ..." Here his lips flick about again, like two smelts out of water, as he babbles on about chemistry and electricity and rapport between two people who hadn't known it was there until one night something or other after coming accidentally together out of some place or other and then *whhht*. "You're taking it like a brick. A million thanks." A million indeed, I think, bitterly. To the penny. "Now I've got to run. Nngaa."

"Nngaa."

I had to look at a job, six rooms and a piano going to Muskegon, and why not, but I had had no lunch, and this being three o'clock I stopped in at the restaurant for which I was in fact headed. Those million thanks still bleeding me internally, I sent two shots of bourbon downhill and then bade the waitress bring me meat that I might sustain myself against the adversities of the day, which were sore grievous, so that mine eyes were weary of looking upon what flesh must yet behold, and so forth and so on. "Anything."

"The fruit plate is a special today," she said, probably pushing something of which a surplus was piling up in the kitchen.

"That will be fine," I said, and was presently returning the gaze of two prunes, half a peach, and several disconsolate grapefruit sections, all reposing on some neurasthenic lettuce leaves and topped with what looked like strands of dental floss, though no doubt to be taken on faith as coconut shreds. This with some river-bottom coffee. By now I was really low enough to walk under a snake's belly wearing a top hat, etc. I tried to convey as much to him who reputedly slumbereth not and never sleeps. "Must thou char the wood ere thou canst limn with it?" I murmured. *Keine Antwort*. I ate what I could, mostly out of sympathy for the waitress, now apparently conscience-stricken over what she had "pushed" as she watched me from behind the counter. Was I sorry I had run into Ambrose? No, it was best that he tell me himself, and straightaway. The news would have rolled downstairs.

As I left the restaurant for my car, parked at the curb a short way up the block, I spotted one of my disciples walking toward me, and darted in the other direction — fully executing the pirouette Ambrose had aborted. Normally I never shirked what I considered my duty to my devotees, tried never to fudge on my obligation to give them *some* kind of observation to brighten their day, some scrap of thought or crumb of wisdom, if possible an aphoristic coinage however modest, whenever they were encountered and in whatever number. It was simply expected of me by my satellites. Today I was drained to the dregs, emotionally as well as mentally, and it seemed nothing could be dredged up worthy of articulation. So I tried to duck out of sight for the moment until this disciple was gone. But as I scuttled around the corner I heard my name called, and checked my pace as the disciple trotted abreast.

We walked side by side the greater part of two blocks, the disciple often turning his eyes to me in dumb entreaty — like one begging intellectual alms.

"All right," I said at last. "Marriage is to courtship as humming is to singing. I turn here."

This was going to be thirty miles of dirt road. When would I run into Snooky next? Into Ambrose again? Was the engagement carved in stone? Whatever would we say to one another? What I saw next was the Prophet, chewing the firmament up the street. I hurried over.

"Ye whores of Pocock, mothers of abomination, housewives wallowing in your adulteries, the Lord will smite you. Lolling in your tubs scented with bath oils, in houses equipped with burglar and fire alarms. But what are ye safe from while imperiling your own souls? For he who said he would come as a thief in the night will do even so, and all your alarms will avail you naught in that hour when ye shall see him face to face. And the Lord will consume your house, he will burn it down with a fire starting in the smoke-alarm system. How do you like them apples? saith the Lord. A short in the smoke-detection mechanism, and up she goes. Then what will avail your microwave ovens and garbage compactor–sanitizer gizmos, Cuisinarts and central air conditioning and CB transmission sets? For in that dread day you shall get the message without a CB, for the message shall get you, and it shall be, that's it, buddy boy. For not all the air conditioning in the world can make you anything but a stench in my nostrils, yea an abomination unto my schnozz. You with your disposable lighters, I'll dispose of *you* saith the Lord. I'll run you through the Handi-Slicer, then I'll stuff you down the Dispose-All, then I'll — Well, I'll think of something. For ye have made Pocock the armpit of the Middle West . . ."

I doubled back to where my car was parked. I had heard this routine before, in fact twice, complete with the prediction about a fire starting in a defective smoke-alarm system, which had in fact already come true, as I had mentioned to Columbine, though maybe the Prophet himself hadn't heard, or read about it in the paper. Faulty wiring in the installation caused a short circuit in the first-floor ceiling of a house on the other side of town, touching off a blaze that gutted an entire wing. The alarm system in catching on fire had apparently rendered itself powerless to turn itself on. But these fulfilled prophecies were getting more than a little eerie. He had also foretold a flash flood and a burst gas main and the Mayor's ruptured appendix, in addition, of course, to one's own modest shipwreck — all likewise represented as vengeful acts of a God fed up with human wickedness, as before the Flood. Some of these disasters had occurred in other parts of the country, and were safely predictable as mishaps that are bound to happen *some*time at *some*time *any*way; but even so, there were those of us who were beginning to think the Prophet had clairvoyant powers. But what a lot of blasting and smiting and holding in derision! And how the Prophet must be enjoying himself. I wondered whether he wrote his material out first or just composed it in his head, and whether he rehearsed it, complete with gestures, perhaps before a mirror.

And it came to pass that at eventide I returned home to find a bill from Doctor Twerp's office: "$25.00, for emergency visit." I telephoned the next day and protested to the nurse-receptionist. "I explained that I was only there with Miss d'Amboise. I wasn't there to see the doctor."

"You were given treatment, though."

"That was necessary only *because* you asked me those questions, about my name and address and so on. It was giving the answers that made me choke, don't you see? To bill me for treatment for something resulting from your misunderstanding is to be arguing in a circle."

"Your life was saved. Don't you want to look on the bright side?"

"You can't have read my book, *New Hope for Optimists.*"

"What?"

"Nothing."

"Isn't your life worth twenty-five dollars?" she asked with a ripple of laughter.

"Not the way things look at the moment."

In the end I gave up and paid the bill. After all, I had learned the Heimlich maneuver, and that might one day help me save some steak wolfer from his just desserts. The receptionist's reasoning made no sense to me. It was *Alice in Wonderland* logic, but what the hell. The Duchess would have loved it.

*S*even

I pointed out to Mrs. d'Amboise that though men of fifty regularly become involved with young women of twenty-two, a youth of twenty-two just cannot be seen taking a girl of sixteen to a dance. This when my actual responses to the bijou contained a noticeable increase in what I had privately come to think of as the icky factor, or, in moments even more searchingly self-critical, the creep quotient. For I now realized that all the early coached vibrations in re the bijou, from the time when she was to be seen roller-skating in pigtails or sucking a lollipop on the front porch as she scratched her mosquito bites, had gone some way toward making a kind of short eyes out of me, a Humbert Humbert latent or otherwise. Now that our berry was ripening along, she grew each month more capable of arousing desire without yet eliminating its old concomitant, half-relished, shame.

I would try to cauterize these erotic arousals (to be laid squarely at Mrs. d'Amboise's door), would try to staunch them, I say, with decelerating, i.e., spiritualized, thoughts about "the rosebud age," or "dew of innocence," correctively murmuring such sentiments along with occasional lust-muf-

fling passages from Holy Writ, like "We have a little sister
and she hath no breasts; what shall we do for our sister in the
day when she shall be spoken for?" — from the Song of Sol-
omon, of course. But perverse variations then perversely
drafted themselves in my mind. "Now our sister hath something like unto twin doorbells there, as in a two-flat hallway,
is it not so? Doth that not seem to be the case? And the twain
would I fain ring, one in each hand, ting-a-*ling*. And unto
what shall I liken the crimson tips upon their crests, save
jujubes? Yea, unto little red jujubes will I liken them, such as
the penny-candy merchant hath and are obtainable in movie
lobbies, and which are sweet upon the tongue. And what
hath now begun to fringe the little gentian there betwixt
her . . . ?" Oh, good God, I would think to myself, you're
kinky as a telephone cord. Where would it all end? I would
breathe deeply in her presence to try to smell her bath soap,
scarcely knowing, as I inhaled her fragrance with closed eyes
and flexing nostrils and wondering what I would think if I
could see myself, whether the creep quotient was rising or
falling, only aware that the aftermath of girlhood bath lather
had a more acute intimacy than the costly perfumes of later
maturity — or was this merely the observation of a latent or
accomplished deviant? Perhaps you have some thoughts of
your own on the subject, and on my fancy that there lingers,
in the natural aura of young girls, certain overtones of milk.
Of course at some point the whole question of the creep
quotient would disappear, say when I was thirty to Colly's
twenty-four, but the memory of such an acknowledged icky
factor in one's past would disturbingly haunt, along with
the fear that it might crop up again anywhere and at any
time in another quarter, bringing disgrace on an outwardly
respectable pillar of the community who had just been
elected secretary-treasurer of something like the local San-
tayana Society. There was no precedent for anything of the
sort in my lineage save for a shirttail kin in Tennessee, a tea

and coffee sampler *manqué*, who took little girls on Sunday botany hikes in organized tours of one, but he was a relative by marriage. He was by my good mother scissored off his wedding picture, so that my aunt stood alone in the red velours frame on our piano top, one of those tall bony women with straight mouths who tell you that something or other won't butter any parsnips, or to save your breath to cool your porridge. No, the only forebear with any claim to sexual flamboyance remains the grandfather who picked up the nail in the fashionable European health spa.

"There is a semantics of numbers as well as of words," I explained to Mrs. d'Amboise, into whom I had again run on the street as I was hurrying toward a favored bar and grill, trailed by a detail of disciples in the first autumn cool. They withdrew a discreet distance, lounging against a storefront while I finished an encounter for which they sensed I had little stomach. The day was drawing near on which some of the d'Amboises had fixed as right for a ritual First Date with Columbine — the Pumpkin Ball annually held on Halloween at the country club to which the d'Amboises belonged. We Peachums did not, the admissions committee frowning on members reputed to emerge from hillside caverns in the spring and shamble along on all fours into the mainstream. Columbine would invite me as her guest if I would but give the sign. "If I were twenty-seven or -eight to her twenty-one or -two, yes, it might wash as a borderline thing," I continued. "But twenty-two and sixteen? She would be with an older man, and I a cradle snatcher." How I lusted for that girl! And what a load of guilt Mrs. d. would be dragging to Judgment Day!

"She'll be seventeen by the time the ball rolls around," Mrs. d. answered, "and she looks older — and you younger. After a haircut, you look nineteen." She went on to hint how, after all these years of my stated or at least implied intention to wait for the bijou (a fiction not to be dislodged from Mrs.

d.'s mind), the bijou had been safeguarded from importuning clods like Doug Haverstick, younger brother of Phooey Haverstick, early drawn into my magnetic field, but now regarded as a rival for Officer Kathy, at least in Vim's determined view.

Suddenly I found myself using a tone I never dreamed I should have taken with Mrs. d., even at her most vexing.

"Look. You must realize that in this day and age you can't expect a fellow to keep his vessels clean, as my Sunday School teacher used to say, until he's ready to get married," I rattled off, furtively pocketing a pretzel I had been munching when accosted. "We all have sex before we're out of high school. Or even into it!" I finished in a voice shrill with fear. Why was I always terrified of Mrs. d'Amboise?

The bells in Christ Church steeple boomed "Demnition bowwows, demnition bowwows," while fresh meteorites fell on Mocs and Pultusk in recognition of truths now to be borne by Mrs. d'Amboise: that adolescents, some of whom might be her own, regularly coupled in parked cars behind the school at an hour when decent folk were still having acid indigestion from orange juice at breakfast time. My eye faltered downward from Mrs. d'Amboise's groaning hat to the sidewalk while fragments of the pretzel crumbled in my fingers, like loose plaster from little Columbine's nursery ceiling in the nearby yet so distant past. Her cheeks went ashen while her lips twitched (evidently a family trait, as it recalled Ambrose when he broke the news about himself and Snooky) and her hands clutched spasmodically at a crewel bag woven of materials supplied by half the crazy string savers in Pocock.

"I quite ... quite ... liberalization. And I suppose some of my own ... Despite everything today about equality there *is* a double standard that remains instinctive with human nature. We don't disapprove so much of the male engaging in premarital nngaa."

"Or extramarital."

There was a silence, in the course of which Mrs. d. could be sensed gathering her forces for an even more conclusive recitative, like a diva drawing a few restorative breaths in an interim provided by an orchestra prolonging a few measures of respite composed for precisely such a purpose. I gazed upward at the sky, like an idler with nothing more on his mind than watching for the return of Christ. A girl ran by rolling a hoop with a stick, something I had never seen outside a de Chirico painting. A puff of wind plastered a page of newsprint to the base of a tree, displaying to advantage a fragment of headline: TOUGH OPTIONS FACE NEW ——, something hardly to be disputed the best of times.

Occasionally choking on a word, as though one might have to nip round and hug her from behind in the Heimlich to dislodge it from her throat, she granted that celibacy was perhaps too much to ask of a red-blooded youth in these days, then hurried large-mindedly on to assure me that my admission of prurience was taken as a show of honesty amounting to *moral* chastity, but that, as for the other principal in our drama, I would in due course, and at whatever age the numerical semantics might be deemed sufficiently resolved for courtship to begin in earnest, certainly be delivered a mint-fresh virgin. That could be counted on. She did everything but tell me they regularly fed Columbine calcium propionate to retard spoilage.

The quickest way out of the Pumpkin Ball was to plead a long shot then, which we actually had booked, eight rooms going to Galena, and then get myself scheduled for the job. Pinky and I loaded it the afternoon of the day before Halloween, to keep in the garage overnight for an early start to Galena, from which we would not return in time for the ball. The customers were moving out of a house on Raymond Street, where with streaming eyes the wife and mother watched the dismantlement of fourteen years of happiness in

Pocock, from which her husband's firm was cruelly transfer-
ring him. I felt guilty being a party to an obviously traumatic
wrench. "He's in aluminum siding," she sobbed, tweaking her
nose with a handkerchief sodden before we got the bed ends
out — which, if you care for arcane information, are among
the first things movers load after such delicacies as mirrors
and lamps are laid to rest in the cupola over the driver's
cabin. They are blanketed and upended behind the first tier.
Anyway. I saw her husband as sealed up inside the wall of
some capacious midwestern barn, his cries growing fainter
and fainter and at last fading into silence behind the aluminum siding he was in. A few disciples hung about, in keeping
with a practice that I be retinued whenever the faithful got
wind of my whereabouts, even loading or unloading a job.
The likelihood of any prickling insights was slight today,
though I did say as I backed up to the tailgate with a trunk
I was humping, "It is not true that some people need less
sleep than others. They simply sleep faster."

I was coming down the front-porch steps with an over-
stuffed chair on my head, slung over upside down in the traditional mover's carry, the back behind to afford a frontal
view, I know all this fascinates you, and had reached the
sidewalk when I heard a familiar voice. "Hey, Ted! That
you? Super."

The chair arms in such a case act as a pair of blinkers cur-
tailing side vision, so I had to turn to the right to bring
Columbine into sight. She was being walked home from high
school by a boy named Chuck Larsen. I had heard of him.
He was a jock rumored to be outshining my own mark on the
basketball court, though no threat to my memory as a stu-
dent, actor and orator. He seemed to be carrying Columbine's
books, for he was loaded down while she carried none. A
length of yellow yarn knotted into her back hair, she wore a
Buster Brown blouse momentarily reviving the icky factor,
and an equally girlish short pleated skirt also contributing

somewhat to the creep quotient. Despite all the cradle-robbing aspects, I felt a twinge of regret at not taking her to the Pumpkin Ball after all. She would wear a full-length frock, of course, no doubt sweep her hair up in adult fashion ... I drew a long, degenerate breath in hopes of catching a hint of body-bath soap, but was rewarded only by a musty whiff of long-sat-upon family upholstery. I shifted the position of the chair so as to ease the pressure of a loose spring against my skull — for the cushions are removed in carries like this.

Colly said: "We're on our way to the library." I was sure then the jock would be her escort tomorrow night. "Chuck has an assignment on General Semantics and doesn't know beans about it. I'll bet you do."

The chair wasn't going to Galena, but down the street a way to a family our customer, Mrs. Halverston, was giving it to, as a sort of goodbye souvenir, and so now Colly and Larsen, as well as the disciples, followed along as I made the short portage, expatiating on the semanticists. Mrs. Halverston drew up the rear with the cushion, sniffling ever more loudly as we approached this particular farewell.

"The first thing you must do is not confuse General Semantics with classic semantics — I. A. Richards and the meaning of meaning and all that," I said. "General Semantics ia a non-Aristotelian system founded by Alfred Korzybski, the purpose of which is to establish a discipline for human communication such as we have through symbols mostly, though not exclusively, linguistic."

"Jeez," Larsen was heard to murmur on my right and a little to my rear, and I had the feeling Colly had taken all his books so he might jot down as copious notes as possible, hoping not to fall off the sled before he had enough for a term paper. The failure of Harvard to take me became daily more incomprehensible. I shifted the chair on my head again and resumed.

"What are some of the Aristotelian principles the General Semanticists have sought to overturn? One is the principle of the excluded middle — the either/or principle. One either is or is not something. Not true, say the semanticists. One might be neither or both. Oh, in certain instances, yes, it would hold. Mrs. Halverston is or is not moving to Galena. With that there can be no quarrel. She *is moving to Galena*." Here another sob escaped the poor woman, louder than any yet. "Any middle here must be excluded. But as to the more essential proposition, 'She either will or will not be happy in Galena,' the semanticists say, 'Nonsense.' The answer must be that she will probably be both, now one, now the other, as it was with her here in Pocock, is with any of us anywhere. So-and-so either is or is not a criminal, says the law of the excluded middle. He may not be in the sense that he has never murdered anyone or committed armed robbery, but he has certainly stolen from the government by cheating a little on his income tax, taking more deductions such as entertainment and so on than he is strictly entitled to — which according to Aristotelian logic puts him in a category with Al Capone. Ergo, the law of the excluded middle, while conceivable on some plane of abstract logic, is not cogent for everyday judgments, where things must remain relative and nonabsolutistic. You may think of semantics, then, as another aspect of the age of relativity. It is Einsteinian rather than Aristotelian."

We had stopped for a traffic light, the house for which we were bound being a few doors beyond the first cross street — farther than I had been led to believe, as my aching shoulders testified. Peripatetic teaching was in this case complicated by my having to keep the weight of the chair lifted enough to ease the pressure on my head, and the strain on my arms and back was beginning to tell. The chair was an enormous wingback, slipcovered in a rather bilious green, which I could not imagine any recipient eagerly awaiting, yet there she was out on the sidewalk waving at our approach, a stoutish woman in a red house dress. The light changed, and our procession continued across the street.

"Another Aristotelian principle is that of identity: a thing is what it is. Again not so, say the semanticists — or, rather, what have you said when you say that? A thing is any number of things to any number of people under ceaselessly changing conditions, so that indeed it can be a number of things to the same person at different times. You might tuck in a little Proustian divagation here," I said to the jock, whom I still could not see but who could in fact be heard scribbling away like mad on a notepad. "The woman waiting for us up ahead," I puffed, "what is her name?"

"Lolly Greenleaf," Mrs. Halverston sobbed, "and a finer, more — "

"To Mrs. Halverston (herself already several different entities to several of us) she is a dear friend from whom she is taking her eternal farewell."

"Oh, my God," Mrs. Halverston wailed afresh, choking in her handkerchief. "Never to have those cups of tea together again, so cozy together, talking things over — "

"There, there," I said. Though nothing on either side was visible to me, I could imagine the scene on my right, where Colly and one or two of the disciples were also "There, thereing," and "Now, nowing," no doubt trying to comfort Mrs. Halverston with their arms around her shoulders. I began to get a little worried. This was not the first case I had seen of a woman becoming hysterical at being wrenched from her nest and whisked off to some strange and distant city. We'd had one actual nervous breakdown, so severe the job was called off. I now regretted having introduced Mrs. Halverston into the elucidation, though on the other hand it was probably just as well for her to get it out of her system. "Could you take another example?" the jock asked. "She's pretty chopped up."

"I was only going to say that the woman up ahead is to Mrs. Halverston what we now know, tea with Lolly and all that, but to her husband something altogether different, of which Mrs. Halverston may not have the slightest inkling — "

"He's a saint," she said.

"Right, right. And to her children something else again, a mother now loving, now stern, now both together. To me, a total stranger toward whom I am carrying a chair I won't have to cart to Galena. Mrs. Greenleaf has a daughter who meets a painter. To the daughter he's an artist with all the glamor invested in the word. To Mr. Greenleaf, a bookkeeper in a hat factory — "

"He's a teller in a bank," Mrs. Halverston said.

"Whatever. These are all hypothetical cases. To him, the artist is somebody who probably won't be able to support his daughter," I said, stumbling up the short flight of stairs to Lolly Greenleaf's front porch, where I dropped the chair and sank into it up to my eyeballs, not waiting for the cushion to be put back, "to the mother, a bohemian with no morals out to seduce her daughter, and so forth and so on. Thus," I panted to the jock, "we have a human entity who is three entirely different things to as many separate people, a far, far cry from the fixed Aristotelian identity of *a thing is what it is.* Korzybski asks that in human intercourse we remain fluidly conscious of abstracting only a partial truth of what we denote with our words, that there is the eternal et cetera, that it is all relative, or, as Alfred North Whitehead put it, a word has no meaning apart from the context in which it is used."

"... no ... meaning ... context ... used," the jock said as he scribbled away at high speed. "Gee, thanks, Mr. Peachum. That's great."

"When the late Justice Oliver Wendell Holmes was a young man, he wrote an attack on Plato and showed it to Emerson, who read it in silence, shook his head, and said,

'When you shoot at a king, you must kill him.' Whether Korzybski has killed Aristotle I leave up to you. But that in a nutshell is his philosophy, as popularized by his disciple Hayakawa, now, of course, a United States Senator. It is resisted in academic quarters that remain strongholds of the Aristotelian discipline, contemporary examples of what I would call the nostalgia for the absolute."

The jock helped me get the chair into the parlor, which involved wrangling it through a narrow doorway on its side. Then we all trooped back to the truck, Mrs. Halverston coming along after a damp leave-taking. That was not the last of the emotion charging the job. Mrs. Halverston spotted another neighbor woman approaching with bags of groceries in both arms, and rushed up to embrace a dear friend she would likewise never see again. On the tailgate, Pinky, half overcome himself, turned away and ejected a stream of chewing-tobacco juice into the street. "This is a dirty business," he said, wiping his chin. Mrs. Halverston stepped back from her friend and exclaimed, "I want you to have something as a memento too. That lamp you always liked. The alligator one we brought back from Florida? Get it out again," she ordered Pinky. "It's the one you put the bulb in its mouth."

Pinky's jaw dropped so far I thought the quid of chewing tobacco would fall out of his mouth.

"Lady, that lamp is in the cupola we call it. *Over the front seat.* It's three tiers back. We'll have to tear out the entire load."

"I don't care." The woman did seem on the verge of hysteria, not entirely responsible. "Get it."

"Lady, let me reason with you."

"Just try."

"I'll show you the light."

"I double dog dare you." Christ, that expression went back beyond my father's day. I remembered it dimly from some play I'd seen.

"Lady," Pinky said, putting a palm against the side of the van and crossing one foot over the other, in an attitude often struck when dealing with intransigents or undertaking a task of rational persuasion, "you're being charged a flat rate for this haul. Not by the hour the way a local job is. If you were paying the per-hour rate for two men we wouldn't care. *You'd* be paying for the extra work taking this whole load apart and putting it together again. But it just ain't fair when the boss is giving you a flat rate where that wasn't anticipated and can't be taken into account."

It seemed good therapy to me, but the woman said: "I want her to have it."

"Send it to her. It'll be cheaper, believe me, because before I tear the seams out of this load and put her together again, I'm going to get the boss on the phone and let him tell you personally the extra money it's going to cost you to dig out an alligator lamp with a bulb in his mouth. Forty dollars an hour for two men."

Here the neighbor woman herself came over, protesting.

"Please, Ev, he's right. It would really be too much trouble. It's sweet of you, but — "

"I want you to have a remembrance of us."

With that, Mrs. Halverston hiked up her skirt and sprang onto the tailgate. She rolled back a barrel with which Pinky had begun the base for a new tier and began to rummage inside it. She undid dish after dish from the newspapers in which they had been wrapped, and a third of the way down came upon what she was looking for, a cut-glass cream pitcher, which she handed the woman from the tailgate. "I want you to have this keepsake. My mother brought it from Sweden."

"I'll think of you every time I pour something."

Another last embrace and the neighbor made for home with the gift riding precariously on the crest of one of the grocery bags. Pinky swiftly recomposed the barrel of dishes while I plugged back into the house for some more base.

Colly and the jock were still around when I emerged with a trunk on my back.

"A third Aristotelian principle," I said, dropping it on the tailgate.

When I got home from Galena next day, about a quarter to ten, a sad but familar scene awaited me. My parents sat at the kitchen table playing out separate hands of solitaire (oh, God, the pity), the rubble of the evening meal between them. Some chicken bones, potato jackets, a heel of pumpernickel. Although we had always dined fashionably late, we ate in the kitchen, like Milton. Pa was cracking nuts with a pair of pliers, something he sometimes enjoyed doing with a monkey wrench, for the unadulterated hell of it, turning the screw slowly till the hull cracked, like a medieval Christian tormentor racking a heretic. He seemed to be trying to extract a retraction from the walnut before it was too late.

He went to the refrigerator and foraged about there for leftovers, returning with a ham end and some cheese, with which he began to build a sandwich. He was fueling up for another seasonal sleep, the indications were there; under his unbuttoned shirt was visible what seemed an especially thick mat of dark hair, to be noted in keeping with the view that at this time of year the density of his outer coat, as well as other signs, offered a clue as to the severity of the forthcoming winter. The evidence, corroborated by what was being said about the woolly caterpillar, pointed to a long and hard one. He heated up a frozen pizza, to be eaten covered with maple syrup.

"Any messages for me?" I asked.

"Listen to him," my mother said. "People like us don't get messages."

"He'll get messages," my father said, adjusting the oven. "You'll see. When he moves to New York. He'll get messages and people will take him to the Harvard Club for working lunches with the other smoothies. And they won't see him come out till two-thirty, quarter to three. Right, Ted?"

While my father painted a picture of urban savoir-faire in which long-legged secretaries suspended buffing their nails long enough to put wretches on hold for my convenience, my mother continued dispensing the gloom to be detected the instant I'd stepped into the house: the aggressive depression of a woman seeing to it that no one in her presence will be happy while she is miserable. That was one of the dependable fallouts of marriage, working the other way around too, I suspected, with a husband in the dumps. "A woman is a glandular disaster," my father explained.

"That's what you always say," my mother said, gathering up her cards for a fresh hand, then throwing them down on the table. Two or three of them landed in the butter. Trying to cheer her up would have been as hopeless as the attempt, before leaving Galena, to buck up Mrs. Halverston, who in the same tendentious gloom had tried to give us half her crockery — "so as much of me as possible will remain in Pocock." Wherever was Mr. Halverston? She had finally forced the alligator lamp on Pinky, partly as punishment for his refusing to dig it out of the cupola in the first place. He said he was going to give it to my mother, who liked nice things.

I don't know why I bathed and shaved in a rush, dressed up, and hurried over to the Pumpkin Ball, except to test my sensations as I peered through a window from the country club veranda at the sight of Colly dancing in another's arms, for some light they might shed on possibly unsavory elements within myself. The result was only to add voycurism to current proclivities. As I peeped in, between scalloped draperies, she was dancing with a dark-haired bloke I didn't know, but when the number was over she returned to Larsen in a manner leaving no doubt the jock was her escort. She was in the expected long dress, an orchid pinned to the bodice, and had indeed swept her hair up, but with the girlish flush on her face the effect was like that of a child playing grown-up. What I felt made me remember a similar twinge of appetite, a few years back, when I'd seen her wobbling along the sidewalk in front of her house on a pair of her mother's high-heeled shoes, a fur around her neck and an enormous bag slung on one arm. I shook my head as I turned and picked my way back across the veranda to the stone stairs. I was losing ground. The prognosis was not good.

Since dress was optional there were as many men in business suits as tuxedos, so I passed unchallenged in my gray pinstripe among the crowd spilling out of the clubhouse for a breath of the unseasonably balmy night, drinks and smokes in hand. With the bash boiling along at this stage, nobody was asked for his credentials, whether club membership card or invitation, and I could mingle as freely as I wished — at least outside. All I had to do was keep a sharp eye peeled for any lurking d'Amboises. And even if I was collared by one of the special police and thrown back onto Schenk Street, it was better than sitting home watching my father scratch himself and listening to his apothegms. Woman a glandular disaster indeed! Where had he picked up that little nugget? Probably some newsmagazine cover story on the menopause in his doctor's office. It had originally been "casualty," but he had raised it to "disaster."

As I strolled out of the light into the shadows of a serpentine gravel path, smoking a cigarette, whom should I see coming toward me, also taking a turn under the stars, but Mrs. d'Amboise, resplendent in an apple-green gown, a tiara in her hair. I ground my teeth till I could smell the friction. The hollow truncheon was in this case of course a ball program.

"I see you got back from Galena," she said, administering the ritual tap on my nose.

"Earlier than we. But still too late to. So I thought I'd. Just for the nngaa."

"Leland hates dancing, and it's hot inside, so I went out for a stroll. What are you doing?"

"Out to tell the rose how the brief night goes in babble and revel and wine."

"Isn't that from Tennyson?"

"More or less."

She tilted her head a few degrees to the left in order that she might look at me askance as, unpursing a tiny smile, she said: "I know you. Just making sure our bijou wasn't being a wallflower, and, satisfied that she's escorted, and not a pathetic little figure huddling all alone on the sidelines, moving along. A gentleman to his fingertips. I've always said it, and I'll say it again."

"You will?" I said, laughing nervously.

"And with the courtly grace to hide the very courtly grace that made him dress up, after a hard day's work, and come all the way over to make sure."

"Don't tell Colly."

"I shan't." Shan't, for God's sake? Did she also say catsup? Probably. Anyone who will say the one will say the other. "It'll be our secret. One that'll make me twice the ally I was, to your cause." Tap.

"That won't be necessary."

"But meanwhile, never fear. This boy means nothing to her. Oh, handsome enough, in the obvious sort of way, and quite the jock at the moment. Just as you were in your day, slam-dunking them in from center court. But really with little else going for him." Mrs. d'Amboise drew a long, open-mouthed breath, one that made me fear she might have sucked in a good lot of the tiny insects that seemed to be pullulating in the year-end reprieve, like a nightjar ingesting its evening meal. "Look, we're running out to Indiana for one last weekend next Friday, if the weather holds good. Why don't you come along?"

"Not by a damn sight."

"Yes, the cottage. Leland was all set to board it up for the

winter, but I persuaded him to let's try for one more weekend, and invite Ted Peachum."

"Colly may prefer Larsen. I mean I assume she'll be
along?"

"He's been to By a Dam Site. Believe me, there's nothing
between them. Zilch, as you young people say. Well, I must
get back in. We leave Friday about three. Leland has booked
no patients after two."

I was mulling over this surprising construction of my motive for coming here, which at least had a limpidity lacking
in my own murky interpretations, and weighing its potential
for deepening my own already confused relations with the
d'Amboises, when I saw in the alternating light and shadow
between the intermittent postlamps a ball of twine floating
toward me slowly at about eye level. Emergence from shade
into a full glow terminated the hallucination I should have
liked to see prolonged indefinitely; for the figure owning this
head of flaxen hair seemed to be still another d'Amboise,
namely Luke, the one threatening to clean my clock if I
didn't do the right thing by Columbine after setting her
a-tremble, etc. But that was a hallucination too. Because it
turned out to be a brother closely resembling him, Islip,
another of the three children who had inherited the father's
towhead rather than the mother's raven locks. He was wearing a dark-blue suit with chalkstripes of a width associated
with someone who had just deposited in the Chicago River
a colleague with his feet encased in cement. Islip, however,
was a strongly conventional middle-class type who owned a
flourishing lumberyard. A man of few words. It was said that
he was so laconic you couldn't tell whether he was speaking to you or not. But he got enough off his chest in this
brief encounter to emphasize that there were definitely two
schools of thought about me in the d'Amboise clan. He had
never cottoned to older boys "taking notions" about, or "having yens" for, young girls. It was against nature, like decaf-
feinated tea.

"Hello, Islip. Nice night."

"Look, fellow," he said. "Colly's here with somebody her own age and speed, see. I don't know who you're here with, if anybody, or just seeing what you can scrounge up for yourself to take into your car, but I'm telling you for the last time. If you don't keep the hell away from Colly I'll clean your clock. I'll fix your wagon, but good."

"Right."

"You dig?"

"Yes, but listen. I'm a decent, hard-working sort with more than one thing on his mind. Just look at these hands. Have you ever seen anything so horny?"

"I'm sure they are, and you just better make damn good and sure you keep them to yourself."

"Check."

So I was to have my clock cleaned no matter what course I took. A fine kettle of carp indeed. He fixed me with a sharp eye as we stood in silence a moment.

"You here with anybody?" Islip demanded at last.

"No."

"I see. Just out trying to scare up some gash for yourself."

"Not at all. Oh, in the long run we all, I mean over the long haul — "

"What's your game?"

"Why, I just thought I'd sort of, kind of, oh, like, drift with every passion till my soul is a stringed lute on which all winds can play."

"See that you do."

"Right. Islip," I said, "there's an old Chinese proverb," and walked away at an oblique angle, leaving him standing there with his mouth open.

Moseying on through the grounds gate and across Schenck Street to a bar, I ordered a stein of beer and began to muse over a boyhood incident connected with the country club. I had gone to it without permission to watch the fireworks, one Fourth of July when I was nine or ten, and come home well after midnight. My punishment the next day was typical for that time of year. "Get into your long woolens," my father said. The temperature was in the nineties, and my memory of that sweltering day was still vivid. My father prided himself on "never resorting to corporal punishment, never laying a hand on a child." Ordering me into winter underwear on hot summer days he did not regard as corporal punishment. It was interesting to speculate on what variant he would have contrived for the winter months if he hadn't been asleep most of the time then, leaving disciplinary measures to my mother, who relied on less inventive devices like confining me to my room or suspending my allowance.

On a relatively empty stomach, the beer plus a bourbon and soda took effect, and I felt rather lightheaded as I backtracked to the club in a vaguely insurrectionary mood. The din of the ball, now roaring on toward midnight, again met my ears as I sauntered through the gate and up the serpentine path. "If you knew Susie like I know Susie," came booming through the open windows. At a turn in the path, my eye caught a glint of metal and the twirl of a nightstick as someone rounded the shrubbery toward me. I recognized Officer Kathy d'Amboise — or rather Officer Arpeggio, as she went by her maiden name — patrolling the grounds in uniform. We had had second breakfasts a few times in Mama Mia's diner, each time with a distinct pleasure in each other's company as we roosted over our coffee at the counter. Parting kisses had each time been more than cursory pecks, at least on my part who aimed for the mouth, and without serious deflection. I could well credit Vim's confidence that there was electricity between us. It must be clear to me if he could sense it as a bystander. Whether Kathy heard woodwinds at the touch of my lips was for her to say, and maybe she would tonight, was the mad thought that seized me. I was tipsy enough to hope we could neck in the prowl car, if she had come in it. She had, with an Officer O'Malley, with whom she was dividing the premises, he on the inside, she out, challenging crashers but mostly on the watch for a gang of punks from the other end of town who often caused trouble at affairs like this, and who had threatened to "start a rumble with the pinky lifters."

"What are you doing here? Somebody's guest?"

"No. I was having a few at Tony's, and thought I'd wander over for the hell of it. Will you have to throw me out as an interloper?" I thought the subtle reminder that we were both from the wrong side of the tracks, my father a mover and hers a garbage man, would do my cause no harm.

"I'll let it pass. But you can't go in."

"Who wants to go in?" I went for broke. "Where's your car? Could we sit in it a spell and tell sad stories of the death of kings?"

She consulted her wristwatch in a delaying motion jammed with uncertainty. Why did Kathy in full panoply, pistol, truncheon, the works, seem only the more fragile and feminine? Something shot along the surface of my heart, like cracking ice, at the thought of all that honey-colored hair bunched up under her patrolman's cap. "Twenty-five to twelve. I guess the punks won't come anymore. Do you know they call themselves the Galahads, of all things?" she said as we cut across the grass to a relatively secluded spot behind some tennis courts where the patrol car was parked. "What's that from again, about 'for God's sake let us sit upon the ground and tell sad stories of the death of kings'?"

"*Richard II,*" I said, my voice hoarse with desire. "The ground will be too damp." I had taken her hand, and now we separated long enough to climb into opposite sides of the front seat. She had discontinued the ponytail and let her hair grow, and bathing my fingers in the soft whorls of gold released when I plucked off her cap was joy in itself. My hands wandered inevitably downward to her shoulders, and my arms gathered her in.

"Jesus," I whispered as I crushed my mouth to hers, which opened like a piece of split fruit, spilling its tongue readily against my own. The kiss must have lasted for five minutes, after which she drew away and gasped into my ear, "You're coming on like a mustang. Not that I — "

"We've had this date for a long time. That's from something too, I forget what."

"A play, yes. Am I a disgrace to this uniform?"

"No. Can we go in the back seat?" I looked madly through the screen separating us from that possible haven, installed for protection against malefactors being chauffeured to headquarters. "It's a little roomier."

"Oh, we can't do that. Ted, for God's sake."

No doubt the drinks contributed to my imprudence, but a long season of frustration, disappointment, uncertainty, confusion and bottled-up desires was mainly behind the rush of emotion that made me want to take her then and there. I unbuttoned her jacket and shirt and drew a breast from its brassiere, and put my mouth to it, circling its hardened nib with my tongue while she lay back in the seat with little moans of pleasure. There is after all nothing like being suckled by a willing woman. I grated my teeth very gently against the buds. "Bite me just a tiny bit harder. Not too much. Now your tongue again. Oh, my God." The sound of the dance band beat like a distant surf. "You're My Everything." Footsteps and laughing voices nearby made us both stiffen alertly, but they instantly receded, and I resumed my importunities.

Deploying my right hand slowly downward along her waist, I tried to unzip her trousers, but first had to contend with her cartridge belt, after which in a supplementary maneuver with my left hand I bruised my knuckles against the butt of her revolver. To be a pistol, oneself, under such conditions is difficult, and certainly poses a strain on the subtleties of amorous persuasion. My contention with her armaments brought a stiff-arm to my jaw that testified to fruitful hours of training at the Police Academy indeed. My tax-payer's money seemed to have been well spent. "Aw, I'm sorry," she said when I let out a yelp of protest, and the lull in her resistance sent me back to the attack with renewed zest. We were now fighting as well as making love, in an amalgam of emotion for which a large glossary is of course now available. The sex war in its most consummate sense, complete with everything including role reversal, the scene would have warmed the cockles of feminist and male-chauvinist hearts alike. Her superiority in pugilistic tech-niques as such, to say nothing of the scale on which she was mechanized, made her the man and me the woman — so the glossary would run — while my sheer muscle-bustin', piano-moving strength kept me very much the man and her the woman, in this writhing, panting, acutely contemporary clash-courtship that sealed, dramatized and encapsulated the truth of Freud's final conclusion: that there is so much of both sexes in all of us that whenever a male and a female make love there are four people in bed together. Or in a prowl car.

What Kathy wanted was to go to bed. I couldn't wait. At the risk of jeopardizing future dalliances between the sheets, *I had to take her in uniform.* At least once. Laughing her own only-half-mirthful laugh, I seized her wrists and pinned them against the back of the seat. "Let — me — go, you nut," she panted. The tussle passed into a sort of frenetic romp as I released one of her arms to unfasten her service belt. Having yanked its buckle loose, I unzipped her trousers, half won-dering what I would find inside them. She arched her back in order to bounce my loins off hers, which enabled me to reach behind and hook my hand around the now unbuckled service belt, where it encountered a pair of handcuffs, a short-wave radio and what I took to be a pad of arrest tickets stick-ing up out of a hind pocket, and with one single determined heave I pulled everything down along with the trousers: revolver, cartridges, handcuffs, radio, arrest tickets, and the sheathed nightstick, everything, with a sense of having made contemporary history. So that no grandchildren could ever ask what I had done during the sex war without getting a solid answer.

In the heat and smoke of this embrace we hadn't heard fresh footsteps, so we were both surprised to see a policeman's head thrust in at the window on Kathy's side.

"Is anything — ? Oh, I'm sorry, I just thought — "

"Oh, hello, O'Malley. Everything is — I was just meeting my friend, for a second," Kathy said, wriggling back into her clothes with a series of gymnastics defter than any seen so far. "Officer O'Malley, I'd like you to meet Ted Peachum."

But O'Malley had turned and was striding away with what I found as perfect an exemplification of law and order as I ever hope to see.

Tidied up, Kathy sat with an elbow on the wheel, her head lowered in her hand, laughing as she shook it. "I should write you up."

My own mood was more troubled. What was the matter with me? First, being turned on by everything about Snooky von Sickle that Schopenhauer deplored, mad for her just because she was a mare and not despite it. Second, I had been harboring unmistakable desires for someone still a child. And tonight I had tried to rape a cop.

Ought I to seek help?

$\mathcal{E}$ight

Everyone loves a plank. Who could not? The proportions are perfect no matter how great the length, the width and breadth being able to meet any challenge to symmetry the length might pose, within reason. A plank makes a hit with one and all. Failure to respond to a plank argues a deficiency in makeup. The satisfaction of seeing a plank, in addition to the purely dimensional, is replete with associations conscious and unconscious: memories of playing in or on or among them in buildings under construction in our childhood neighborhood; of using one to improvise a teeter-totter on a rock, or a bridge across a muddy stretch of barnyard, or to prop a closet pole sagging with the weight of clothing that might otherwise fall to the floor in a heap, causing marital discord and even rupture and divorce as blame is apportioned and recriminations fly, possibly even the use of firearms. "Oh, my God. What have I done? But it wasn't the last straw. Well, I suppose it was, but giving me a bran muffin with a candle in it for breakfast on my birthday, that started it, the day. I just grabbed his shotgun and then everything went blank. Oh, my God. And on my birthday." A plank opportunely wedged under the closet pole might have prevented all that.

Gangplanks and diving boards are among the images with which a plank is subliminally aswarm, I continued to my disciples, for the reader will have guessed that the disquisition begun above was one I delivered while in fact carrying a one-by-eight across town one afternoon a few weeks after the attempted rape of Officer Arpeggio in the prowl car, an incident radically elevating the creep quotient in my plunging estimate of myself. The board was of a length requiring me to stand back some distance from the curb as we waited for a traffic light to change, which let me note that only three of the faithful had come clustering when the word was out that I was about. Evidence mounted of rather an apostasy among my disciples, who complained that my stuff was becoming too discursive. It lacked the pithiness of the early, vintage, Peachum. Nevertheless, I resumed the comments, as I did the trip to the widow woman from whom I had borrowed this lumber.

Everyone will turn to watch a man carrying a plank down the street (I dilated). In addition to the above factors, there is the uneasy hilarity of his possibly smacking somebody in the face when rounding a corner, evoking the rich jumble of silent-film–farce memories. That happened now as we swung right on Pocock and struck out along Wilcox, even to the ritualized sequence of hitting a second victim when turning to apologize to the first.

A plank has an elegance of proportion forever denied a two-by-four. A plank always comes off, not true of a two-by-four, a far more plebeian thing, wholly lacking in linear finesse. Planks protruding far out over the tailgate of a truck, a red flag fluttering from their extremities, have something a similar load of two-by-fours do not, say what you will.

Everyone loves to carry a plank on his shoulder, or to see another doing so —

"You said that," protested what I now perceived was the only remaining disciple, the others having fled like Byzantines. He gave notice by delicate but firm insinuation that he was only sticking because he was going my way anyway, and even so might choose the other side of the street to keep out of earshot of such turgidities. Turgidities! I do not find them so, how about you, all you Jaspers out there? He urged that I hop my material up a little, firstly cutting it *away* down, sharply gingering up what was left. This stuff about planks really drug in the middle, however esoteric I myself might think it. For hacks, he would as lief be home curled up with Deuteronomy. Even boiling it down to an apothegm wasn't anything on which he pinned any particular hopes, since my zingers themselves had fallen to the level of Chinese fortune cookies. "Advice is wasted on him who will not heed it," were my words as remembered from a few weeks before when I was going the other way with the same plank, having just picked it up at the home of the old lady from whom I had borrowed it.

Chief among the pleasures of carrying a plank across town is the exhilaration of sensing its equilibrium within oneself, with which one toys, removing one's hands and letting it ride unsteadied on one's shoulder. All the laws of physics are embodied in the figure pedestrians stop to watch pass. They would like to be carrying the plank themselves, or another like it. Look at them all, standing back to get a better view. A plank never misses . . .

When I reached the small cottage on Diamond Street for which I was bound, I learned to my regret that the woman had died. Her brother, a one-legged railroad-crossing tender *manqué*, was the only one about. He had lived with her for the past mumble mumble. They had been close all their mumble mumble. Ever since as little children they had lived together, growing up in mumble mumble Minnesota. From what I was able to piece together from other sources later, for I was interested, he was reputed to have been himself responsible for three accidents at his crossing, and had then been retired on half-pension by the railroad company.

"Keep the plank," he said.

"Oh, I couldn't."

"I don't want it, and she has no use for it, now."

"That's true enough."

"She'd want you to have it. You seem to like planks."

"I have a thing about them. This one's walnut, and that's valuable lumber these days," I reminded him decently.

"What did you want it for?" the brother asked curiously, shifting his weight off the wooden leg. I wondered whether he himself mightn't have been a victim of one of the mishaps his negligence or incompetence had precipitated. In a way I hoped so, since that would greatly have mitigated the burden of guilt he must carry through life, until he went to join his sister in Fairlawn.

"To wheel a heavy lawn mower into a station wagon, which I also had to borrow from a friend, to take to a repair shop," I said. "I had one plank at home and needed another like it, to make a sort of skid to load and unload this heavy mower. Roll it in. I saw this board leaning against the side of the house here, and stopped and asked whether I might borrow it."

"Well, you keep it. You may need it again."

"That's true. I've got the power mower back, but I never know when I'll have to have it repaired again after I start using it come spring. It's a lemon."

"I'm sorry to hear that."

"Well, thanks. I'll be running along now. I'm sorry to hear about your sister, you being so close and all. She was a good woman."

On the walk back, I picked up a couple of fresh disciples, newcomers who had not yet got wind of my decline — a slump certainly traceable in part at least to the tension and confusion bedeviling my sex life in practically every quarter. Before much could pass in the way of verbal intercourse, we ran into the Prophet haranguing a street crowd of seven or eight, and stopped to listen. I set the plank on end, holding it so on the outer rim of the crowd.

" 'Up yours,' saith the Lord God of hosts. 'I've had it up to here with all you dingbats.' Now learn a parable of the dishwasher," the Prophet said, striking what had become a new note. "It hath completed a cycle and is full of clean vessels, purged of all the *coq au vin,* beef stroganoff and cherries jubilee with which you have been stuffing your heathen guts in your mad determination to outdo the Roman Empire. One taketh this out of the dishwasher, another that, a cup and saucer, a bowl, some spoons or forks, *without unloading it.* Others then put back this used plate, that fork, and so on, till half the load is clean and half dirty again, and it must all be run over. Thus in the frailty of human resolve our souls are soiled no more than they have just been cleansed, and none of us is not filthy in some wise. Partially purged are we at best, through our own efforts, and all stand in need of that divine redemption by grace which I bring unto you."

That was certainly an apt enough metaphor for my own state of affairs at the time, no more tidied up here than mucked up there, and applied well enough to human life in general, if it came to that, all you Jaspers out there. While not in the Prophet's best vein, it showed that his stuff at least wasn't sagging, or wanting in point and concision. Whether he would make the big time — Isaiah, Jeremiah, and all that bunch — remained to be seen. He might land somewhere among the minor prophets, provided his material held up, with a few really top-drawer moments, as we get in Micah, not on balance an oracle of the first order. But a rather ominous note was being struck here with the talking in parables, along with such references as that to divine redemption, "which I bring unto you." If the comparison deliberately invited became chronic, it might mean he was bucking for messiahship. I had always thought trying for minor seer, hoping to land, say, somewhere between Obadiah and Habakkuk, was the more prudent course, like that of movie actors who enter the Academy Awards competition by weighing in as featured players rather than principals, to increase their chances of winning an Oscar. But we would have to see.

The Prophet moved off and I shoved along too, each with his straggle of followers.

"A plank has a geometric felicity all its own," I told the new recruits, now carrying the board on top of my head as we threaded our way at a brisk trot through the dispersing crowd. By shifting into second, so to speak, I was deliberately testing the loyalty of the novitiates in attendance. Also, the suspicion that I had an appointment for something or other that afternoon nagged at the back of my mind, but I couldn't for the life of me remember what it was. "Enforcing posture, it confers an elegance on the bearer by transmitting to his limbs a sense of equipoise both fore and aft, and whether carrying it on his shoulder or otherwise. That is why everyone loves to carry a plank. Two buckets of water just drawn from a well suspended from either end of a pole balanced on the shoulder is the archetypally beautiful *functional* sight among the ancients — " I paused in midflight, sensing something wrong with the sentence, taking the occasion also to stop and see who was still listening. Only a single diehard flanked me, and he was muttering something about the set piece being an improvement on fortune cookies, but not much. Then he was not all that new, being privy to recent deteriorations? I couldn't place him. The face didn't seem familiar. But his attention was clearly flagging. Perhaps a little Freudian filth would pick us up.

"The vaginal symbolism of the fortune cookie must not have escaped even the Chinese bakers molding them into that suggestive shape, or certainly not the mandarins who sat tittivating by their mountain pools, or on the Yangtze studied out their beards," I said, throwing in a little Wallace Stevens as a vindictive gesture aimed at Ambrose, that self-appointed authority on the poet. (He claimed even to understand "The Emperor of Ice Cream," whose meaning had eluded the likes of Edmund Wilson.) "Mark that the dough is folded over not once, but twice, so that the synonymous crevice is not lost on even the most abstracted muncher as he breaks it in his fingers to discover the secret within . . ."

The disciple had gone, pleading some just-recalled business as he made off obliquely up a side street. All that was listening was Mrs. d'Amboise. She lacked a tubular truncheon with which to tap me on the nose to emphasize her point, but as she stood in my path her face was a study in scarlet distraction.

"We've been looking all over for you. Didn't you get it straight — that we were to leave at three? It's nearly half-past now."

"Leave?"

"For the lake. Dam Site."

"Oh, that's today. I knew there. Then it completely. Things have been so. I'm terribly sorry. I guess I thought it was next week."

"Leland and Colly have the car all packed and ready to go. Your mother said you had to go to Diamond Street to return a plank. That's in the other direction."

"The people from whom I lent it gave it me." "Gave it me" was Mrs. d'Amboise talk. It went with shan't and catsup, and filled me with self-loathing.

"Then you're going home," Mrs. d'Amboise said, now falling into a fresh gallop beside me as we turned a corner and headed on up Pocock. There was no unquixotic question of making her adjust her stride to mine: it was I who was put to it to keep up with her, a dedicated jogger in the trimmest fettle. We settled into a stride tolerable to both of us. "I suppose all you need do is throw a few things into a suitcase. Why, what was it you were talking to yourself about when I bumped into you? Something about fortune cookies and old Chinese by their mountain pools, and what not."

"It was nothing. Will Islip be there?"

"No, no. Just the four of us. Plenty of room to rattle around in. The water will still be warm, though the day isn't the brightest."

We cantered along in a silence unbroken save for our measured breathing. Long peripatetic habit had made me instinctively consider anyone flanking or tailing me as a devotee awaiting the next pungency. Rolling an eye at the rows of tidy cottages between which we sped, I observed, "And just to think that not so long ago all this was overrun with howling redskins."

The weather was, indeed, not up to weekend scratch. Skies were of that gray associated with oyster stew and sweatsuits. But the air was warm enough. One had no kick coming, considering the time of year. Colly and I sat in the back seat of the capacious station wagon in which we tooled southward out of Pocock through suburbs bearing names you know to have a greater cachet — Winnetka, Evanston, Wilmette — struck out along Chicago's waterfront Gold Coast, swung northward beyond the city limits up around the penis tip of Lake Michigan, and headed at last into the Indiana dunes, near which nestled the fabled By a Dam Site, or BADS, in the acronym that had fixed itself in my mind. On my left, in a crisp print dress, Colly smelled fragrantly again of bath soap, which I inhaled with the old depravity as she chattered away in the charming effort to prove herself a grown lady.

"You could tell Mother's not a midwesterner, right?" she said, "by the way she pronounces Michigan." Mrs. d. had just been extolling the splendors of the lake. "You and I and Pop

all say Mishigan. She puts that 't' in it that lots of, um, east-
erners do. And prolly Europeans."

"Auden pronounces it Mitchigan too," I said.

"Oh, really? I hadn't realized that. You prolly heard him
on one of his records. Our English teacher played some of
them in class, but I don't remember that."

"Can you recall the exact line?" Mrs. d. asked, twisting
around in the front seat.

"No, but I'll look it up," I said. "I'll definitely check into
it. You're in good company anyway. In fact Auden would
probably say Tchicago too, as lots of people do. Why don't
you do that, Mrs. d'Amboise?"

"I used to, matter of fact, but Leland put his foot down.
Didn't you, dear?"

"I certainly did," Leland said, intent on his driving.

"I've mended my ways there, and I shall on Mitchigan."

"Oh, don't, Mother. We like you to stay quaint. Don't we,
Ted?"

"Hell, yes."

After two hours of conversation of fluctuating literacy, we
veered right to a small town five miles east of the lake, on
the outskirts of which stood the resort cottage, an eight-room
shingled house on the bank, sure enough, of a stream with a
dam said to have provided a millrace for an eighteenth-century flour mill. There was no sign of any mill now, but of
course the dam had been grist enough for the creative powers of the bygone property owner whose whimsies were to
enthrall generations yet unborn. And of course the hurrying
water made a pleasant sound, though I had to fight the phonetic rendering *shrdlu, shrdlu* which got its obsessive hooks
into my head.

After I had been shown into the sole downstairs bedroom,
the d'Amboises all trooped upstairs to bedrooms on the second floor, along which ran a deck forming part of the ceiling
of the large studio living room. There being only showers up-

stairs, Colly used "my" tub for the hot bath in which she liked to soak before dinner. "God, she takes two or three baths a day," Leland said as he squatted at the hearth to light a fire against the expected evening chill. No wonder she always smelled of soap. "The cleanest girl I know," Mrs. d. called from the see-through kitchen, probably to deflect Leland from discoursing on the psychological significance of bathing habits. The positions in sleep had long since been exhausted as conversation fodder, along with gestures and body language in general (there is apparently no human posture safe from psychoanalytical sleuthing) but ablutions might be open to exegesis.

"I think bathing a good deal is a healthy sign," I said, my own thoughts far from deserving that adjective as I listened to the water drumming into "my" tub, and imagined the bijou slipping out of her terrycloth robe and into the gathering suds, for she had taken a bottle of bubble soap with her. What a sweet little aquarelle was being enacted behind that closed door! And wouldn't I have liked to have had a hand in its execution. "We're told schizophrenics hate water," I continued, lathering the slim young flanks as I knelt beside the tub, spreading the luscious foam over the apple breasts and then, oh, downward into the virgin cleft with gently fondling leisure. What a Filthy McNasty I was, and no use blinking it. What an out-and-out incontrovertible crumpot. A sicko if ever there was one. I lost the thread of what I was saying to Leland, and gave my head a shake as though physically to divert this mental millrace into a more respectable stream of thought.

"What's the matter, Ted?" Leland asked.

"Nothing. I just had this kind of dizzy — something. It's nothing. Where were we?"

"You were talking about schizophrenics hating to take baths. That's interesting in the light of what I was reading the other day about paranoiacs. Apparently they . . ."

The sound of singing floated through the house. Colly would have one leg extended as she trilled out the verses of "Billy Boy" in her girlish soprano, holding the flower-stem limb aloft with one hand as with the other she ran a dripping sponge upward along her calf, her thigh . . .

"— because there's something sexual in it," Leland said. "Do you think there's anything in that theory?"

"Very much. Very much indeed. How is Islip these days?"

"Oh, Islip," Mrs. d'Amboise answered for Leland from the kitchen. She hated his lumberyard. All those planks!

After the day's harried hurry I certainly wanted a bath myself before din-din, and I found the tub spotless when I bent to run water into it. The kaleidoscope of images continued, this time of my predecessor still naked as she knelt to scrub it clean for me, me! Did women — girls — think about us in as intimate detail as we did them? Did they fantasize about us twenty ways to Sunday; were we similarly not only denuded as we made our way across a room, but dissected, plucked and eaten? I have never been able to get a woman to answer me frankly about this, though the way so many flick their eyes at your middle when you stand talking to them may indicate the wind blows generally in the same direction. More to the point, did my own erotic scenarios exceed the normal permissible febrility, let alone how I acted on them? An incident occurred that inspired once again the suspicion that I might be a borderline degenerate, or was studying to become one.

When I reached to the towel rack after stepping onto the bath mat, I saw that the towel Columbine had used was still there, damply wadded over the bar alongside the two neatly folded ones. I dried myself with it instead of taking one of the fresh, pausing now and then to hold against my body what had just been pressed to hers, savoring the furtive intimacy with a deep and secret excitement. I tried to keep it clean by clinging to the general idea of her morning girlhood

transmitting its benediction to myself, the delicious damp I
felt being the dew of her innocence, etc. That sort of thing.
Yet the icky factor would not be exorcised. Was I a creep?
Nonsense. This was how a creep would behave, I told myself, and by way of demonstration loitered where the fabric
had been most intimately pressed to the girl, at the same
time kind of rolling my eyes in a mooning way and making
moaning and gurgling noises, drooling some. There, *that* was
how a creep would behave, a Faulkner cretin, say. Wasn't
there a Snopes who broke into a woman's bedroom and nuzzled an undergarment he stole from her bureau drawer? At
least one assumed it was an underthing, also that he probably
made whinnying noises such as I did now as I nuzzled the
towel — to show that this was not my speed, not my speed
at *all*. I whinnied and slobbered some more to show how utterly alien this sort of thing was to my nature, totally out of
character. Not my line of country at all. I was just this red-
blooded young blade with a profoundly tender side. Oh, sailing a bit close to the wind at times perhaps, to be sure, but
thereby only proving the more this basic lyricism girls-wise.
How about trying to rape the cop? Hey, how about that, trying to haul down the whole arsenal preparatory to taking
silk? Well, that was a whole nother bucket of worms. The
cop was a grown woman, and the assault only semantically
that, since it involved merely a greater measure of ardor, and
therefore vigor, than is usually the case when a bloke normally tries to take silk. No, I was not your bona fide odd-
ment, sent downriver for an offense while the neighbors
stood in puzzled knots telling reporters for the six o'clock
news what a nice chap he had always been, quiet, even
teaching a Sunday school class. Yet a question troubled me
as I finished with one of the other towels and then scrubbed
out the tub with a brush and scouring powder kept on its
ledge. Would I have used Columbine's if she were still
twelve? The answer was "Probably." That was how Mrs.

d'Amboise had bent the twig. What was the age of consent in Illinois? Indiana? ...

Columbine went to bed early after a fine spaghetti dinner made with clam sauce, and when the three of us adults were alone, I sensed that Mrs. d'Amboise wanted to talk about something. Leland had poked the fire up and thrown on another log or two. She glanced upstairs to make sure the door of Colly's bedroom was closed, and said, rubbing her palms together as she walked the floor, "Colly has come a long way, thanks in no small measure to your wholesome influence." I disclaimed credit with the two-handed motions of a man waving off the last of the summer's flies, at the same time muttering something unintelligible even to myself. "She has far fewer allergies. They're down from eighteen to a mere five or six. They no longer include camel hair, kapok, sisal, pyrethrum, and gum tragacinth."

I lowered my head modestly. "Tell me about gum tragacinth."

"I think it's gum traga*canth*, darling," Leland said, thoughtfully pacing the floor himself as he looked down at his feet. The weekend was in part dedicated to determining whether a new pair of shoes he'd bought were too tight and should go back, or had only the snugness common to new footwear, and would be O.K. after being broken in — a common enough dilemma for all of us. He had to confine his steps to carpeted areas, so the soles would remain clean and the shoes returnable without resistance from the merchant. Wearing them outside was out of the question until the problem was resolved. The suspense was unbearable. Could my heart stand it?

"Yes, tragacanth," Mrs. d. agreed, "and that includes candies, cheese both processed and spread — you remember the maladventure with the double Gloucester — chewing gum, oh, some medical creams and ointments as well as salad dressing. Of course she's on maintenance — an injection every two weeks, finally maybe three or four, should do it permanently."

"What about that other? Pyre-something?" I asked.

"Pyrethrum. That's in insecticides. Now we can spray our houseplants again without the poor dear going into fits. Of course we outgrow a lot of allergies naturally."

"Get on with what you want to tell Ted, darling," Leland said, treading the carpet border with an expression of the most intensely focused uncertainty.

"Yes. Well, Colly's developing beautifully."

"She's filling out very nicely," I concurred.

That was disingenuous, as she was nothing of the kind. I was just agreeing courteously with what I thought a doting mother meant. Colly would always be slim-hipped, with a figure ideal for a boy riding a dolphin in a public fountain, and her breasts were doorbells, and doorbells would remain (not that that isn't to many masculine tastes). I had once remarked as much to a group of my "peers." I was now thoroughly ashamed of the metaphor, by which a nickname had been inadvertently pinned on the sweet girl. Little Miss Doorbells the local louts now called her, and every time I heard it I hated myself. By uncontrollable association I thought of Snooky's ripe melons and equine amplitudes, and the pang of remorse over Colly became a twinge of desire. The muse of guilt again, ever at our shoulder (to trot out Auden again). This entire train of agony was unnecessary, as Mrs. d'Amboise hadn't meant what I'd thought at all.

"No, no, I mean developing as a person, though, yes, she's given notice of the sylphlike figure she can always be proud of. What I intended to say was, she's been brought to the threshold of young womanhood, and now her attachment to you has grown to where it has pitfalls as well as blessings. You see, her attitude toward sex had an unfortunate shakeup during early childhood." Mrs. d'Amboise paused and said, facing me, "I don't know whether you've ever heard, but, you see, she was violated by Santa Claus."

"Oh, come now, Evelyn," Leland put in. "That's a bit drastic. You make it sound like one of those books where someone is ravished by Satan. No, she was *molested* by Santa Claus. That's as strongly as you can put it."

"All right. She was molested by Santa Claus."

"You mean she was molested by *a* Santa Claus," I interjected.

"What's the difference? Since she was a little tyke at the time, with all her illusions intact, it came to the same thing. There was a Santa Claus and he was it, this vile old thing in the department store. Took her on his lap when she was the last in line, and — but what's the use of going into details. He was a disgrace to his uniform."

She said this with such a straight face I could hardly keep my own. I covered a threatening smile with both hands, elbows on the arms of my chair, and shook my lowered head. "Imagine that."

"You don't have to imagine it. Such things are. The world is full of degenerates."

"True, true."

"You never know."

"Never."

"Creeps and freaks freely roam the streets."

"Freely."

"You don't dream who's warped. It could be somebody next door, and when it comes out, the neighbors stand around shaking their heads and saying what a nice person he was."

"Never hurt a fly. Taught Sunday school — "

"Kind to old people — "

"Helped them across the street — "

"And then *kaboom*." My hostess brought her palms together like a tympanist climaxing an orchestral crescendo with a cymbal crash.

"The monster inside all of us, clanking his chains and snorting to be let out." Unnerved by the sight of Mrs. d'Amboise planted firmly in front of me, I got out of my chair and began to pace the room, too, looking down at the floor somewhat in the manner of Leland himself, as though my own shoes, though purchased years ago, were still under review. The traffic in the room was now quite heavy. "What happened to this bird? This Santa? Did you prefer charges?"

"We debated long and hard over that, and Leland and I finally decided that putting Colly through all that, the report at the police station, the trial, would have made the trauma even worse. He was promptly discharged when we told the department store manager what had happened, but not preferring charges did make us feel guilty. Fortunately he committed another offense, and was sent up. I don't know whether he's in or out now. Animal."

"This other offense, was that in uniform too?"

"Yes. It was soon after. That must have been part of his twisted mind, the perverse satisfaction of besmirching something sacred. Defiling Christmas." Mrs. d'Amboise gave one of those sharp sighs of hers which seemed to slice off the end of a conversation, or some phase of it, in order that you might go on to the next. "So we've been grateful for the example of purity you've set. The distance that must be necessarily observed between a grown youth of known interest in a little girl can be of great value in that girl's development, especially when it must be corrective."

"It was nothing."

"She's had the sense of being a, well, china figurine on a pedestal, and that has purged sex for her of its disagreeable elements. But the ticklish part is still ahead." Mrs. d'Amboise smiled in response to the blank look I gave in return. "The actual physical part and all that. I know you'll handle it skillfully."

I don't know what response would have issued from my open mouth had there not been an interruption just then. An upstairs door flew open and Columbine appeared on the balcony in her nightgown squealing, "There's a mouse in my room. Can someone get rid of it?"

I looked at Leland, poised on a border of the rug. If he ran across the intervening stretch of bare floor and up the wooden stairs, the shoes would have been "committed," since the scuffed undersole would have rendered them unreturnable. I myself snatched up a short hearth broom and pelted up the stairs into Colly's bedroom, having to push the door open again because a tilt in the second floor kept all the doors swinging shut of their own accord there. "You won't need that," Colly said as I went past her, "I mean to chase it or anything. The mouse is dead. It's in a trap in a corner near the bed."

I found it readily enough, picked it up and threw it, trap and all, out of an open window. Then I stood, alone a moment, in the middle of the room. The door had again swung shut. I had heard the latch click. I thought again of the Snopes who had broken by dark of night into what-was-her-name's bedroom. Narcissa. Yes, in *Sartoris*. It all came back now. He had done something else besides nuzzle Narcissa's garment and steal the packet of letters. He had thrown himself into her bed and writhed about in it, moaning into her pillow. There was a silk scarf hanging on the back of a chair here, which I reached out and touched. A reading lamp burned on a table beside the bed, the covers of which were flung back, revealing a hollow where its occupant had lain. I took three steps toward the bed and dove face forward into it, wrapping the pillow around my ears to make a sandwich of my head and breathing deeply of some sachet scenting the slip, again to emphasize the sort of thing that simply wasn't up my alley. It felt distinctly inappropriate, I could take every confidence in that. This was assuredly not my métier.

I rose, trailing a hand where she had lain, got the broom, which I had propped against the wall, and went out. Colly being now wakeful, we all trooped into the kitchen and had a cup of hot chocolate. Still dubious about his shoes, Leland removed them and got into his bedroom slippers. As we sat around the table, Colly in a flamboyant quilted bathrobe, I told a story about an uncle of mine who had bought a pair of shoes in one store and returned them to another where they charged a higher price for them, so that he got two dollars more for the shoes than what he had originally paid for them.

"Didn't they ask to see the sales slip?" Mrs. d'Amboise asked from the stove where she was heating the milk for our cocoa.

"He said he lost it. They trusted Uncle Woodrow I think his name was. Said he had an honest face."

"And did he?"

"I don't know. I never saw him, except for a picture in a family album, one of those red velvet–bound things with brass clasps so appropriate for encasing the concept of human continuity" — just listen to Motor Mouth knocking them dead — "and he looked to me as though he might have stolen a horse or two in his time. We didn't have much to do with that branch of the family. The — what was their name again? Snopes, I believe it was."

For a moment there was no response. Then Mrs. d'Amboise turned her head around while continuing to stir the milk in the pan, and smiled, pleased both with my literary joke and with herself for having caught it, so that, smiling conspiratorially at me, she was also smiling to herself. This was the sort of chap she wanted to marry into her family.

Did Mrs. d'Amboise think my compatibility with her, whether fancied or otherwise, was sufficient ground on which to base a marriage with her daughter? Was she off her rocker? Was I off mine? What you do with a rocker is hang it upside down on your back (I mean if you still have this consuming interest in furniture movers' esoterica), you hook the overturned rocking chair onto your shoulders by the curved runners, you see, leaving both hands free to carry something else to or from the truck — in my case two loaded Gladstone bags making a sincere effort to tear my arms out of their sockets. This was going to be a relatively dry-eyed job, since the people in question were only moving into a house across the street and down two or three addresses. Not, in other words, worth loading the truck for; that sometimes happens. "Going to Jerusalem" we called an across-the-street or down-the-block move. Pinky and Buster were the rest of the crew, and they dollied the heavy stuff that had to be two-timed out of the house and then into the new, such as dressers and sofas, using ramps handily provided by driveways at both ends, which avoided the nuisance of curbstones to trundle the dolly over. At one point, on this Saturday morning a week after the jollifications at By a Dam Site, there was a procession crossing the street consisting of Pinky and Buster dollying a highboy; the husband toting a bushel basket full of kitchenware on his shoulder; three small children with armloads of toys and books; the wife and mother carrying a pair of table lamps, along with a fourth child inside her; and me with the aforementioned rocker and Gladstone bags, plus a hatbox lashed for good measure onto the top of my head by means of its tying bands knotted in a bow under my chin, like a maiden of the olden time wearing the bonnet itself. A few down-at-mouth disciples traipsing in my wake brought up the rear.

"If we can think of this vast and in many ways incredible country, which I love with every other fiber of my being, put it that way," I was saying, "if we can think of it as polarized between two pairs of James brothers, Jesse and Frank at one end, and at the other, of course — "

"You've already said that," one of the disciples protested. "We've all had that routine."

"It bears repeating. And speaking of bears, Delmore Schwartz's probably best poem, with an epigraph from Whitehead about 'the withness of the body,' likens our mass of physical needs and hungers to a bear itself, in 'the scrimmage of appetite everywhere.' That's how it ends."

"You've recited that to us before too."

Had he emptied his quiver? Was he scraping the bottom of the barrel? Such were doubtless the ruminations of my disciples as they shuffled off afield, around noon, little suspecting that I entertained precisely such misgivings about the caliber of satellite I seemed to be attracting of late. It was a Saturday half day, and as I wandered off to lunch alone somewhere, letting Pinky and Buster take the van back, I wondered why I was sticking around Pocock. Why hadn't I long ago moved to New York, as planned? Was I afraid of not making it as an actor? Or still hopefully hankering after Snooky? Or Kathy? Was I really waiting for Columbine? It was hard to know. I was poured so many ways. In the high West there burned a sulfurous star. It was mine, holding sway over my increasingly jaundiced destiny.

I was on foot, and as I was debating with myself whether to break into a trot so as to get in a little jogging, I was startled by the sight of Columbine herself hurrying along an intersecting street. She had crossed against the light, and after scurrying out of the path of a honking motorist, she resumed the long-legged stride characteristic of her. Dressed in scarlet slacks and a purple jacket, she drew the attention of a group of mailbox loafers, of the kind I myself had once been, though beginning to draw into my orbit the first of the rather more creditable disciples of my early period. As she disappeared behind a corner building, I noticed the louts looking after her, laughing and talking among themselves. They were still at it when I approached them. One of them said something

I thought I had caught, but I wasn't sure. I walked up to him, a stocky kid with skin like pizza crust.

"What was that remark you passed?" I demanded. "What did you call her?"

"Miss Doorbells. Like everybody else."

"Well, I'd advise you that next time I hear you say it, you miserable little punk, you goddamn well better be sure of the size of your fists. Is that clear?" I helped myself to a handful of his coat lapel. *"Is that clear?"*

"Jeez, I was only — "

"Never mind what you was only. Just remember what I said, or I'll hand you your head. Understand?"

"Sure, I was just . . . I didn't mean anything."

I had come within an inch of actually belting him. It was a rather complicated moment in one man's moral history. Because what would I have been socking him for? For using a coinage I have myself apparently slipped into the language (the reverse of your Miss Twin Peaks, for the likes of Snooky), and as a nickname for a girl on whom I had myself unintentionally pinned it thanks to my gift for imaginative metaphor, as evidence of her undesirability as a mate. The least I could do was ask her to marry me. Such must be the course taken by any chap with a shred of decency, and I rather think I had that.

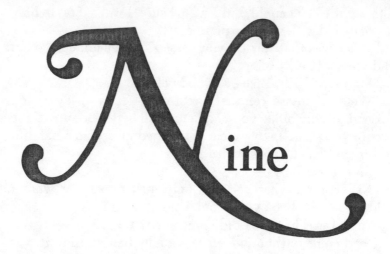

Nine

My next sex offense was to kiss a bride on the mouth. Even with Snooky von Sickle, *especially* with Snooky von Sickle, five minutes after she had become Mrs. Ambrose d'Amboise, should I have limited myself to the customary congratulatory peck on the cheek, I know, I know, but when it was my turn in the long queue, something came over me.

Shuffling forward toward the reception line — we are again at the country club — I had been both nervous and excited, in an emotional tumult easy to understand. How beautiful she looks, I thought, more Junoesque than ever, it would really have torn it for old Schopenhauer. Ah, those swelling flanks, those billowing breasts and hemispheres, that mare of a girl I had so often so deliriously mounted. Now there she stood in her bridal gown, skin like honey, her mouth like a, what was that flower again? Gloxinia, yes, like a gloxinia opening to take your kiss . . .

Only one disciple had been invited, Phooey Haverstick, trailing me at the necessarily snail-like pace. I was currently under strain from many quarters and must be forgiven for counting the buttons on people's clothing, the slats in a picket fence, even the ridges on a quarter, or trying to. My disciples themselves were under a pall of gloom, partly because I was not much abroad, and not up to scratch when I was; partly because the ostracism of one of them had been distressing to a degree. He had been drummed out of the group for what we called *ejaculatio praecox*, premature ejaculation over — anything. Everything. A new writer or painter still unproved, a film not all that good, maybe a new girl in town with a surface glamor not surviving closer scrutiny. "Wow!" "Hey!" "Gosh!" "Neat!" Such callow ebullience was not to be tolerated among accredited cool cats, if the race was to be nudged along.

The wedding guests inched forward. Hand in trouser pocket, I pressed a dime under a fingernail until I drew an admission of pain from my finger end. I knew Phooey expected a trenchancy.

"Modesty is often a mask for inferiority," I told him over my shoulder.

"That's better," he said. Yet his approval was grudging, I could sense that. His pickle-slice eyes had that inheld glint of men who are defecting to the West from satellite Balkan countries. Did he have his gaze on Kathy d'Amboise, for whom I was still considered his rival?

I am approaching the von Sickles and then Leland and Mrs. d'Amboise. You're next, says the latter's look. Her old hunger. Who can blame her? I am personable, I grant, agreeable, though a louse, and I would never belt a dame. There are those who do, in seemingly swelling quantity. Totally incomprehensible to me.

At last I creep toward the nuptial pair. I congratulate a couple of bridesmaids on how lovely they look, and now stand face to face with Snooky, while Ambrose, just beyond her, is engrossed in hearing out another congratulator. The old electricity is still there. That much is certain from the first contact of my lips on hers. Does she hear woodwinds

too, in a kiss mixing memory and desire like the very April
in which all this is taking place? In a heartfelt burst of felici-
tation I fling my arms around her. "All the happiness in the
world," I say, tears in my eyes. I can feel her brassiere
through her bridal gown, can even discern the two hooks,
like a safecracker with the sensitive fingers required for that
exacting profession. I am vermin, I know, I know. An abomination. Yes, yes, true. But being a sicko has its own nuances,
its own finely shaded discriminations. Oh, Snooky, what'll we
do? "Thanks, Ted. Thanks." A sweetly tremulous smile over-
spreads her flushed face. "I hope you'll come and see us if
you get to New York. We're moving there soon — we don't
know exactly when." My left hand is still in hers when I
wring Ambrose's with my right. "All the best, old man. I hope
you'll both be very nngaa." I embrace him and then hurry
along to the punch table for some desperately needed irriga-
tion.

There are nearly a hundred guests. The d'Amboise clan is
out in force, of course, including Luke and Islip, keeping an
eye on me for opposite reasons. Which one will get to clean
my clock in the end? Nothing unusual in the paradoxical
bind in which I find myself as a result of two mutually can-
celing motivations, the very universe itself having been con-
cocted out of what Eliot has called the "balance of contrarieties." I choose a point midway between my tormentors,
which lands me in conversation with a Mrs. Peartree.

"How is your husband's diverticulum?"

"He can't eat a thing with seeds in it, like raspberries? One
could get caught in a bend of his intestines and cause no end
of infection."

I must get out of the country. That much is bleeding clear.
I spot Columbine and make for her as fast as possible. One
of the bridesmaids, she's wearing a gown of apple-green taf-
feta. I steal a line from *The Scoundrel,* what Noel Coward
says to Julie Hayden.

"You belong to the dawn of time."

"What a nice thing to say."

"You're exquisite, Colly."

"You look pretty good yourself in that jacket. Look, Ted, I've been wanting to ask you something, O.K.? Did Mum and Pop give you all that about Santa Claus and me one time?"

"They did rather give the impression — "

"And that the experience was traumatic, bollixing up my psyche and one thing and another? Most of that is nonsense. It never harmed me at all, or made me unfit for normal blah-blah-blah. It's my mother it was traumatic for. The incident was completely forgotten. He was just another flake."

"And no two are alike."

"What?"

"Nothing. I'm relieved to learn no great harm came of it. No great harm will ever come to you, Columbine. I'll see to that personally."

She laughed into her glass of punch. "You will? How?"

I drained my own glass. "Well, I guess to fulfill that promise I'd have to marry you, wouldn't I? Eventually. Sometime."

The Bambi eyes again lowered to the glass she was holding, now in both hands. She smiled and said in the breathless whisper characteristic of her, "I kind of promised Chuck Larsen I'd wait for him, O.K.?"

I stood in dumb disbelief. What the hell was this? The house of d'Amboise turns me into a cradle snatcher over the family jewel and now the jewel is going to wait for a wet-eared jock whose homework I have to do for him. The mesomorph who doesn't know from Aristotle.

"Wait for him?"

"He'll be a long time getting through premed, then med, and then intern in some hospital, maybe more, and then setting himself up in practice somewhere while he pays off his educational loans, before he can even think of supporting a wife."

"That's true," I said with a serenity I personally found insane. Could this conversation really be taking place, or was I hallucinating? What did her mother think of this? Not that I'd have been churlish enough to ask. But I was curious — did Mrs. d. know we had this whole new pail of snails on the table? Maybe it would all blow over in another ten years, which was about how long it would take the Svensk to get through all those schools, if I was any judge. Anyway it squared me with Islip, and maybe with Luke too, if he were told that I had at least *proposed* to his sister. Vim was rather another problem. Colly went back to the punch bowl with me when I suggested we refill our glasses, but once there, I lost her in the crowd, or rather was plucked out of it and to one side by Vim. This was a Saturday cocktail reception with a buffet supper afterward, for which I doubted I was going to stay after the following passage with Vim. I felt I was ready for a decompression chamber.

"Kathy tells me you two keep having lunch and stuff together at Mama Mia's, and that you were together at the Pumpkin Ball," he said. "Ted, she's right for you."

"I tried to rape her."

He spread his arms as at the crystalline simplicity of it. "What could better prove it?"

"I tried to rape her in her own prowl car."

He reasoned with me as patiently as ever before. None of this made any difference, he stressed. Phooey Haverstick was not her line of country, he was beginning to see that now. I was. And if the incident — by itself or together with possibly other unsavory elements in my data mix — gave me pause about my fitness as a husband, there was always the fact that, like Presidents about whom doubts might be reasonably evoked upon their election, I would grow with the office.

"Well, I'll see," I said.

I had graver matters on my mind.

Columbine's response to my "proposal," off the wall though

it had been, disturbed me more than I would have thought possible. Disappointment at the results of what had been half playacting on my part made me actually seem like a rejected suitor. It showed what my feelings for her were — and had always been. I realized they went back to the time when she was thirteen and fourteen. I regretted the child on roller skates, the one peering through my telescope. The d'Amboises had made a kinko out of me — that was the real pail of snails we now had on the table. All the talk about waiting for her had worked its subtle poison, fostered a latent inclination for unopened buds that might otherwise have lain safely dormant till middle age when, seasonally adjusted, as economists said about industrial statistics, it could have been more acceptably expressed in entanglements with twenty-three-year-old office secretaries or messes with waitresses or (if theatrical ambitions were realized) a fling or two with scatterbrained juvenile leads. That was how the speculation would run. Well, I refused to believe it, and I would not take this lying down.

The first order of business was to prove beyond a shadow of a doubt that I had no interest in moppets, at least over and above Maurice Chevalier singing "Thank Heaven for Little Girls" in *Gigi*. I would spot a sprite of ten or twelve in a department store and walk as close to her as possible, smiling down as I patted her on the head, avuncularly of course, smiling at the mother, too, and nodding my appreciation as they shopped for toys or pretty clothes — a man showing universal human satisfaction in all the world's childhood. I next took to following them down the street; and then one warmish day in May I turned into the park when I saw a girl wandering there alone, carrying a Frisbee.

"Hello, little girl," I said, falling in beside her. "Nobody to play with?"

"No."

"That's too bad," I said, dropping a hand on her shoulder.

Words cannot describe the tremor of pleasure that went through me at the realization that I felt absolutely nothing. Nothing at all. This would put to rout all gnawing suspicions. The conditions for verification were perfect. To a warpo the child was in her prime. Maybe thirteen or fourteen, with fine blue eyes and silky yellow hair. To prolong the sensation I had initially found so reassuring, I moved my hand gently upward under the gold locks, fondling her neck. Negative. I moved it back along the bare shoulder, exquisitely round and smooth as marble. Negative. All, all negative. No, this was not my speed. It was wildly out of character, from that I could take abiding comfort. It allayed all my fears. This was not for me any more than the Faulkner shenanigans had been. I wasn't a Humbert Humbert any more than I was a Snopes.

I glanced back to make sure I wasn't being observed, and saw a cop hoofing along the gravel path behind us. My mind worked with such lightning speed as to check the very reflex of removal that would have aroused suspicion. Instead, I steered my companion openly onto the grass and said, "How about a catch with the Frisbee?" The child was delighted, and so we were soon pitching it to one another with gay abandon. Without looking directly at the cop, I kept him in view out of the tail of my eye. He continued his patrol without a glance in our direction, picking 'em up and laying 'em down in the immemorial gait of the constabulary. What were we paying him for, for God's sake, if not to look alive?

The child was all shrieks of delight as we frolicked in the sun, and I had never felt more wholesomely happy in my life. I helped her get the hang of flinging the Frisbee, and catching it on her finger and then twirling it a spin or two before tossing it back. Once I flung it over her head and it sailed into the bushes and disappeared. Her search for it proving in vain, I ducked into the shrubbery after her. It was then I heard a woman's voice shouting, "Ernestine! Come here this minute!" and, parting the foliage to peer through it, saw the mother running over, followed by the cop at full tilt, billy at the ready.

The poor child was pulled out of the bushes and scolded in words that can be imagined. "Why didn't you wait for me on that bench by the gate where I told you, you naughty girl? And why do you talk to strange men, like I said you shouldn't? I warned you."

"I didn't talk to him. He talked to me."

"What about?" the cop interjected, and, alas, I now recognized the Officer O'Malley who had seen me wrestling with Kathy the night of the Pumpkin Ball. "Did he say anything that wasn't, well, nice?"

"Of course not. He just asked me whether I had anybody to play with, and when I said no, he said he would."

"Oh, for Christ's sake, O'Malley," I said, "didn't you know I knew I was in plain view of you? You remember me. Ted Peachum. We met the night of the Pumpkin Ball last fall. I was with Officer Arpeggio."

"Yeah, now I remember." He gave me a quizzical look. "You certainly get around, don't you." Then he turned to the mother. "Do you want to make anything of this? I mean it's up to you. If we want to question the child at headquarters, or write anything up."

"Heavens, no. It would be too traumatic."

"What?"

"It wouldn't be a good idea. I'm sure from what she's already said there was nothing . . . nothing out of the . . . And he looks all right. Just a little indiscreet. Too indiscreet to be anything worse."

"I can give you a letter from my pastor," I said with acid irony as she dragged the child off, her charge chattering about "a nice man." I turned to the cop. "Would you like to play a little pie, O'Malley?" I asked sardonically. "The Frisbee is still there in the bushes somewhere."

*   *   *

Straight into the jaws of death I ride. For here comes Mrs. d'Amboise toward me along the sidewalk, fresh from another exhibition. This by an artist up to then principally emphasizing sales graphs and pie charts to be hung unaltered, except for his signature, on gallery walls, but whose work has now taken a new and exciting turn — the railroad timetables and steamer schedules embedded in Plexiglas of his mature period. Are we not all embedded in Plexiglas, gazing wistfully at one another while locked within a medium ostensibly transparent through which, nonetheless, we can never really reach out to touch one another? Mrs. d'Amboise herself had called us all "prison-pent," which sounded like another heist from T. Wolfe. She again carried a rolled-up catalogue in her two fists, but there was to be no tap on the nose today. Today was a brute, not to be got through with the lubricants of playfulness.

"I'd like you never to show Columbine any more attentions whatsoever, ever, from now on," she said. "I'd like you to cease and desist."

"What brings on this reading of the riot act?"

"You know very well. The incident in the public park."

Then O'Malley had been flapping his lip, the oaf, laying the episode open to snowballing misconstruction he himself knew to be unfair.

"That whole thing was a total and absolute misunderstanding, and I intend to sue the officer in question and the whole damn police department for at least a million dollars for slander and character defamation and libel and I don't know what all," I said, seething with an instinctive determination I knew sober reconsideration would moderate. It could only make matters worse. Better to forget it, and let everybody else do the same.

"I should have suspected it from the first," Mrs. d'Amboise said. "An interest in a girl that young."

"You always said the potential was there, in my case."

"Nine years old."

"Colly was ten when you started stirring up my —"

"The shocks and surprises we get."

"Life isn't a bowl of cabarets."

"And you already what at the time? Sixteen."

"And advanced for my age. I mean a real short eyes even then."

"A what?"

"Short eyes. It's what convicts call twisties like me. Prison jargon."

"Oh, yes, I believe I've heard that expression. There was a movie with that title. Curious term."

"I think it carries the general connotation of somebody taking a short-sighted attitude toward something, and not the long view. The mature one. We of the criminal class are known for our ingenuity in creating slang, of course. Take a powder, go South, the slammer, stir, bum rap. There's no end to our inventiveness. We have a feeling for words. What the Germans call *Sprachgefühl*. Americans have that in abundance — not even the British can touch us — especially with slang. That's our long suit, and I might observe," I continued, as though Mrs. d'Amboise were a disciple, "or you may have observed it to yourself, that linguistic inventiveness is in inverse ratio to the social level. The lower orders produce more than, say, the bourgeoisie, and when you get to the presumable top, say college professors, the contribution is zilch. Well, this has been pleasant. We must have another of our chats soon."

I didn't intend to hold my breath until I was invited to tea. Instead, Mrs. d'Amboise sighed, and regarded me with a more sympathetic air.

"Leland tends to be understanding about it. Says there's something like that in everybody."

"Just as there's a little larceny in all of us," I agreed, wishing that my telepathic powers were keen enough to transmit to Mrs. d. a reminder of some of her own literary snatches, as remembered from the days when, sculpting me as Shelley and the Discobolus (clutching a Frisbee for verisimilitude), she had first put the bee in my bonnet about waiting for Columbine.

I dropped a book I was returning to the library, and as I stooped to retrieve it from the sidewalk she asked what it was.

"*The Phenomenon of Man,* by Pierre Teilhard de Chardin," I said, displaying it. "You've probably read it. It offers a philosophy supplying an answer to one of the great hungers of modern man. What Camus has called the nostalgia for the absolute. I'm sure you've read *him*," I added, fixing her with a level gaze. "Well, good day, Mrs. d'Amboise. It's been nice talking to you."

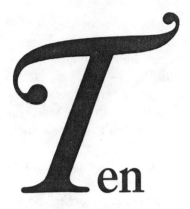

Ten

"The road to good intentions is paved with hell."

I sloped across town with my dwindling band of devotees at heel, finally shaking them off by pleading an important errand on which I was bent as I turned a corner, making for a Chinese restaurant known as the Ping Pong to pick up something for family dinner.

It must by now be axiomatic Americana that egg foo young, char shew ding and pu pu platter all taste like cardboard by the time you get them home, and I thought of Sydney Carton as I scooped out the containers onto supper plates at home, musing how what I was doing was also a far, far better thing than I had ever done, though I was hardly headed for a better rest as a result. I mean my decision to stay on a while to ease howsoe'er I could a rapidly worsening situation between my parents, instead of choosing this moment to leave it all behind and at last light out for New York. These were my good intentions, and the pressures to which I consequently remained subject in Pocock, the hell with which they were paved. Thus my remark had had a point, and was not a jejune frivolity flung over my shoulder as I shook the entourage.

The next crisis was one of the worst, and was precipitated unwittingly by my poor dear mother. In a fit of whatever rage or despair had been the latest in whatever chain of frustrations had been boiling up inside her — yes, yes, chains boiling, let it stand — in whatever climacteric storm of the hormonal catastrophe my father said a woman was, my mother bundled up all the comics in his den and threw them out. She was cleaning house on an Augean-stable scale. When my father awoke and saw what had happened he was horror-struck.

"Do you know how much those things are *worth*?" he exclaimed. "Thousands! Some of them are collector's items. It's what they call nostalgia. Ask Ted. Ain't they, Ted?" he appealed to me, for I happened to be on hand at the moment of discovery, eating my breakfast.

"Are they?" my mother asked, her voice shaking with fear.

I could hardly bear to look up from my eggs. My mother's eyes were a dog's eyes. What had she done to deserve this, after a lifetime of drab diligence relieved by nothing but a spot of slap-and-tickle with Pinky Montmorency and the new-neighbor welcome parties to which the d'Amboises had not come? I thought of the buffet porcupine bristling with toothpicks on which were impaled the chunks of cheddar and Vienna finger sausages, and bled quietly to death.

I cleared my throat with a shrug and shoved my chair back.

"Oh, worth something, sure. Few hundred bucks maybe. What's that?" I knew better, and my mother knew I did.

She sank onto a kitchen chair and sat there with a stunned expression. One hand lay upturned in her lap, as it did when she ate at her supper parties in accordance with instructions given her in etiquette manuals. With the money the comics were worth they could have bought a new "parlor suit."

"Where are you going?"

"To the dump." I went for my coat. "You bundled them up
I suppose, Ma? I mean the way we do old newspapers?"

"I bundled them up real nice."

"When did you throw them out?"

"Day before yesterday."

"Oh, then they're probably still there. I know where to
look."

That was the Sunday after the Chinese takeout dinner. I
got into the car and hurried off on my rescue mission. What
a dump, one might say in praise of our model wasteland, so
ecologically organized. Glass went into a trailer gondola
here, metal into another there, while old newspapers and mag-
azines were loaded into an enormous van. Garbage worthy
of the name was dropped off in a "garbage pavilion," where
it was bulldozed into hoppers for incineration elsewhere. I
was familiar with the complex from a number of past deposits. Pocockians were supposed to cart everything but their
garbage away, but few complied with this utopian dream.
Most just left even their baled newspapers for their sanita-
tion drivers to include in their hauls. That was what my
mother had done with the comic books — which were to
seem precipitately less funny from here on.

The dump is just behind the police station. I parked at the
driveway entrance, across which now a heavy iron chain was
slung, for it is officially closed on Sundays. I stepped over the
chain and made for the wastepaper van. When I reached it,
my heart sank. It was loaded to the roof and nearly to the
back end.

I stood there hesitantly. How long — how many hours of
Herculean toil — might it take me to haul out those bales of
old newspapers, the strings of some of which would no doubt
snap in my hands, before I reached the pay dirt I was looking
for? And then to stack, or at least hurl, them all back in? If
the treasure was embedded somewhere in that thirty-foot

maw, where? How far back? I thought of Pinky being asked
by the weeping Mrs. what-was-her-name, the one we moved
to Galena, to dismantle half a van load to retrieve a lamp
from the cupola. How much were the comics worth? A lot.
Not hundreds, as I said to soothe my mother, but probably
more like thousands. I'd read a piece about that. Collector's
items! Nostalgia! My father had kept every damn one of
them.

To some, much is given. Others have to buckle in with a
bit of a grin. I laid my coat over a nearby barrel and rolled
up my sleeves. I had carried out thirty or forty bundles, two
at a time, and begun a systematic stack on the ground behind
the trailer, when I saw a police car whip across the station
parking lot and slam to a stop behind mine. A policeman got
out. Or, rather, a policewoman. It was Officer Arpeggio.

"Hello, Kathy."

"Ted, what in God's name are you doing here at this hour?
This place is closed Sundays. Can't you read that sign? It's
against the rules to be here. I could write you up."

"Please do. Make me immortal with a ticket. Christ, you
look nice. Especially with that pepper pot sticking out of
your holster. Tumescence itself."

"Thanks, but satisfy my curiosity."

I explained my mission as swiftly as possible. She was
shaking her head before I was half finished.

"Won't do you any good. They won't be in there."

"Why not?"

"You'll more likely find them at my house. My parents'
house I mean."

"What the hell are you talking about?"

"Papa's by now a real hepcat to anything valuable people
throw out." I struck my brow. In the confusion it had completely slipped my mind that her father was our garbage
man. "He's got that book, *Treasure in Trash,* or whatever it's
called. It's his Bible. Comics are one of the first things he'd

know about. And aren't they now legally his property? If he wants to latch onto them?"

I sighed, making a gesture of helpless consternation. "You got me." I eyed my outside stack and then the van irresolutely. "But you're sure they won't be here."

"Pretty. So now it's hell and high water at home?"

"It's a pool of blood. Look, what about phoning your father and asking him —"

She laughed. "Do you think he'd tell you if he's got them? *'Caveat emptor,'* he keeps saying, which he thinks means finders keepers. But you've got me curious. Let's hop in my car and drive out there. They'll probably both be at eleven o'clock Mass, and we can sneak a peek. Just for the hell of it. I know where the outside key hangs. Or maybe all we'll have to do is look in the garage. Come on. Chuck these back in and let's go."

We had not driven very far when a constrained silence fell between us. This vehicle held uneasy memories for me — and I thought I sensed what else Kathy was thinking. Pretending to be taking in some sight or other on my left, that required my glancing diagonally past her, I saw out of the corner of my eye that she was smiling faintly. She spun along for another block or so, gripping the steering wheel at the bottom. Her radio crackled out a message for another squad car, and was silent. At last Kathy spoke.

"What was Lewis Carroll's real name again?"

"Charles Something-or-other Dodgson."

"Yes. He liked little girls. You could write another *Alice in Wonderland.*"

"Do you really believe that ridiculous story about me?"

"Of course not, you sap. If I did I wouldn't bring it up, even as a joke. O'Malley is a chatterbox. I hear you gave him holy hell. He's made a pitch for me, not that I ever tell on a

man for that. I just mention it to reassure you he may have
some kind of animus against you. So don't you repeat it."

"Don't worry. I'm a gentleman to my fingertips. Which is
where it ends, as you know from personal experience. You
know what sort of helped turn me on that night at the country club? This is going to sound kind of flaky."

"Try me. We're a very esoteric police force."

"That pistol-packin'-mama bit. I suppose a textbook explanation would give me role reversal as something that can
hop sex up between two people, but it doesn't *make* you masculine, only seem more fragile. And all that other stuff your
loins are girded with. Christ, look at it all. Walkie-talkie,
flashlight, that salami to club people with, strip of bullets,
handcuffs. No wonder I wanted to pull it all down and get
to the silk. I mean the sheer contrast. Does this make sense
to you?"

"I think. The challenge, the —"

"It's like storming a citadel. I get the same feeling when I
see one of those new girl conductors they've got on trains.
They've got almost as much festooning their middles as you.
Have you ever seen one? Ticket punches, big clanking bunch
of keys, to open God knows what all with, change pouches
hanging there like outside uteruses, containers backside left
for this kind of ticket, backside right for that, and then another gadget I've never been able to figure out. Do you know
what I want to do whenever I see one of those railroad
nymphs?"

"Pull everything down and take her in the aisle."

"The more to pull down the better, prior to taking silk.
That's how I want to churn her butter. I have this thing
about pulling everything down — you're *razing defense
works.* I'm a pulling-everything-down buff. I want to ravage
all that armament till the ticket punches and keys are strewn
the length of the coach and the chicken feed spills in every
direction in a silver ejaculation. An orgasm of nickels and

dimes and quarters." I paused, breathing heavily as I licked my lips. "You know what else does it to me? This is the real blast. Those new telephone lineswomen. Now there's something really aphrodisiac. What hangs down from them is virtually uninventoriable. Telephone, pliers, hammer, flashlight, screwdriver, ratchet wrenches, potato masher, eggbeater, name it. Do you know what I want to do when I see one of *those* dames shinny up a telephone pole?"

"Shinny up after her."

"Shinny up after her and pull the whole works down — get this — pull the whole goddamn shebang down *from behind and underneath*. How does that grab you?"

"Perfectly understandable. There'd be no other way to do it. There's only one thing."

"What's that?"

"You're seeing things if you've watched women climb poles to work on power lines. They don't have them — yet."

I looked at her in surprise, rather alarmed at this evidence of hallucination. "Are you sure?"

"Sure. But don't worry. You're probably clairvoyant. The day will come."

"Do you think I'm going crazy?"

"Of course not. You just like the New Woman. Well, here we are, and there looks to be nobody home."

We entered through a back door with a key hanging from a nail outside the garage, stepping into a kitchen with another door affording a view of the garage itself, which a quick look revealed not to contain the missing treasure. I felt like a burglar breaking and entering, though to Kathy it had taken on the proportions of a lark. She giggled as we stepped out of the kitchen into a passage leading to the main part of the house. We made our way over thick wall-to-wall carpeting through a paneled dining room and parlor crowded with what could fairly be called low camp, or perhaps high borax:

massive chairs and sofas with paroxysmic scrollwork; lamps with bases like blunt instruments ideal for impromptu murders in fits of domestic passion, surmounted by tasseled shades; bombastically carved cabinets replete with agonizing chinaware and vacation-souvenir bric-a-brac, and a grand piano across which was spread a fringed shawl with a somebody-threw-an-egg-at-the-fan sunset (or sunrise) on it, and under which lay a ceramic black cat you knew in your heart of hearts was wired to have its eyes blink when a switch was flipped.

"Is this too rich for your blood?" Kathy laughed. "I think I married to get away from the furniture."

There had been still no sign of the comics. She opened the front-hall closet long enough to glance into that, fruitlessly.

"Could they be in the basement?" I asked. I was now torn between wanting to find them, with all that might mean in the way of a lost cause in a probably disagreeable dispute, and tackling the damn van all over again.

Kathy held a finger aloft, to indicate she had an idea. She led the way back into the dining room, and paused before a closed door just off it. She stood soberly a moment with her hand on the knob. "This is Papa's den. An office actually. If they're anywhere, they're here."

She opened the door and there they were, stacked against two walls in such a way as to make the room uncannily reminiscent of my own father's placental snuggery. All it would have needed was a bed to replace the desk at which Mr. Arpeggio attended to his bookkeeping and other business.

Kathy gestured to the cache. "There you are. Just as I guessed. No dumbbell Papa."

Her gesture had been an invitation to enter, which I did. I was bending over the bonanza of *Archies* and *Blondies* and *Captain Midnights* when a car pulled into the driveway. Her folks were home from church.

"Now what?" I asked.

"Now the confrontation."

She seemed progressively more amused by the whole adventure as my own stomach for it dwindled. She said to wait in the parlor and, closing the study door, went to greet her parents, adding that the patrol car in the driveway wouldn't have surprised them as she often dropped in for coffee on Sundays.

I was sitting in one of the thronelike chairs, my arms disposed along its arms, like Abraham Lincoln in the Washington memorial, admiring a mantel statuette of Venus with a clock in her stomach, feeling like an uneasy blend of housebreaker and gentleman caller, when the three entered. I sprang to my feet, grinning like a stuffed wolverine. How in hell had I consented to this?

"I'd like you to meet Ted Peachum — if you don't already know him, Papa."

They were one of those look-alike couples with which the world is stocked in rather amazing quantity. (My explanation isn't that people "grow to look like one another after years of marriage" at all, but that they have from the first unconsciously selected each other for their idealizing resemblance to themselves. I had once observed as much to my disciples in the days before my decline, adding that all the young couples and newlyweds who look alike proved my point. Well, no matter.) The Arpeggios had greatly different colorings, though, and it was obviously from her mother that Kathy had inherited her fair hair and skin. Arpeggio had a thick short black mop sprinkled with gray. Both were dressed in their Sunday best, he in a dark suit, his wife in a zebra-striped dress that seemed to have been selected to go with one of the lampshades. I wondered if they were aware of Vim's and Kathy's intention to separate once a suitable husband had been found for Kathy — a plan that continued to remind me of those "Now Renting" signs for apartments to be erected on sites where the buildings they are to replace have not even been torn down. In that case the Arpeggios might think me a suitor being trotted out for inspection.

Kathy set it all straight in as few words as possible. "So his mother threw them out without knowing their true value as collector's items," she concluded. "You probably do, Papa. Have you got them?"

"Me?" He shrugged, at the same time rolling his eyes as if in humorous dismissal of any notion that he was a connoisseur. "What would I know?"

"You've got that book about treasures in trash. You know what's what." As Kathy said this, Mrs. Arpeggio darted her husband a look not to be missed, and which he must have sensed without seeing her, as if by marital radar.

"And even if I got," Arpeggio said, "Mr. Peachum knows what *caveat emptor* means."

"Finders keepers," I said.

"That's a right."

It was a ticklish moment in the discussion. I had instinctively fallen in with Kathy's realization that Arpeggio must not know he had been caught with the goods red-handed. He must be let save face by yielding them up voluntarily, in a kind of moral catharsis. Anything more would mean the collapse of the negotiations. With that in mind I said:

"I perfectly see your point, Mr. Arpeggio. It's just that someone in this case, a good customer who always paid her bills, threw something out in good faith and total ignorance — "

"I once found a stamp collection in the trash can," he said. "Can you believe it? Not worth a million bucks, but something."

"He gave it back," Mrs. Arpeggio put in. "After a soul struggle. He knew some kid didn't know what it was worth. It wouldn't have been right."

"She dwells on things," Arpeggio said with a jerk of his head at his wife.

"That was swell of you," I said, "and, but as I was saying,

somebody discarded something in total ignorance of its value who has been a good customer of yours for — how long?"

"Seventeen years. Yeah. I know. I took 'em. Kept 'em I mean," finger aloft to emphasize a fine point of casuistry. "I stored 'em in there. They're in there." He pointed to his office. "I just been to church and it's been on my conscience. Take 'em back. They're yours."

Mrs. Arpeggio, who had been following all this as one definitely in the know, and possible accomplice, clapped her hands in a kind of religious ecstasy. "Lord of mercy! I knew he'd do the right thing. He never done anything else but the right thing, with me or anybody else. He knew it would have been on his conscience."

"See how she dwells on things?"

"Don't they all," I laughed, as though we were both seasoned husbands all too familiar with the changeless nature of our women folks. So great was my relief at having probably saved my own parents' marriage that I gratefully pumped Arpeggio's horny hand in my own and invited him to take his pick of the treasure trove. "Say the first issue of *Batman*. That must be worth a lot of money."

"Three hundred bucks," said Arpeggio, who had obviously already looked all this up.

"Or what was the very first comic book printed, in nineteen thirty something. *Action Comics*."

"That's worth a thousand bucks. There are only a few around. That's the most valuable of all. But no, I wouldn't. I don't want no reward. I wouldn't feel right."

"Lord of mercy!"

"Don't dwell. But I'll tell you what. I'll take some of those *Mutt and Jeffs*. I always liked them. Just to read. My favorite funnies. Well, let's get them bundled up again. Not that I untied them all. Just a few. But the *Action* number one is there. That's a very rare."

We retied the bundles Arpeggio had opened while, giving up the dwelling, Mrs. Arpeggio ran to the kitchen to fix us some coffee. Arpeggio and I toasted our worth with a glass of Chianti. He helped us load the comics into the patrol car.

"Enjoyment of something, how much more a worth than mere monetary," observed the quenchless dweller as she watched from the lawn.

The back of the car was full and I held two bundles on my lap as we made off, waving our thanks to the sterling Arpeggios.

"They're dolls," I said.

"That they are."

"And I'm a mile deep in your debt. If you hadn't come along I'd still be plugging away in the van."

I was really thinking about Kathy as a product of the household of whose integrity and composure I had just had a glimpse. What a wife she would make for the right man! She was pretty, amusing, a feminist while also femininely dependent. She was independent while also being considerate and reasonable, and she would not dwell. What was wrong with Vim? Or between them?

"Marry me."

"Oh, Ted. It's sweet of you. And sweet to hear too, like a bell on this Sunday morning. But it's too late. I'm pregnant."

"Ah. I'm so happy for you. And Vim. How does he feel?"

"He's tickled pink. You see, it's Phooey Haverstick's. You knew I'd been seeing him?"

Wasn't this the signal to pack my bags? For what was my story so far? I had salvaged my parents' marriage, for a while at least, but himself he could not save. Ambrose had got Snooky von Sickle, Columbine would wait for Chuck Larsen, and Phooey Haverstick — my Judas — was going to marry Officer Arpeggio as soon as she got a divorce. Pocock, Illinois, had nothing more to offer me, nor I it. It was clearly time to leave and mount the assault, already too long delayed, on the East. I set my face like flint for New York.

Eleven

"When in doubt, massage your gums."

I called this to a cluster of damp disciples through the window of the airport limousine which was to take me to O'Hare, from where I would wing my way on to the Apple, and they nodded, laughing among themselves in the gray dawn drizzle in which they had loyally turned out to see me off. This, while not vintage me, was nevertheless the old Peachum: skewed: *Weltschmerz*-drenched: not a little reminiscent of the cosmic gibberish itself. Perhaps not a little marked by the ennui Magritte claimed to have been the motive power behind his paintings. I may get back to you on that later.

"He who seeks his fortune with a high heart has already found it," I shouted as the limo glided away, and the half-soaked cult laughed again and nodded, this time in recognition of a parody of the fortune-cookie phase I had happily climbed out of, as evidenced by my previous *saillie*. Try *that* in a fortune cookie! The customers would pick up their teapots and throw them at the silk-screen mural depicting a procession of people, one, an old man, carrying a sack on his shoulder, crossing a bridge toward a pagoda set amid fruit trees in fragile bloom.

By nightfall, with its sense of new beginnings, I am lurking in a Greenwich Village doorway, a cigarette burning in my fingers, enacting a bit of business. It's good practice for an actor. Chaplin never gave off doing bits of business for the amusement of friends or guests — on street corners, behind trees, anywhere. The routine I was rehearsing now is a cliché familiar to all moviegoers. There is dirty work afoot for which one character flashes a signal to another. Say a potential victim is leaving a saloon, or an armored truck marked for robbery rounds a corner. At least one of the confederates between whom the signal is flashed wears a snap-brim hat, pulled down over one eye, and smokes a cigarette. They are both in shadow, one usually pressed into a dark doorway. The one smoking a cigarette always flips it away after giving or getting the signal, and then, hunching his shoulders, moves on. That was the bit I enacted now. Nodding almost imperceptibly to my ally that the sign had been received, I stepped out of the doorway, snapping my cigarette away.

"For Christ's sake, Mac, watch where you're shooting cigarette butts, can't you?" a voice rang out in the night.

The lighted stub in its trajectory had apparently struck a passing pedestrian at about chest level, judging by the way he was slapping and brushing himself down there. He struck a note of genuine anger in the pantomime he enacted of "putting himself out," so to speak.

"Oh, I'm awfully sorry," I said, hurrying over to help tidy him. I slapped at his necktie, to which a spark or two still adhered. I drew him toward a street lamp, by the light of which I assured him that no great damage had been done his toilet, reiterating my apologies the while. He was a stocky man in late middle age, well dressed in a dark pinstripe suit and Homburg. There seemed to be a teensy perforation on one of the stripes of his tie, of which I made little.

"Maybe I can buy you a drink?" I said, having noted a certain rubescence to the nose, with tiny excrescences on either side such as are known in the South as grog blossoms. "Could do with one myself after this contretemps. I was about to head for that tavern over there, matter of fact."

"After this what?"

"Contretemps. An inopportune, or embarrassing, occurrence; a mishap."

"Well . . ."

We strolled along side by side toward a street corner where a sign reading Tic Tac Toe Club gave promise of refreshment.

"My name's Ted Peachum."

"Frank Candlestickmaker." He gave me a handshake that, injury for injury, left him even-steven and a little better. My metacarpals would no doubt be shipshape after a few weeks in splints, but if I was a concert pianist, forget it. Doctor Einhorn and I have been over these X rays together, and we have every confidence that as a page turner . . .

"What do you do, if I may ask?" I said.

"I'm a producer."

I was silent a moment, in hushed gratitude, if provisional, not daring to press my luck. At last: "Of what?"

"Movies."

I fairly trembled. This was too good to be true. Could it be my big break, coming mere hours, nay minutes, after settling into the small but moldering hotel from which I planned to wage my search for more permanent, if not more savory, digs? I would not immediately divulge that I was an actor; the disclosure coming so swiftly on the heels of our meeting might make the nature of it seem devised — a gimmick on my part as cinematically threadbare as the snicked-away butt. I hurried on with some more questions to forestall his asking what I was.

"What have you produced? I'm not as familiar with that end of . . ."

Here he reeled off half a dozen or so titles, none of which

I recognized. I soon gathered that he wasn't an executive or creative producer so much as a screen-struck financial backer. Nothing wrong with that. We marched in step toward the Tic Tac Toe Club, which on first entry struck me as some sort of low mecca for commuters who had just been routed by a raid, for the deserted tables seemed occupied only by attaché cases — a dive whence all had fled. Candlestickmaker explained that those were backgammon sets for the amusement of customers, and that no thickly painted ladies lurked behind the curtained doorway. We took a corner table, where he watered his grog blossoms with three or four bourbons, telling of his past activities and present embarrassments. A tycoon a little short till Saturday is not a reassuring entity; in any case he had lost his shirt on a recent film flop d'estime, while also taking a bath in the market, so now his usual position was reversed. He had an option on a theatrical property for which he was trying to *get* backing from others. I observed that our meeting had thus been for me, an actor, a sort of deus ex machina, only coming at the beginning of the story rather than the end.

"Deus what?"

"Deus ex machina. In Greek or Roman drama, a device or events unexpectedly introduced to resolve a situation, actually brought in by stage machinery to intervene in it. Literally, 'god from a machine.'"

Candlestickmaker looked around the now rapidly filling café, and suddenly realized he hadn't had any supper. His stomach thought his throat was cut. "They have wonderful pastrami sandwiches here."

The hole burned in his necktie being on close scrutiny much larger than at first realized, I sprang for one of those too, ordering the same for myself. I noticed that he ate his with a knife and fork, after asking the waitress to fetch them. This was to be explained later on when we had become "a quarter to nine" — his term for a relationship as close as the two hands of a clock are at that hour. He held out two fingers to illustrate. But the bond began to form even now.

"What is this property you've got an option on?"

"Three one-act plays all having to do with yearning," he said, gesturing with knife and fork after swallowing a mouthful of pastrami large enough to inspire a mental brushing up on the Heimlich. "Human yearning."

"Right."

"One has to do with a trapped housewife who longs to return to her ballet dancing. Another with a cop who's dying to crack a big case. The third with a youth craving to get to what he calls 'the big city and the bright lights.' He's lived all his boyhood on a New York street on the Lower East Side."

"And he yearns to get to midtown Manhattan."

"No, no, Chicago. That's the touching part. Chicago is to him the Big Town. He's been weaned on old period movies with like Edward Arnold taking the ladies on railroad trips to the Windy City to buy them dresses and hats, in *Come and Get It.* Western turn-of-the-century people longing to take the iron horse there, whole families dreaming of getting the hell out of Fargo and going *east* — to Chi! City of the big shoulders, hog butcher for the world!"

"People are quoting Sandburg at the turn of the century?"

"No, no. The character in the play. He's had him in school. He spouts him, to the consternation of his family."

"Sounds delightful. I'd like to read for that. Speaking of yearning."

"Go ahead." Here Candlestickmaker put down his eating utensils and drew a sheaf of manuscript from his breast pocket. "I happen to have a copy of that one with me." He flattened down the pages, which had been folded lengthwise. "Here's the weenie, this main speech of his right in here, the heart of it. Go over it a minute and then take a heave at it, if you want."

"Here?"

"Sure. You're not afraid of an audience, are you?" Candle-stickmaker laughed.

He finished his pastrami, with yet another bourbon, while I hastily read through the speech, which took nearly an entire single-spaced page. Then I indicated that I was ready to begin, cleared my throat, and did.

"No, stand up and do it the way it is in the scene. See, here's what I have in mind for that scene. He's standing at the window in a pose reminiscent of that painting of Renoir's called 'The Song of the Lark.' You remember it. The girl stands in the field listening — transfixed. Is that the word I want?"

"That's it," I answered, deeming it wisest not to add that "Renoir" was hardly the other *mot juste*. "Read it that way, as though the Big Town calling to him in his dreams is *his* Song of the Lark. The thought of one day fulfilling his destiny there kindles him, has him on fire. You can stand right over there," he said, indicating a fortunately rather secluded corner window next to our table. "But I want three things out of this." He ticked them off on his fingers. "Smoldering intensity — "

"Smoldering intensity."

" — underlying sadness."

"Right."

"And ethnic ambivalence."

"Got you."

I rose and circled toward the window behind Candlestick-maker. The back of his neck was creased in squares the size of the wire mesh in detention screens on the windows of mental institutions, just large enough for the occupant to put his fingers through while hollering, "Let me out of here!" A light fall of dandruff on his coat collar reminded me that snow flurries had been predicted. Through an unwashed pane of glass I could see two men engaged in earnest argument on

the sidewalk, apparently panhandlers pooling their take for
a bottle of wine. I struck a stance, head high as called for in
the scene or as high as possible consistent with having to read
the script, which was consequently held almost upside down,
free elbow back, as remembered from the painting, whether
accurately or not, my entire frame expressive of rapture.

"I'm going there one day — I'll get there," I read. "You'll
all see. To Chi. Just watch." Here a twisted grin left open the
question whether I was promising my family a show of
achievement of which they would be proud, or indicating my
need to get away from people whose guts I hated. Candlestickmaker, who sat switched around in his chair so he could
see me, nodded approval, as I gathered from a glance darted
downward at him. I returned my eye to the script. "I want so
much what's out there, waiting for me, I can taste it. The
organ rumble of the City itself, sophisticated people, money,
sure, money with which to buy furs and flowers for women
with bodies like racehorses. Chocolatcel Ecstacy in the afternoon! Ecstasy at night! The sleek flanks of expensive cars
purring along the old Boul Mich! You name it, I'll have it!
Moonlight on the Wrigley Building — "

Candlestickmaker cut me off with a flourish of his fork.

"The part's yours."

"You mean it, Mr. Candlestickmaker?"

"You give it most of what I'm looking for. The ethnic ambivalence is there, so is the underlying sadness."

"What about the smoldering intensity?"

He made the oscillating-hand gesture by which we indicate dubiety. "Not quite, but it'll come. It'll come as you grow
in the part. You'll do all right."

Broadway! Cradle of a thousand dreams. Graveyard of a
thousand hopes. The ineffable single most bewitching magnet
of the American dream.

"When do we start rehearsal?" I signaled to the waitress
for the check. "When do we start on that?"

"Well, that's the thing," Candlestickmaker said, plucking seven or eight paper napkins from the container. Through these he said, "What we're going to need first is money-raising auditions. There'll be a lot of them. It's the kind of production that won't attract one or two big angels, but needs a lot of little investors buying small shares. Half shares even. I've got a few of those lined up already. Do you think you could get yourself letter-perfect for an audition a week from Friday?"

That was how our association grew. Backers' auditions had got to be a sort of social fad that year, a theme for parties. Producers with musicals or revues on the front burner had no trouble finding after-dinner or cocktail-party audiences for a few songs and sketches; those with plays found ample hearings for essential scenes, or even an entire act. Hostesses got free entertainment. Of course potential investors also had the entire script available for private perusal. We did the three-character playlet in which I had the lead, over and over again in New York apartments and town houses, and I did grow in the part, Candlestickmaker even agreeing that the smoldering intensity, originally lacking, was soon unmistakable, permeating the entire role. We remained a quarter-to-nine, though he sometimes called us three-fifteen, which, of course, comes to the same thing.

Through those months I made new friends. I kept in touch with home, by mail and phone, corresponded with others in Pocock and elsewhere, keeping abreast of the gossip. I learned that Snooky and Ambrose were moving to New York, that Columbine had shown an interest in fashion modeling, and had had a response from a Chicago agency. Leland had thrown his back out while administering chiropractic treatment to a patient, and was under the care of an osteopath in hopes of shortening the interval till he might once again be profitably manipulating others. Kathy and Vim had their amicable divorce, and she and Phooey Haverstick were married and expecting their baby.

I often dropped into Candlestickmaker's Broadway office informally, now that we were a quarter-to-nine, and one morning learned the reason why he so frequently used utensils on foodstuffs most of us normally bite into. He was cutting up his midmorning Danish with a large pair of desk shears, snipping off a bit here, a corner there, washing each mouthful down with coffee.

"I have capped teeth," he explained, clacking the scissors, "these teeth are capped, and all of us with capped teeth — including Clark Gable I'm sure, whose were famous — live in constant fear of the jackets breaking off at inopportune moments, resulting in a contretemps. It's happened to me several times, once in a restaurant with friends, another time at a banquet, mind you."

"I understand," I said. "I have a couple capped myself, and had a jacket crack once. So you minify the strain on your teeth by eliminating the bite factor whenever possible."

"I what the strain?"

"Minify. That's the correct use of the word. Minimize, which people always say in the context in which I just used it, is wrong. That means to belittle. To reduce, or *keep*, to a minimum, for that minify is the correct usage."

He shook his head, snipping off another edge of the Danish. "If everybody talked correct English like you it would be the end of human communications. Would you like my secretary to bring you some coffee? It's the real. She has a percolator out there."

"That would be nice. Black, please."

"Good. Because we have something to talk about. You were down last night."

"I sensed it myself. I wasn't getting the subcutaneous melancholy."

"The what?"

"Underlying sadness. And the smoldering intensity wasn't so hot either. I was delivering my lines too fast, because I felt the hostess wanted to get on with the party, flitting around with cordials the way she was. Gertrude Buffalo was down too."

Candlestickmaker shrugged. "All actors are, once in a while." He ordered my coffee over an intercom. "Anybody can be down."

I agreed, having heard the term so often that I was beginning to think a lackluster performance now and again was the hallmark of a good actor. After thanking the secretary for the coffee she had brought, I quoted Max Beerbohm on the subject of fluctuating quality. " 'Only mediocrity is always at its best,' Max said."

"He the one who produced *Garter Street*?"

"No, no, this is a writer, talking about writers. Being uneven and stuff."

"You better be up Saturday. It's some people with real money, I understand. They could kick in with the, say, fifty thousand we need yet to get rolling. Get a good afternoon's rest, and I'll pick you up at nine-thirty sharp. The showcase is set for ten."

He was as good as his word, and at nine-thirty I climbed into the cab in which he called for me, dressed in the clothes I had to wear for the role: a T-shirt reading "Emma Goldman," a pair of painter's overalls, and soiled sneakers. When Candlestickmaker had given the driver an upper East Side address, I leaned back and asked: "Who are these people tonight?"

"A fairly young couple who just moved here from the Middle West. She's got the money, apparently. Inherited brewery money. Old German family. But the married name is fancy French. With a small 'd' and an apostrophe and God knows what all. I keep having to learn it all over again." He drew from his breast pocket an envelope on which the name and address were jotted: "d'Amboise."

"Let me out. Driver, stop."

"What's the matter with you?" Candlestickmaker said.

"I'm sick. I'm going to be sick. I can't go on tonight. Get my understudy."

"*Under*study for Christ's sake! Who do you think you are, some Broadway star with an understudy?"

The driver had in any case pulled to the curb by now, and I scrambled out, climbing past, not to say over, Candlestickmaker. I swung the door shut behind me but Candlestickmaker caught it and pushed it open again. "What the hell is this all about?"

"I know these people. They're intimate friends of mine. Too intimate. The wife and I once — but never mind that."

"So? Isn't that all to the good? Among friends?"

"Not in this case. You don't understand. You can get somebody to read my part. Or read it yourself. The very thought of — " I normally never drank before a performance, but I'd had a few tonight, with a Greek dinner that itself didn't seem to set very well. All that, together with the shattering nature of Candlestickmaker's revelation, brought on a few premonitory heaves, but nothing substantive. I hung over the gutter just in case.

"I don't get this," Candlestickmaker said, sitting on the edge of the seat and leaning out the door, which he persisted in holding open as though he might be going to be sick himself. "It turns out you happen to know these people and that's a *hazard*? It should break the ice, make everything easier."

"There are special circumstances which would make it very sticky in ways that I simply can't go into now. I'd be excruciatingly uneasy, and give a bad performance."

"Look. A thing like this, a popup, whatever, is exactly the test of whether somebody belongs in the theatre. Are you a trooper?" I knew from an office memo of his I'd seen that that was how he thought it was spelled. "The audition must go on. So get back in this taxicab."

"Not if he's going to barf his Twinkies he don't," the driver put in.

"You hear that? *He* knows the score. He knows the show's got to go on. If that doesn't shame you into a sense of your professional responsibilities I don't know what will."

"You've got the two other scenes. I've often gone on with one of them missing, or read another part myself," I argued.

"But this is *important* tonight. So are you a trooper, or a goddamn frigging poltroon?" That was another word I had given him, correcting his impression that it was some kind of bridge. Candlestickmaker flopped dramatically back in the seat. "You're a poltroon."

"Tu quoque."

Nothing was said for maybe an entire minute, as we all three remained frozen in time: Candlestickmaker slumped as though in an amateur elucidation of Despair, the cabbie with one hand on the wheel and his cheek resting on it, watching me, and I hanging over the curb in a tableau of arrested illness. Then Candlestickmaker, his head rolling on the back of the seat as though half decapitated by an executioner who had bungled the job, began softly to misquote Shakespeare.

"The coward dies over and over again. The valiant never die but once."

"Check," said the cabbie, straightening up. "To which strictures I will add that the meter is ticking away. I don't think he's going to upchuck. He's not green anymore. Hop in, Barrymore. But keep the window down."

Candlestickmaker added his good offices to the invitation. Leaning out the door again, a hand extended as though in Christian fellowship, he quietly resumed urging my return, this time like one trying to coax an animal back into its stall or a suicide off a ledge. "You been playing this role for over six months now. Actors in the other parts have come and gone, fallen by the wayside or going for fat salaries in soapies, but Ted Peachum has stuck. We just celebrated your fiftieth

performance with a party." That was true. Candlestickmaker
had asked several people down to the Tic Tac Toe for a supper that had only cost me a hundred dollars. "Tonight's the
biggie. The last, if these friends of yours come through and
invest. Don't vomit. *Triumph. Excel.* Show them what you've
got inside you."

"That's what I was afraid he was gonna do," the driver
chimed in, "but I think the danger's past. He looks all right.
Come on, climb in. You're gonna be just swell."

Candlestickmaker shoved over to make room as I got re-
luctantly back in. "He's right. You'll be just fine." He reached
past me and banged the door shut, waving to the driver to
hurry along. He laid a hand soothingly on my knee as we
shot away into the traffic. "What was that too something you
called me when I called you a poltroon? For which abject
apologies. Too something."

"*Tu quoque.* It's Latin for likewise you. You too. In other
words, a retort accusing an accuser of a similar offense. You
called me something and I called you the same thing right
back, by using that term."

"We say things in the heat of an argument that we don't
really mean. We'll let bygones be bygones. Well! What a
beautiful fall evening."

"It's also used in the nominative sense, as in 'They had a
tu quoque.' Hence a recriminatory altercation between two
people."

"What a command of the English language."

We were soon deposited before a new white-brick apartment building of clearly the luxury variety. It was on York
Avenue in the Seventies, overlooking the East River. Candlestickmaker tossed the driver a tip no doubt covering the
angst-making interval, and then a doorman in plum-colored
livery opened a glass door admitting us to a large, airy lobby.
A security guard announced Candlestickmaker and friend to

our hosts through a telephone, then an elevator shot us up eighteen floors to the top. A penthouse? A former suitor comes to play the jester at the princess's table, I thought, again following my avowed philosophy of self-pitying stoicism. A wandering minstrel, a thing of shreds and patches. And queasy to boot.

The dinner party was in its dessert stage at the table, and a maid showed us into a breakfast alcove off the kitchen where the other actors were being fed coffee and cookies. They were five in all, plus Hopalong Bunshaft, the director, so called owing to a hitch in his gait marginally reminiscent of Walter Brennan, but not so pronounced as to make the nickname in any way uncharitable. He called himself that, say, when he phoned you. "Hopalong here." We were chattering away in undertones, my back to the dining-room doorway, when I heard footsteps behind me, and there was Snooky in a long, peacock-blue hostess gown, full and flowing. Her face fell into a hundred dazzling pieces when she saw me.

"Ted, for God's sake! *You!*"

"Me, Snooky," I said, rising to take her embrace. "I had no idea till the last minute when Mr. Candlestickmaker here — Or I'd have phoned, of course, to ask whether it was O.K. If you minded — "

"Minded! Of course it's O.K. I knew you were trying to get work in the theatre here. Ambrose and I talked of looking you up. He's heading the eastern office of the brewery business, you know, and that's why we — Ambrose!" she called into the dining room. "Look who's here. Surprise! Excuse Ambrose a sec, all of you. No, you come on in, Ted." She snatched my hand and towed me into the dining room. Ambrose threw his arms aloft, rolling his eyes to heaven, as he rose from his chair at the head of a long candlelit table at which fourteen guests were finishing their baba au rhum. He shook my hand in both his, and then nothing would do but that an extra chair be dragged up so I could be wedged in at a corner of the table beside him. He introduced me to the guests, most of whom were young, a few early middle-aged, who must think what they must of my Emma Goldman T-shirt. Hopalong Bunshaft was for changing it, as few people now remembered the Russian-born anarchist of two generations ago. Wait till they got a load of Gertrude Buffalo's shirt with its "68" on the front and "70" behind. She only slipped it on for the auditions.

Snooky explained that she herself was working for an Off-Broadway group called Pegasus — as were some of the guests — and the interest tonight centered around the possibility of their incorporating *Yearnings* into the season's bill of fare.

"You're looking terrific," Snooky said from the far end of the table. "Ted was a furniture mover," she explained to her guests, "hence the gorgeous muscles. No wonder he wears a T-shirt for the part. Look at those biceps."

"I still am — part-time," I said. "How do you think actors live when they ain't working, which is most of the time? I'm on call with the Mercury Movers, and keyboard man for their piano crew."

"What's a keyboard man?" asked a red-haired thirtyish young woman with a mouth like a ripe plum, whose juicy pulps I had already in spirit tasted.

"The guy, usually of a crew of three," I answered, knowing I was going to do this butch, "who handles the keyboard part of an upright." I sucked in my stomach while for the rest swelling up like a blowfish. "There's the top man, alone above as you go up or down the stairs, and underneath the fiddle," I continued, hating myself for slinging my occupational slang like a hardy son of toil, "the heavy corner man and the guy at the keyboard — the lightest part. It's like being third banana. But of course we share the weight."

"Well, take care of your body while you've got it. You know what Auden says. In his Yeats poem."

I knew very well what Auden said, in his Yeats poem, but

I wanted to hear it from the burst-plum lips as, very gently, I parted her thighs by wedging a knee persuasively between them. I was beginning to be glad I had come after all. Her voice was low, a voluptuously soft, thick contralto, and made me think of ripe figs being hurled at high speed into a pan of gruel.

"What is the Auden you're thinking of?"

" 'Time that is something or other, and indifferent in a week to a beautiful physique.' "

"Ah, yes. Well, hard work is better than all that boring exercise. I'll remember what you said."

The show went on about fifteen minutes later, in an enormous living room overlooking the river fantasy, where the party had their coffee and liqueurs. The tinkling of spoons and clatter of cups were by now a familiar nuisance. I tried to give my role, particularly a long sort of soliloquy, my best, but I was distracted by Snooky's and Ambrose's being there. Also acutely aware of the succulent Auden-quoter. The three bits went about as well as usual, and, not to presume, I left with the rest of the troupe, and then went to a bar and got drunk with three of them, two girls and another man.

The next morning I awoke looking like a police sketch of myself put together from conflicting sources. There was the same unconvincing linkage between mouth and chin, the same blurred improbability about the eyeballs, as of revisions inked in under instructions from uncertain informants, all these further possessing a sort of scrambled relationship to brow and jawline, completing the overall sense of a whole assembled from contradictory impressions of someone fleeing the scene of a crime. "That does it," I said, turning away from the bathroom mirror. "I'll never touch another drop of the stuff." Except for a hair of the dog, of course, the efficacy of which is known of old. I would resist Cyril Connolly's dictum that a tuft of the dog was even better. I had a slug of jug wine from the refrigerator, then let a breakfast of ham and eggs work its restorative blessings. The telephone rang and it was Candlestickmaker, asking me to come up to his office "about eleven sharp."

I had inferred from some of last night's responses that the last of the needed money was assured, and the Pegasus group would stage the production. This could only mean that a contract awaited my signature, a supposition enforced by the sight of Hopalong Bunshaft in Candlestickmaker's office when I arrived. Candlestickmaker was scissoring up a prune Danish as I was shown in. He came right to the point.

"Peachum, we feel you've gone stale in the part."

"Stale."

"Yes."

"From doing backer auditions." I would eat this outrage slowly, savoring every morsel of it. I would gorge myself on outrage. Stale in the part and we hadn't even opened.

"Months of them. Hopalong agrees with me. You were down last night."

"Mechanical," Hopalong said. "You walked through it," he added, getting up out of his chair and sidling around toward a window behind Candlestickmaker's desk, possibly seeing some glint in my eye he didn't like. "You peaked about your twenty-fifth performance. That time on Beekman Place. Great. Last night was the first time I've seen it since then, and you've gone stale. Candy's right. In the long, crucial soliloquy particularly, you were in the basement. You stood there like the girl in 'The Song of the Lark.'"

"But he told me to do it that way! Didn't you? That night in the Tic Tac Toe. Didn't you, Candlestickmaker?"

"Yes, but not so mechanically. So we were thinking that maybe somebody like Corky Kramer, who *is* ethnic . . ."

I took three steps toward Candlestickmaker's desk and hunched toward him with my knuckles resting on it, like an ape.

"Now you listen, Candlestickmaker, and you listen good. And you tune in too, Hopalong. I been beating my gums for nothing for more than — "

"You've been given a half share in the property. You'll keep that, of course."

"Screw your half share. I want a contract, with a run-of-the-play clause writ in stone." I picked up the shears and began to clack them menacingly in midair, which caused Candlestickmaker to get up out of his chair and Hopalong to edge away from the window toward the desk, which they both began to circle in reverse, keeping it between them and me as I slowly pursued them around it. "The feast is finished and the lamps expire, the captains and the kings depart, and we'll go no more a-roving, plucking the strings of our insipid lutes. That right, boys?" I banged the desk with my fist. "Is that right!"

"Sure, Peachum, anything you say," Hopalong answered in a quavering voice as Candlestickmaker replied, "Not at all," in the same placating tone. They both feared they had a maniac on their hands, best humored, an advantage I pressed. The scene was going well. It moved. One wasn't down this morning! Every inflection told that we were no longer a quarter-to-nine — we were more like twelve-thirty.

"Now you both get this. I'll go to Equity with this — stale on investor auditions, ha! Who would believe *that* theatrical first. I'll go to Equity, and if that doesn't do any good I'll go to a lawyer. A whole firm of lawyers. And then I'll go to court. If necessary I'll go to the Supreme Court. And when I've sued you both for every nickel you've got, why, you know where I'll go then?"

"Where, Peachum?" they asked, still backing terrifiedly around the desk.

"I'll arise and go to Innisfree, and a small cabin build there of clay and wattles made. Nine bean rows will I have, and a

hive for the honey bee, and live alone in the bee-loud glade.
How does that grab you?"

"I see your point."

"Whatever turns you on."

"I'll stand there with the wind in my hair, and, of course,
vice versa."

The intimations were by now clear to both. If I heard any
more of this crud about going stale in the part — we'd see
about that in rehearsal — if I heard one more word, my expression said as I inched slowly toward them, still porten-
tously clacking the shears, I would cut Candlestickmaker up
like a midmorning Danish and have his guts for garters, while
by the time I got through with Hopalong *both* legs would be
shorter than the other, and not just one.

"I shan't be gone long — you come too," I finished with a
hideous grin.

"How's Equity minimum and say an extra fifty a week?"
Candlestickmaker said.

"And a run-of-the-play clause," Hopalong said, a pale
green by now.

That didn't mean too much, as the show was only a moderate success, running three and a half months. The notices
were all right, with a few of the actors singled out for special
mention, not including me.

A more significant upshot of the whole period had to do
with the relationship between Snooky and Ambrose and me,
as now renewed. We were shown to be still very much a
viable triangle, and what was more, our triangle was going
to work because we were going to *make* it work.

Twelve

"Two's a crowd."

I had no women disciples, and no wish to be talking to Snooky as though she were one — it wasn't meant that way at all. It was not a matter of throwing her a trenchancy or two, a few obiter dicta to beguile a misty autumn afternoon, rather of honestly answering questions she posed as we strolled up Second Avenue. I had an armchair on my head, one we had picked up from a small repair shop where she'd had it restored. I of course held the eighteenth-century silk rep *fauteuil* in the traditional mover's carry, upside down with the back behind so I could see where I was going, as of old. She was worrying, or at least wondering, about the progressive erosion of marriage in our time. As there had once been whirlwind courtships, there were now whirlwind divorces. She had friends splitting up after two years, a year — six months. Dustups and bustups to right and left of us. I read into this some unvoiced anxiety about her own union, now a little over a year old, but I could have been wrong. So I was giving my views. I sensed a few magnetized New Yorkers collecting about me, though of course they could have been merely pedestrians going our way anyway, rather than pickup disciples eager not to miss a word. It made no matter.

"The capacity for tight grips and close quarters, living in one another's pockets, seems to be waning in our time," I discoursed as we forged steadily northward. "Is it the declining willingness to cope? Or is it simply the relaxation of moral rigidities that in previous eras alone held together marriages equally not worth the enduring? Are we breeding too sensitive an organism, less and less up to the clasp and clutch of entwined existence? Has the liquidation of Mosaic thou-shalts struck from our wrists the fetters that alone chained our forebears to those awful double beds?" I seemed to be asking questions rather than answering them, perhaps a new phase. It was, in any case, time for a declarative sentence. Telepathically, I seemed to sense impatience for a pearl in an eavesdropper on my right and a step behind — possibly a peripatetic recruit, for he had remained in step when we had veered right toward York and the d'Amboise apartment. Shifting the *fauteuil* some, I said, "Irritation levels and boredom thresholds are now so low as to be flush with the floor. Two has, in our hypersensitized, narcissistic time, become, indeed, a crowd — while three may, not inconceivably, be company."

As the generalissimo opened the apartment-building door to admit us, the now clearly perceived aficionado, a thin blond man with a cat-scratch mustache, smiled and waved as he passed in and out of my life, with a grateful nod of approbation for the gem flung out upon the public afternoon, into the public domain. There was also the recognition that, were things otherwise, he would sup with me and I with him. If he knocked, it would be opened unto him; if he asked, he would receive.

The generalissimo let us take the *fauteuil* up on the passenger elevator, instead of the freight lift in back, and so presently I was slogging ankle-deep in shag rug toward the master bedroom with it. I set it down in the spot Snooky indicated, plopping into it myself with a hearty "Whew!"

"You deserve a drink after all that."

Our hero ran a delaying eye around the room. It was decorated in a "tweed" beige wallpaper neutral enough to accommodate without collision the conglomerate riches it enveloped: the Empire bureau and matching dressing table, the Chagall with its villagers afloat in midair, the teardrop chandelier, and the twin beds decked in rich cream-colored brocade beneath which one caught glimpses of drum-taut peppermint-striped sheets. Oh, Snooky.

She could not have failed to read my thoughts.

"I suppose all this looks familiar to you."

"You've moved practically everything out of your old bedroom. It's not the first time I've sat in this chair, is it?" I fondled an arm of it with my palm, smiling ruefully with the little-lost-boy look used to such advantage in times past. Were things otherwise, she would have been tousling my hair by now. "Yes, I've been here before, in Pocock, and you know they were among the happiest hours of my life. I realize I'm a clod to say it, now."

I wish I knew what she was about to reply, because as she opened her mouth to speak the door buzzer sounded, and, excusing herself, she flew to answer it. I shot over to the dresser and after rummaging in a couple of drawers found a pink silk to nuzzle with one tenderly inclined cheek, while making the whinnying noise now definitely recognizable as Not My Style. The evidence was mounting. Again there was the most satisfyingly jarring sense of behaving absolutely atypically. I was enacting the cretin I was emphatically not. This was wildly out of character. I was not a moron, and should not have had to go to such lengths to certify as much. But the muffled sound was not unlike the little whimpers of pleasure characteristic of Snooky herself when making love.

Charming, charming. Grace notes. In the horsing-around epilogues of the old days I would often, in lieu of one of her hats or a handy lampshade, make a cap of her underpants, pulling it on over my head as I capered around the room for her amusement. Or I would draw them on properly when, she in something of mine such as a shirt, we went down to the kitchen to forage for snacks. We liked to put each other's things on. What memories. Snooky laughing gently as I reached my peaks, with a woman's deep, deep joy at bringing a man to such ecstasy. Snooky drinking off a last lingering dewdrop, squeezing it forth like sap from a flower stem. She said she plagiarized the gesture from *Lady Chatterley's Lover*, though I have scoured my copy in vain for the precedent.

I thrust the garment back into its drawer and hurried down the hall to the living room just as she entered it carrying a parcel the doorman had brought up.

"Are you going to audition for *Stars of a Summer Night*?" she asked as she set it down and made for the liquor cabinet. It was Thursday, and the maid was off.

"I'll have nothing more to do with Candlestickmaker."

"Why not?"

"He should get slivers under his fingernails from scratching his head."

"I see. Bourbon and water, right? Hey, no, there's a half bottle of some great Burgundy Ambrose bought in the icebox. What's left of our second bottle last night." Had she almost said "battle" and corrected herself?

"That sounds good. Why, I was walking to the theatre with Candlestickmaker one afternoon during rehearsal, and a man coming toward us saw him and ducked around a corner. Candlestickmaker said, 'My nemesis. He owes me two yards, so he scrams every time he sees me.' That's what he calls a nemesis. Somebody who ducks around corners to avoid him."

I shook my head. I had followed Snooky into the kitchen,

where I again lusted for her as she poured the remainder of some Bâtard-Montrachet into two large glasses.

"You should find things like that rewarding. He once told me something about being in the dulldrums. Well, maybe that's the way it should be pronounced. Is two yards two hundred dollars?"

"Yes. Once he spoke of keeping an ear peeled for funny sounds in his car on a vacation trip. Keeping an ear peeled." Again I shook my head at the wonder.

I sat on a sofa. She started to take a chair, then changed her mind and joined me, probably deciding the other would have been too obvious a gesture of avoidance. We clinked glasses and drank. "Good old Montrachet," I said. "You can feel those fumes going up into the crevices of your brain. Like incense. Is Ambrose liking running the New York office?"

"Oh, sure. It leaves him enough freedom to bustle around for the Pegasus rep group and what not. We've become patrons of the arts. Can you imagine anything more stodgy?"

"You stodgy never. I have a good shot at something in a new soap opera. *The Adrian Family.* One of the brothers. Stuck in a bank but yearning for self-enrichment. At the audition the director said he wanted a smoldering intensity. Smoldering intensity is large this year. If you haven't got it don't bother to get up. Well, I have a callback on it for tomorrow."

"Oh, great, Ted. I hope you get it."

Snooky had set her glass down on a coffee table, and with her last words she had instinctively laid a hand on my arm — a friendly gesture. I took it in mine and pressed it gently. I am ordure. I am an abomination to myself. Still, she laid her other hand over the top of mine. I set my glass down and tilted her face upward by her chin, lowering mine to kiss her. Undeserving of the good will of others, worthy only to be cast out. I sent the tip of my tongue out on a patrol mission, and was rewarded by feeling hers flickering responsively against it. An insect, to be flushed down the sink.

She drew back with a sharp sigh. "I couldn't deceive a man in his own house. Like violate the marriage bed."

"Of course." I settled into a corner of the sofa. After a moment of silence, I reached for my wine. Then I heard the top of my head blow off.

"But maybe I'll come to your place."

"Oh, baby."

"I mean it's something that exists anyway. It wouldn't be anything new. I think Ambrose has some kind of obbligato going, somewhere. Said she with a touch of self-justification."

I am of two minds about myself — at least. I have this crush on myself — but the feeling is not returned. It's not mutual. I don't know to this day whether I'd have gone ahead with Snooky, my affection for Ambrose being what it was, had my conscience not been eased by her news that he himself was up to something extramarital. Nor do I know whether she'd have gone back to bed with me without the balm of that extenuation. But here we were, threshing about in one another's arms again, in my Village digs.

Again, we struck every note on the keyboard. She moaned with her mouth full of me as I sipped the nectar from her flower. Then more quadruped love, and what a thrill it was to have her on her knees, goring her between those great globes, the melons of her breasts gripped in my palms. Later we basked in one another's arms, drowsing, one of my knees wedged between her spicy thighs. What a mount!

When apart from her, my fantasies had of course always been erotic — imagination well documented by memory! Now it was the reverse. As she snoozed I wool-gathered about domesticity with such a one. What would it be like to live in one another's pockets, our clothes hanging in the same closet, winter and summer, day and night? I was thinking of real marriage, or at least cohabitation, not just playing house, as now, when we rose for the icebox-raid ritual.

"Allow me," I said, helping her into my shirt. She rolled the cuffs up, then started to button it. "No, leave it open."

"If it's Sodom and Gomorrah time, here," she said, picking up her earrings from the dresser where she'd left them, and screwed them onto my lobes. They were large gold hoops, and she snicked one with a finger as she said, "In any buddy system you'd be the butch fag, wouldn't you, you teamster." I simpered some macho. She led the way into the kitchen, looking pleasantly ridiculous inside my flapping shirttails. She always liked this switchplay, more than I did, once even wanting to make me up. I had protested when she actually started digging lipstick and a compact out of her bag. The subject seemed to fascinate her. "And I suppose I'd be the bull dyke?" She made a question out of it with the expression of smiling inquiry sent over her shoulder.

"Like hell. You're too gloriously all-woman, though I can see members of the sisterhood getting a good yearn on you."

"It's nice with you too, Ted." We were now side by side in the kitchen, my arm around her. "There's just one thing, if you don't mind."

"What's that?"

"I've always hated my nickname. How it got stuck on me in high school I don't know. Nobody here calls me that."

"Consider it buried forever. Do you prefer Sandra or Sandy?"

"Either one."

"Done and done, Sandy," I said, remembering that Ambrose called her Sandra, probably also under optionalized instructions.

"Good God, here's an apple with one bite out of it." She was bent over, peering into the icebox. There was some good lean prosciutto, and I scrambled some eggs to go with that

"Did you know a few people have called me Peachy, including Candlestickmaker of all people? That was when we were a quarter to nine, and not like now, half past twelve. Well, twenty after."

"He's coming Sunday afternoon with a playwright and a couple of actors, to read a script to a bunch of us. Why don't you drop in? Bury the hatchet."

"I may just do that."

Here we were chatting across the kitchen table, just like husband and wife. One of the earrings dropped into my scrambled eggs, and she fished it out and screwed it back onto my ear, after wiping it off with her napkin. We traded stories about objects falling into people's food, like the time a broken clasp sent a rope of pearls cascading into her mother's spaghetti at a church lap supper, and a clip-on bowtie fell into her brother-in-law Vim's soup at a formal banquet. This, then, was marriage? Where the strain? As Sandy talked, I felt secret quivers of pleasure at the sight and sound of her eating the scrambled eggs, tucking forkfuls of it sensuously between those wide, red, rubbery lips, smacking them as she gulped her coffee. I often have that experience at dinners, particularly when sitting beside a woman with whom I am huddled in progressively more intimate conversation. If the woman is pretty or at least sensuous, there is almost no limit to the responses seething inside a man experiencing such moments close up. She can talk as she eats and eat as she talks, who cares, the chewing and salivating become a kind of crescendo of stimulation, genuinely sexual, the reverse of the grossness it might be under other circumstances. If there are strawberries for dessert, I want her to hold one poised in her teeth and then, leaning slowly toward me, ever more tantalizingly as our faces meet, slip it voluptuously between mine. Of course such a suggestion is not practical in polite society, especially if you have just met the lady, but these are often my thoughts as my partner or my vis-à-vis spoons a berry into her mouth and I imagine it — see and *hear* it — being chewed, the red juice running from its bursting pulp over her tongue, mingling with her saliva, slipping through the crevices between her teeth before sluicing down her throat and into her bloodstream. *Yech,* you say? So much the worse for you. Once a creep, you add? Go boil your socks. I want to run howling to the hostess's escritoire and start a poem with lines in it like "the liquors of thy mouth" for the partner or vis-à-vis (a woman of forty-eight with three grown children yet) to tuck in her bosom for later perusal at home. Oral exchanges of strawberries and grapes and other tidbits had always figured in Sandy's and my love play, but I thought I'd better draw the line at scrambled eggs. These were runny, as we liked them, but, oh, I had such a sweet sense of the purity of the flesh as I watched her lustily put them away. We had a glass of white jug wine later, and frolicked with an oral exchange of that, laughing over the hydraulic problems entailed as she wiped her chin.

"Is it your father you said keeps a wad of prosciutto in his cheek, like chewing tobacco?"

"No, that's Pinky Montmorency, who works for us. Yes, he'll tuck a quid of it in his jaw, couple of strips, and leave it there, spitting the juice out just like it was cut plug. I got into the habit myself once, for a while," I said, adjusting one of my earrings at a mirror. "When we were near an Italian delicatessen somewhere, he'd go in and buy a few slices and stow them away. I tried it when I was a kid on the truck, firing a jet out the cabin window just like the men."

"Part of your butch side."

"I guess. Christ, there goes the other earring. I guess my lobes aren't thick enough." I removed its mate and set them both on the table. "Are we going to waltz again?"

"I have to go soon," Sandy said, taking my extended hand in both hers. "Ambrose used to wear one earring, didn't he? In high school. Like a pirate."

"Yeah, when it was a kind of fad with the kids. My mother used to say, 'As long as he don't wear two.'"

She shared my laugh only to the extent of smiling, and then only half-heartedly, lowering her eyes to the table as she let go my hands. "Ambrose had a great capacity for friendship, or has, I should say. I was only thinking of the past, with you. In your experience."

"None loyaler. That's why I feel kind of sticky about this. Only you led me to believe that he . . . I mean it's up to you. It's your moral bookkeeping."

"Do you think he's double-jointed?"

I assumed she meant in the anatomical sense, which in fact was the case with Ambrose, who could crack his knuckles and bend his fingers into incredible shapes. Then I seemed to hear a kind of high-frequency *ping* at the far edge of my mind. I pretended not to realize the turn the conversation was taking, and answered, "He's certainly that. He can bend his middle finger back nearly flat along his hand. It always gave me the willies."

"His friendship with Mack Turner — you know, the photographer who took the pictures for your play — is getting a little rich for my blood." Did she really think he had one foot in that denomination?

"Nonsense. It couldn't be thicker than his and mine, and we're both straight as tamaracks."

"I suppose." She sighed and rose. "I don't, in any case, have much stomach for deception. So . . ."

"Oh, God, Snooky, I — Sorry. Sandy. You mean you want to break this off? Please don't tell me that."

"No, I mean I think I'll tell him."

"Oh, Jesus, don't do that."

She nodded, as though to herself. "I think I will." She bobbed her head a moment longer, in confirmation of her decision.

"What if he hits the ceiling? It would kill us aborning. We couldn't make love in a shambles like that."

"I don't think he will." She started slowly back to the bedroom, taking off my shirt. "Something he said once, about us now, makes me think he can live with it. I'd find it hard to live with this — and besides, we promised there'd be no secrets. Absolutely open, free, and honest. So come Sunday, it's three o'clock. Maybe Candlestickmaker will let you read with the others."

Thirteen

Candlestickmaker arrived in an overcoat of a plaid so loud that when it was removed and shut in a closet a hush seemed to fall over the house. Sandy and Ambrose being busy in the kitchen with refreshments and other preparations, I had gone to answer the door. Neither his actors nor any of the guests had arrived yet. I led him into the living room. Once over his first disgust at seeing me, Candlestickmaker became more relaxed. "Back begging again," he said, dropping a script on a table.

"Oh, don't look at it that way," I said. "Your money raising isn't eleemosynary."

"Isn't what?"

"Eleemosynary. Relating, or devoted, to charity or alms. So you shouldn't regard yourself as a mendicant."

"A what?"

It was like old times again as we fell naturally into the cadence that had always been characteristic of our conversation.

"Beggar. With a tin cup, or perhaps wooden bowl, clutched

in a wasted hand outstretched to heedless passersby hurrying through the marketplace, while flies buzz round your suppurating sores in the Oriental sun."

"Jesus H. Christ. O.K., what's suppurating?"

"Generating pus, or a puslike condition. Except for those lesions that, of course, have undergone suberization."

"That's bad."

"No, that's good. Suberization is the conversion of the cell walls into cork tissue by the development of suberin, as when a callus forms over a wound."

"So I'll pull through."

I gave the flat-handed wag by which he had so often expressed doubt over my performances. "It's touch and go. There are possibly maleficent signs of a recrudescence of the dorsal putrefactions."

"There's one I'm genuinely curious. I've often wondered. What's a recrudescence?"

"It's a sort of loganberry, related to the — Excuse me, there's the door. The d'Amboises will be right out."

"You're very thick with them." I heard him muttering the name of the Lord again, along with something about living to torment him, as I hurried to the vestibule, in time to collide with Ambrose, also on his way to the door. I deferred to him and went back to the parlor — into which actors and guests were presently pouring.

The play opened with a man in tattered evening dress panhandling on a winter afternoon. He has seen better days. Much better, the formal garb being not tuxedo but white tie and tails, no less. Between approaches to pedestrians, which are done with a sidling, hangdog air, he plucks at strands of his threadbare coat, or makes fidgeting adjustments of his white tie, which is filthy dirty, as is his vest. He is trying to mooch enough for cab fare to get back to his nearby country estate. "Can you spare a quarter, buddy?" he whines, palm up. "Give a guy a break." No wonder Candlestickmaker had begging on his mind when he came in. He let me read the part of Clodstrup, a patient in the mental sanatorium which the estate turns out to be, who thinks he is a seal. I flopped about the living room on my knees with great gusto, my arms held close to my sides so my hands would simulate flippers, waddling along with that sense of hamstrung diligence that seals seem to elucidate, climbing arduously up onto chairs and sofas while the other screwballs read their lines. Seals in repose are blobs of gelatinous inanition, until they suddenly get up and act as though they have a thousand things to do. I felt myself getting stale in the part after five minutes, diverting myself by mentally resisting the temptation to nuzzle my way up women's laps. I am swill. Scum. There is no denying it. The script was of course black humor, with the premise that delusions are even better than illusions at making life bearable. The crazier you are the luckier, as shown by contrasting the state of mind of the patients with those of the staff. It had a lot more quality than such a probably unfair résumé sounds, though I doubted anybody there was going to put any money into it. The reading was over by five, and after that it became a cocktail party till seven or so. "I liked the penultimate scene best," I told Candlestickmaker, dropping us back into our preordained rhythms. Finally there was nobody left in the apartment but the maid in the kitchen and Sandy and Ambrose and me in the parlor chattering up a smokescreen around our collective self-consciousness. I was sure she had told him about "us."

"I didn't think much of that piece of schnitzel," Ambrose said, the familiar twitch of his nose making his glasses jump. He sat with one leg up on an ottoman, his small frame slumped far down in an easy chair, and he kept twirling and untwirling on his finger a piece of twine he had picked up somewhere. "The guy in threadbare evening dress was good, but the character wasn't developed."

"I doubt we'll take it on at Pegasus," Sandy said, "but look.

What was all that about the Deerfield glint the doctor kept talking about. That went by my left ear."

Ambrose came to life, heaving himself upright in the chair.

"I remember about that from when I looked at Deerfield with my father. It's what the headmaster there used to say he looked for in a boy. He might not be scholastically up to snuff, but if he had the Deerfield glint in his eye, he'd take a chance on him. Like a banker will on a loan applicant even if he doesn't have the collateral. That's the Deerfield glint."

None of us had it here, God knew. The air was thick with evasive deception. When would we stop avoiding one another's gaze?

"What is the matter with Candlestickmaker?" Sandy said. "I don't dig him."

"I just figured him out, Sandra, honey. He's what used to be called an immitigable blatherskite. That was when people knew how to talk."

"The days when they said 'damnable,' " I threw in.

"The way you and he talk together. This kind of antiphonal conversation. It's like an Episcopal ritual."

The maid dismissed, we made a snack supper out of the rest of the canapés, and on the second of Ambrose's bottles of thirty-dollar Montrachet (thank God for beer breweries) we showed every sign of thawing out for the confrontation. Our minds would melt into amiably funny shapes, like silly putty. Midway the second bottle I was repeating my seal triumph. Hands once more bent into flippers, I waddled across the floor on my knees, barking hoarsely. There were gales of laughter as I tried over and over to flop up onto a couch. "All right, have it your way, you heard a seal bark," Ambrose said to Sandy as she went, smiling, to the kitchen to get some more butter. My mouth snapped at something imaginary in the air. The circus trainer was throwing me fishes as rewards for feats well accomplished. My mouth began to work at horn bulbs arranged in horizontal sequence.

"He's playing our song!" Ambrose called to Sandy, who shouted from the kitchen that she understood.

"Hoink, hoink, hoink," I said, in tone pitches leaving no doubt that I was playing "Brighten the Corner."

"I know about you and Sandra."

"Hoink, hoink. Hoink, hoink, hoink." Someone far from harbor you may guide across the bar. Brighten the corner where you are!

"Fella." I waddled past him, making for a chair, my shoulders wagging busily from side to side, all abustle. "I want you to know that, while to me it's nngaa, not the greatest thing since sliced bread, I understand. I'm not going to snort and paw the ground and lock antlers with you."

"Thanks, old man." *What?* I thought in the chair, nursing my by now rather chafed knees. "Thanks, old man." That was worse than "Look here, we don't want your sort in this club, Tremayne."

"Call it a preexisting nonconformity.

"*What?*"

Sandy returned in time to be civilized with us. All three of us, together, civilized. Well, *being* civilized at least. Not quite the same thing.

"Ambrose is a brick," she said.

"Why, a preexisting nonconformity," Ambrose dilated, "is an irregularity, such as a house on one acre in a two-acre zone, or a commercial structure like a tavern or dress shop in a residential area, that *predated the municipal ban against them.* You two were lovers before Sandra and I were, so it's as though nothing new has come in to disrupt the picture."

"That's right," Sandy said. "My fondness for Ted doesn't qualify my love for you. I think I've got enough to go around. You get no less heat from a fire because a friend is warming his hands at it. I told you about it because, while I might do something wrong, I won't do anything sleazy. Deceptive.

This is an open marriage, we'll both be free. No lies and no chains."

"All right, let's really be free," Ambrose said. "Let's all go to bed together. We're drunk enough."

I had to do it. There was no way of getting out of it. Weren't we free, to do as we pleased? Absolutely liberated agents? Or did we just sit around making a noise like emancipation? The Eskimos . . .

We bathed and dried Sandy together, on our knees, then took quick showers ourselves. Ambrose had her first, while she breast-fed me, somehow, because it was close quarters. She wanted it that way. After her first crisis, she wanted an interval with each of us kissing a breast, all four of our hands roaming her, one of hers caressing each of us, moaning softly as she came into fresh excitement. For me, she was quadruped, on her hands and knees with Ambrose being suckled on his back, underneath her. After these gymnastics, and a few others, we all lay quite depleted together, on the floor of course, a twin bed not being large enough to accommodate all this.

She murmured lazily, "Do you boys think you could take me *en sandwich?* I read the term in a book once. I don't quite know what it means."

"We can figure it out," Ambrose said.

"I've got it doped out already," I said. "But think of the position this puts Sandy in."

"But not now."

"You want to know something?" Sandy said.

"I've always wanted to."

"You're neither of you very big, until it gets angry. Then you leave nothing to be desired. A girl is quite filled up."

"Well, that's the thing," Ambrose said, rolling onto his side and propping himself on an elbow. "It's a phenomenon. The bigger it is the less it swells. The smaller it is the more it does, when the time comes. An inch or two can get to be six, but six won't get you twelve."

"I love you both, I truly do. Ambrose a little more than Ted, but I hope there's enough to go around. Didn't Hemingway and Fitzgerald have an argument once about the sizes of their dingdongs? How silly it all is. Like women and their breasts. I'm still hungry. Let's see what's in the kitchen."

Drawing on his bathrobe, Ambrose said: "This was all predicted by Pascal. Pascal said that the loss of God would lead to two things. Megalomania or erotomania, or both."

"He was bound to come into it," I said.

"He did with Ted's nervous breakdown. Here he is again."

It continued for months, a year or more, our idyll. Until suddenly, one day, I fell madly in love with a set of triplets, and they with me.

ourteen

I met the first of the Peppermint Sisters in an East Side bar.
It was mid-November, and the rose, as the maid of Amherst
put it, was out of town. I had got the part of the banker
brother who knew there must be something else out there, in
the new television serial, and was pulling down fifteen hundred dollars a week. Back in Pocock, my parents were "making a go of it," the Prophet was still chewing the firmament,
Kathy and Phooey Haverstick were enjoying their little son,
Dr. Leland d'Amboise had again thrown his back out while
chiropractically manipulating a patient, and was once more
in the hands of an osteopath who "made no bones" about
thinking Leland might need spinal fusion. Columbine had
dropped out of college and was making good money as a
fashion model, enough, I was secretly suspecting, though
without documentation, to help Larsen through his own
school years. If she continued in that career, there was every
likelihood of her turning up in New York. I was totally un-
decided about whether in that case I wanted to see her again.
Days when I wasn't busy at the Long Island studio where

the soap opera was shot, I took what work I could get at the Mercury Movers, partly to keep in shape, partly because I liked moving furniture (frequently with a quid of prosciutto in my cheek) and sweating honestly with other men in an ambiance wreathed in the good coarse close sex musk of burlap.

I was roosting at the bar over a beer, dressed in a tan corduroy jacket and a life-affirming tie, eye-sparring with a girl in a raspberry-colored coat seated in a nearby booth. The only other customer was a man two stools away with as sullenly resentful an expression as I have ever seen. From time to time he muttered to himself under his breath. At last he finished his whiskey and slunk out with the look of a disinherited cat.

I slid down off my stool and walked over to the booth where the girl was sitting. My claim to resilience lay in leaving my beer on the bar till we had seen how this overture materialized. But I was quite smitten by the luminous blue-green eyes, gold curls and peaches-and-cream complexion.

"I'll buzz off if you'd like," I said, ardently.

"Park your carcass."

I got my beer and returned. "I won't tell you you're beautiful," I said, sliding in across from her. "You already know that. When you finish that drink say the word. What on earth is it?"

"Scotch and skim milk. Now what?" She leaned with her forearms on the table, her fingers folded backwards up to the second knuckles.

I took a pull on my beer and said, "Flee into some forgotten night and be of all dark long my moon-bright company. Beyond the something of Paradise come, out of all something make our home. Seek we some close hid something for our lair, hallowed by Noah's mouse beneath the chair wherein the Omnipotent, in slumber bound, nods till the piteous Trump of Judgment sound. There of your beauty we would joyance make, repeat joyance, a music wistful for the sea-nymph's sake."

"That's rather a large order."

"Walter de la Mare, a not sufficiently appreciated poet of the old school."

"It's terrific. It goes through you, like band music. Especially the part about the Omnipotent."

"Nodding till the piteous Trump of Judgment sound. Doesn't that send a charge up your spine?"

"You can probably spout the stuff by the gallon. Nobody's ever recited poetry to me before. Makes a girl feel — old-fashioned."

"Imagine anybody saying 'joyance' today. Christ, they'd lock him up. I think we should all be a lot cornier, don't you? Let it out. Promise me you and I will always be corny. Like, this is already 'our place.' Right?"

"And put some money in the jukebox and we'll have a song."

"Are there any more at home like you?"

"Yes. Here comes one now,' she said, and in walked an exact replica, except for hair tinted Titian instead of blond, who said, "Hi," and slipped in beside her.

Mine was the classic confusion of the suitor in love with a twin, who when he sees the other must love her as well— except that I experienced this sweet bewilderment in triplicate. Because the third tripped in minutes later, brunette-haired, and there they all were, eerie photocopies of one another, identically dressed for an audition in a nearby theatre where a musical was in preparation. The Peppermint Sisters was the professional name taken by three Wallace girls named, in the order met, Trish, Chelsea and Mona.

They all drank Scotch and skim milk and they all smoked Kools. There was an extended unanimity in our all four hating math and believing that you only live once. Notes were compared that soon verged on the intimacy miraculously attainable by strangers, while withheld from intimates with whom one has lived for years. I sensed a readiness in all of them for a good round of rosebud gathering, and I found myself trembling with anticipation. I told them the fact of Time's wingèd chariot at our backs could not be too strongly emphasized in a world full of peanut butter and jelly and hundred-mile-an-hour winds, or too sedulously borne in mind. After explaining what sedulous meant I hurried on to stress the desperate importance of a woman enjoying her beauty whilst she had it. I leaned across the table, my face burning with urgency. "I mean all over the world there are old men living in Fort Lauderdale with beepers in their pockets that beep when it's time for their one o'clock pills, then their three, then five, let alone when it's time to pick up their wives, and so on, lolling back in their lounge chairs with their hats down over their eyes talking about crack trains and molten mamas. That comes soon enough. Soon enough the snow turns to slush and then the slush swirls off into the gutter and down the sewer. So let's throw nonchalance to the winds and become downright Dionysian!"

"So *cool*."

"What a smooth article."

"The epitoam of suavity."

"When kwee start?" This from Chelsea, the Titian, glass at lip.

My eyes must have bulged as I took in the implications (and challenges): I was to have them *en bloc*. Dionysian indeed! They had to run now, for the audition, but a rendezvous was set for Saturday afternoon.

It occurred in the hotel room I made my digs while looking for a new apartment. We were biped, quadruped, supine, prone, upside down and inside out. Those first conjunctions can hardly be recollected even in tranquillity — *especially* in tranquillity — but think of Rube Goldberg constructions *vivants*. For them I had to summon up the strength for exer-

tions I'd wot not of. I was a priapic stunt man. I scarcely
knew into whom I sank, initially, but it was one of those
orgasms that unjell the eyeball, rattle the windows of the
Chrysler Building, and cause thousands to cancel their *Grit*
subscriptions. Then, "Is it twirly tweet?" "No, it's not twirly
tweet. I'm starved." Food was sent up by a room-service
waiter who was an exponent of stertorous breathing, and who
interpreted as he must the noises from the bathroom where
the three graces were secreted. Chicken and shrimp salads,
and then it was back to the drawing board. We managed a
quadrilaterally synchronized swoon that unstuck the wallpaper and derailed a train near Perth Amboy. "You all knock
my socks off," I announced as I collapsed under them in a
moist jumble. I lay there for some time with one arm across
my eyes, like one flung there in a game of living statues.

"Kwee come back next week? Kwee do this again?"

"We'll see. Maybe the week after. Alternate Saturdays
might be best."

Hands clapped amid squeals of delight. Being swarmed
over by the luscious trinity made one feel like those cartoon
explorers being ministered to by grateful Polynesians in a
hammock slung between two trees, natives to be described
in their notebooks as seeming friendly. They lay wreathed in
one's arms, purring like electronic cash registers. The third
conclusion was nothing much in either intensity or duration,
doing little more than startle a few pigeons on the windowsill
and dislodge an inlay in a molar.

"Wit in a man may save a marriage. Wit in a woman, de-
stroy it."

But they were not disciple material.

The next animal act took place two Saturdays later. I was
beside myself, which made five of us in all, you might say.
Half the time I seemed to be doing my seal imitation, for
though much of this could be conducted on the double bed
a lot of it took place on the floor. At one point we had to

maneuver around a framed color print propped against one wall, for I have a peculiarity — a phobia if you will — about which I will tell you. The first thing I do when checking into any hotel room is remove the Utrillo hanging over the bed and set it down somewhere else, for fear of the nail's coming loose in the plaster and dropping the picture on my head when I'm asleep. Mona had the knack of adjusting the cliché that lies in wait for the most esoteric of us. "This thing is bigger than all four of us," she puffed prettily at one point.

How to get that across to one's menage à trois, if the digression were discovered? Peachum had a scenario, rehearsed to the last haggard detail, a scene in which he would justify himself to the woman he had betrayed. "I'm in love with triplets, y'all. They're crazy as toenails, but nice. You'll like them." As to that, the triplets all had Morton's toe — where the second toe is longer than the great — and had it in common with Peachum, as noted by Trish in some sweet configuration or other. To be corporately ushered through such multiple delights by three who singly left nothing to be desired was a Moslem paradise indeed. They racked him with tactile and labial delights that had him begging for more, and then for mercy. Such travels on cusp and curve and hollow, such ceaselessly ranging bliss. He wished he had six hands with which to graze on derrières whose checks — rarest of phenomena — were dimpled.

Thus they romped and lolled, slept and woke and romped again. Such sweet ease took they of one another that flocks of songbirds might have caroled them to their riots and their rests. Fussing over our Peachum, his triumvirate would twine their fingers in locks of his hair or trail them across his cheek like pink sea anemones, or tenderly scold him for the way he groomed his nails or had his sideburns cut, always with the familiar "the natives seem friendly" tableau. They murmured and cooed in amiably rival proprietorship, their breath conveying the odor of warm fruit and their voices like dulcimers

in his ear. In such sweet jumbles lay they abed, till they were
faint with joy. Then the tinkle of a room-service cart would
bring its furtive music to the delinquent afternoon, let it cost
another fifty bucks. "Bring me wine and figs that I may refresh myself," he would say, and they would bring him wine
and figs in the guise of beer and chicken salad, in pantomime,
like the lovely actresses *manquées* they were, slithering and
sliding like temple dancers up to the bed where he lay, and
their voices and their rhythms reminded him that his own
talent wasn't the greatest thing since zippers either. Then
hurry, laggard Monday, pick up your feet, dawdling Tuesday,
and so come delirious Saturday to the appointed hour and
levitate us into heaven once again. Then shall the ham and
cheese be lark's tongues and mangoes and juicy gobbets of
roasted ortolans dealt him by three nymphs out of Mallarmé,
yea glimpsed by a faun on a hot afternoon. Suck the pulp
from the grapeskins, drink wine from the one cup only. Lick
your fingers — lick one another's fingers! Be off with you,
desiccated scruples, wipe away the moral sweat and *Live!*
Thus the truth struck home to Peachum, that he not only
must tell Sandy, but perfectly easily could. The rehearsal
again. "Look, I've fallen in love with triplets. They're crazy
as toenails, but nice."

Of that awful insipidity that envelops the closing hours of
legal holidays, the worst must be the pall that descends at
Christmas dusk. The sheer glutted sensibilities, both gastrointestinal and emotional; the inevitably frustrated nostalgia
provoked by memories of irrecoverable childhood; the pleth-
ora of overfed relatives each with his own cud of recollection
to chew, and all leaving behind fresh deposits of scarves and
neckties you wouldn't wear to a dogfight; the surfeit of carols
whose subtle nausea has in fact been working its spell since
Thanksgiving (whose vesper torpor is second only to that of
Christmas itself); all this, together with some itching resent-

ment at not being able to believe the myths under pretended celebration, makes for a mood of letdown harder to shake each passing year. And how guiltily one remains haunted by all the returned or exchanged gifts from misguided loved ones — tie clips, orange mittens, volumes of Longfellow, albums of best-loved overtures. Ah, the ghost of Christmas presents.

The d'Amboises were as sodden as I with the goose and Montrachet they had invited me to share with them. It was a quarter to five. Blue shadows on the snow. The amethyst cuff links they had given me were handsome, quite justifying the switch to shirts with French cuffs which I must now make, and they had exclaimed over my volume of Vermeer prints. It was no old-fashioned Christmas, but for Sandy it must certainly be better than her mother's reminiscences of Clydesdale horses with braided tails drawing beer wagons through the streets of Milwaukee. What marred the glazed stupefaction into which we had sunk was their obvious wish, Sandy's particularly, to bring up a subject needing no clairvoyance on my part to guess. The maid was off. At last Sandy spoke up.

"You've been a stranger lately, Ted."

"Yes."

"Is it another woman?"

"Not exactly."

"Oh. Then you've just lost interest."

"In you, Sandy my dear? Never."

"Then what is it?"

"You know I adore you. It's just that I've — well, you yourself admit that you can love more than one person. You'd be hardly in a position to deny it," I added with a gently wry smile.

"Right. Then it is another woman."

"Not exactly, as I said."

"Then what, for God's sake? Another man?"

"Three, actually."

"Three men?"

"No, no, three women."

"What the hell are you talking about? Nobody can be mixed up with three *other* women at once."

"These are triplets. I've fallen in love with triplets. An entire set of them."

Their bugging eyes made me hurry on.

"Now just a minute. Look, it's not as mad as it sounds. We all know about the courting swain in love with a sister who has a twin, and he rings the bell and the twin answers the door and he doesn't know but what it's his sweetheart. Since they're facsimiles, if he is smitten by the one he must be smitten by the other. They are interchangeable. I've just got that in triplicate. If they were quintuplets I'd have to love the lot of them. Equally. They're a sort of job lot, don't you see. A shipment of open stock. Since they're identical there's no additional emotion involved. Just a duplication. I'm not cheating on you three times, just once. And nobody here is in a position to complain about cheating qua cheating."

Sandy raised her glass to her lips and, finding it empty, held it out to Ambrose to fill without taking her eyes off me. He poured out the last trickle of his bottle of beloved Montrachet into it. Sandy drained it off, her eye floating a long look at me. Ambrose made patterns on the tablecloth with a fingernail, wearing a familiar expression recalling what is termed in early Greek sculpture the "archaic smile." It is a stylized smile, three-cornered, a kind of classic simper which can be approximated by turning the ends of your mouth up, the lips slightly pursed as though about to pronounce the syllable "urr." Ambrose continued engraving the tablecloth.

"Do you make love to them, I mean, in rotation or something?"

"No, all together."

Sandy did not bat an eye, but it seemed the inverted

equivalent of rolling them to heaven while flinging her hands up.

"You must have your hands full."

"Yes. They are the hottest little pieces in Christendom."

"Who are they?"

"Have you ever heard of the Peppermint Sisters? They're singers. Not too good, I gather. Also tried their hands at acting and dancing. You'll like them."

What in God's name had I said? I'd meant to speak wholly in the subjunctive — "You'd like them." Surely we could not all meet!

Ambrose said, "Well, we'll have to talk the whole thing over like" — he counted on his fingers — "six intelligent people."

Sandy put her napkin down on the table, with an odd look from one to the other of us. "I'm afraid it's gone beyond that. There are four of us here."

"What do you mean?" Ambrose said.

She dropped her bombshell.

"I'm pregnant. Not to take the play away from the Nativity we're supposed to be celebrating now."

We looked at her with the same stunned expression, and the same thought in our minds.

"Whose is it?" we asked simultaneously.

"Wouldn't I like to know. Let's have some brandy in here."

We staggered into the living room where we sat about in a daze of naturally conflicting emotions. Ambrose was again sunk in an armchair with one foot on an ottoman, Sandy and I on either side of a sofa. Nothing was said for perhaps live minutes of brandy sipping, and then we all began grinning rather stupidly, as though we were a trio of naughty children who, caught out, nevertheless relished among them the prank for which grownups were trying to decide on a just punishment.

"Maybe we'll never know," Ambrose said at last.

"That's right," I said. "I don't think the tests for paternity are foolproof."

"Unless it looks definitely like either Ted or me. Then that would settle it beyond a reasonable doubt. If it takes after Sandra, we'll never know."

"What you can know now," Sandy said softly, "is that I'm not promiscuous. There's never been anybody but you two who ever meant a hill of beans to me."

"Look how beautiful she looks," Ambrose said. "We should have guessed. All lit up from within."

It was the maternal glow for which I had so fearfully looked when scuttling from cover to cover in the supermarket to get a close-up of her. Now it excited me. I had never desired her more, and Ambrose must have felt the same — eager to get me out of here. I reached to take her hand and said, "You've knocked us for a loop, but there'd be something wrong with us if we weren't also thrilled." Ambrose impulsively took her other hand, and as she gathered us to her, kneeling, our heads coming to rest at last on the folds of her housecoat, her face had a madonna look.

This tableau was interrupted by the ringing of the telephone. It was Mrs. d'Amboise calling from Pocock to wish them a Merry Christmas, including me when she learned I was there. After a few minutes of this, Ambrose's manner turned sober as he asked his mother about Columbine. There was a long string of "Mm-hms" as she filled him in on something. Sandy leaned toward me to whisper, "You've heard about Colly?"

"No. What is it?"

"The affair with the Larsen boy blew up. He apparently broke it off, and she's crushed. Sort of a nervous breakdown. You know what anorexia nervosa is?"

"Young girls starving themselves."

"They can't get her to eat anything. Her weight is down to —"

Ambrose held the phone out to me. "My mother wants to say Merry Christmas, Ted."

Mrs. d. had written me a letter apologizing for her response to the rubbish about the park incident, which had been corrected by the facts. Officer O'Malley had evidently eaten his words, clearing one's name.

After an exchange of greetings, I asked after Columbine. The situation was roughly as Sandy had said: serious malnutrition.

"Can you put her on the phone?"

"Oh, she's in the hospital, my dear boy."

"Where? Can you give me her room number? I'll write. No, wait. I'm going home for a few days next week to see my parents. Tell her I'll be on hand to wish her a Happy New Year."

Mrs. d. had a way of putting her fingertips to her mouth when surprised, whether happily or otherwise, like an actor miming *mal de mer* in a shipboard movie. A sort of gestured gasp. I could see her executing it now, even with the phone in the other hand.

"Oh, you will? That will be wonderful. It will mean the world to our bijou."

That was how it added up, then. A jilted girl-next-door on the rebound, a set of triplets, and my best friend's wife with child. All in all, a rich, full life.

Fifteen

I rode to Chicago on a bus with mice. And some damn secretary-treasurer had her valise on the only seat left, necessitating my asking her to remove it. The expression of pious self-sacrifice with which she lifted it up and organized it on her lap, under her shoulder bag, argued officership in something like an organization of madrigal buffs, or the Society for the Prevention of Deplorable Conditions. Refreshments will be served. Let's make this a banner year. Also, she was in the aisle seat, indicating a thrown-stone phobia, so there was hell's own amount of discommoding before everyone was settled. How do we get through this life, as one of the girls in *Little Women* observes. Clark Gable and Claudette Colbert were across the aisle and a few rows down, headed for something happening one night. Or, alternatively, perhaps not.

"Going far?" I said to the woman I'll call Mrs. Fondue, striking up a "conversation."

"Just to Allentown."

"That's a nice town. I once met somebody who lived there, and if he was typical of your element, it leaves nothing to be desired. Pleasant people, plenty of cultural activities. You

look like a cultured woman to me." Why am I such a crud?
I am offal of scum, spawn of vermin, worthy only to be
flushed into oblivion. "Engaged in cultural activities?"

"I do a little of this and that. Help liven up the community.
Women's Club, raise money for the local arts center."

"Ah."

I decided to make a disciple of her.

"Born in New Bedford when it was still a whaling port,
Albert Tinkham Ryder was the youngest of four sons of a fuel
dealer," I said. "The family moved to New York when he was
in his early twenties, and an older brother turned restaura-
teur helped see him through art school. Ryder first lived in
Greenwich Village and later in a West Side rooming house,
where he slept huddled beneath piles of threadbare over-
coats on a floor heaped a foot and a half to two feet high,
authorities differ, with assorted filth such as yellowing newspapers — they will yellow — empty tin cans, cheese rinds
and mice months dead in the traps he had set for them."

Mrs. Fondue was leaning so far away from me that I
thought she might topple over into the aisle, looking at the
bus driver as though she was going to call him. Her expression was both resentful, apprehensive and bewildered. That's
three "boths," but I want to give you your money's worth,
you old tassel-fondler you. Sensing time was running out for
me as an enfant terrible, I hurried along.

"Troubled since early childhood with weak eyesight (and
later by both gout, anemia and kidney disease), he stayed indoors during the day and roamed the streets at night, dressed
in tatters, often pausing in a reverie to stare at the moon for
minutes at a time. As I have explained to the other eleven of
my disciples, it is no doubt his faulty eyesight that gives his
paintings their mystic quality, for a mystic can see anything
in a fog. Oddly enough . . ."

The woman now looked as though she was definitely going
to bolt out of her seat and report me to the driver. He would

make a citizen's arrest and hustle me to headquarters, where I would be lucky to get off with any charge less than aggravated erudition. Slumped away from her against the window, I lapsed into a reverie of my own.

People should do more surface traveling. Who sees anything of this wonderful country from a plane? Bowling through Pittsburgh, I glimpsed a sight I had never seen before — a woman window washer clinging to the rock face of an office building like a mounting yak on an escarpment too sheer even for him. I craned around till she was out of sight, so exhilarating was the picture. Positively aphrodisiac. I mean those loins were *girded.* What a lot of citadel to storm! Belts and straps and buckles and brushes and hooks in a mélange of metal, leather and wood till hell wouldn't have it. To say nothing of a bucket and squeegee, all of it hanging there, to be brought down in one gargantuan heave, before plucking silk with a gesture gentler than the culling of a flower. I daydreamed an orgy with three New Women, no, four: a window washer, a railroad conductor, a cop, and a telephone linesperson pole climber, equipment clanking across the hotel-room floor in every direction as I pumped on to one of those sonic booms that suck the marrow from your pelvic bones and cause housewives for miles around to look up from their knitting and say, "What was that?"

The Fondue had by now got off, her seat occupied by another damn secretary-treasurer, this time unmistakably of the Rotary Club ilk. Giving financial reports at the Tuesday luncheons at the Holiday Inn, he said "fully cognizant" and "increasing awareness." He must be given a glimpse of something better.

"If we can think of this great country of ours as polarized between two sets of James brothers," I said, slouching down in my seat like those old men in Fort Lauderdale reminiscing about crack trains and molten mamas, "Frank and Jesse at one end and Henry and William at the other, why, we begin to get some sense of the enormous spectrum in between."

"That's what I always say."

To stretch my legs a bit I rose and strolled up and down the aisle, pausing here and there to drop an epigram into a conversation appearing in need of it. A youngish couple in denims and sweaters were discussing a friend, apparently a playwright, who had been through hell and whose recent work showed a new dimension as a result. *"Owl's Regret* has a depth and perception Jack never showed before," the man said.

"A writer is like his pencil," I said. "He must be worn down to be kept sharp."

On the other side of the aisle a man was paging through an art magazine, at the moment open to a reproduction of a painting showing a fried egg floating through a revolving door. I bent to ponder it with him.

"Surrealism," I said at length, "may be the last of the may-onnaise of Romanticism oozing from the disintegrating club sandwich of the Western psyche."

The man made a sibilant noise through his teeth, like a repressed hiss, or as though he had uttered the name of the Galilean with the vowels missing. Moving on a bit, I found myself standing over a woman with her hair skun back into a yam at the back of her head, who was reading a copy of *Exile's Return.*

"Malcolm Cowley is the Pope for those of us who are catholic in our tastes . . . Now, are there any questions?"

"Yeah, why don't you zip your lip?" an oaf piped up from a back seat.

"Yeah, why doesn't he go home and tell his mother she wants him?"

"Yeah, get Marathon Mouth over there. Some of us are trying to sleep."

"Are there any other questions?"

The sullen looks on people's faces dramatized the need for stimulation, more urgent than I had thought. Yet one woman put her fingers in her ears as we swayed crazily down a long twisting stretch of road. I hovered over a man reading through pince-nez a copy of *Forbes: Capitalist Tool,* his mouth crimped into the tight seam of those who Will Not Listen.

"A rather interesting phenomenon of our time is the male feminist, don't you think?" I reflected. "It is my theory that most such commitments spring from a deficient relationship with the mother — a compensatory correction, you see. Perhaps more of Auden's 'the muse of guilt.' Rimbaud offers an enlightening case in point. He was a champion of women who nevertheless called his bigoted mother 'as inflexible as sixty-three helmeted administrations.' That's a lot of helmeted administrations. Even two or three would be formidable enough, God knows. So. Rimbaud wanted to become a worker principally in order that he might strike . . ."

The likelihood of picking up any apostolic recruits here was slim; few if any would arise and follow me, seek to sup with me and I with them. In fact at the next café-and-restroom stop there was a general rush for the door the instant the driver lurched into the parking lot. It was odd. The stampede left only one other passenger on the bus, a man with his arm in a sling. A vestigial tuft of hair just about his forehead made him look as though he had a shaving brush embedded in his skull. I sat down behind him and, leaning forward over the back of his seat, began to murmur in his ear: "Born in Both Feet, Utah, at an early age, of poor but dishonest parents, I was seized quite soon with a sense of vocation almost pentecostal in its intensity, the conviction that I must drench my fellowmen with facts and fancies of a breathtaking range and variety. You may have detected in me one of those driven spirits whose terrible mission it is to strew the world with aphorisms . . ."

He heaved himself to his feet, mumbling about harassment and breathing threats of reprisal as he tramped toward the door, where the driver helped him down by taking his good arm. He said something that sounded like "Flesh and blood can stand so much — if that." Off he stumped into the café, where the other passengers were swarming around the coffee counter. I stepped out for a breath of air myself, the driver moving watchfully back as I passed him. A stocky good-looking man. A touch of macho suggested by the cigarette clamped in the teeth, rather than hanging from the lips. He removed it after a deep drag and said: "Look, I've been getting complaints. People resent being force-fed all this whatever it is you're dishing out. What the hell is it? Can you give me an example?"

I leaned on one shoulder against the side of the bus, folding my arms as I waited for three lice-infested black-jacketed motorcyclists to roar past at sixty miles an hour. "A woman is only a woman, but a good cigar is a smoke."

"Yeah. Well, you're a little rich for the people you're traveling with's blood, so soft-pedal it some. Don't try to keep the conversational ball rolling so much."

The others began dribbling out of the café, eating peanuts and gnawing candy bars, and soon we were on our way again. As we tooled along farmlands, I could see a wide expanse of blue sky. There was one enormous white cloud from the fringe of which fragments drifted away, like tufts plucked by an invisible hand from a great wad of cotton. I can hardly think you give a damn, and I don't either, really, but I just wanted to remind you of my gift for metaphor.

I found my parents in an unexpectedly buoyant state of mind. My mother was definitely having it on with Pinky Montmorency, while my father was having an affair with a housewife he'd met on a job, eight rooms coming from the other end of town. With both of them happily fooling around, their marriage seemed secure, at least for the time being. My mother said my father "stayed up till all months."

I would not have recognized Columbine had I not known it was her room in Pocock Memorial. Wasted down to eighty-

nine pounds, she lay like a wraith in the bed. Her cheeks
were so hollow the bones all but showed through. Yet the
clean beautiful jawline was still there (Mrs. d'Amboise had
always had the wrong Hepburn), the great doe's eyes still
luminous in their sockets. My heart broke in two at the sight
of her. I knew that if I didn't at least ask her to marry me I'd
never be able to look at myself again. That face in the mirror
would be a composite sketch of every louse that ever lived.
At the same time, I guessed that a solemn, or even sympa-
thizing, tone was to be avoided, for her own good. Columbine must not be let sink farther into whatever self-destruc-
tive mold is behind one of the most baffling of young women's
diseases, even for fashion models obsessed with staying thin.

"You're letting yourself go," I said. "You shouldn't do that.
Cut down on the starches, lay off the fudge sundaes and thick
shakes." That was the tone to take. "You're getting to be a big
fat slob."

She turned her head away, and two tears rolled from under
her closed lids. She creased her lips into the twisted pleat
women make of their mouths when trying to keep from
crying.

"Marry me."

I must be mad. Who in his right mind would turn a phrase
like that? Yet there the words were, hanging in the air, like
the Chagall villagers in Sandy's bedroom. She turned farther
away, burying her face in the pillow.

"You feel sorry for me."

"Of course. For myself too. For everybody. Christ, don't
make me talk like a high-school sophomore again."

"You like Snooky, and I have no breasts."

"Neither do I." Grasping her shoulder, I drew her around
onto her back again. "Look. Let me say this for all girls who
think themselves so cheated. There are melons, there are apples, there are pears. There are peaches and plums. There are
even cherries. But it's all fruit, and, baby, it's all paradise.

Now let's stop this nonsense and eat. Here comes your lunch, and I'm hungry if you don't want it."

I spooned some soup into her, the first nourishment she'd had in three days. I even managed to get most of a pork chop and some mashed potatoes down, as well as a little applesauce. Yes, yes, I remembered the custard she'd brought me when I was myself prostrate, for reasons I could now only dimly reconstruct. It had happened to somebody else, long, long ago. The Santayanan calm at last. I felt my own deus ex machina, brought to resolve all the mad action in a bus from New York.

"You don't love me."

"I asked you to marry me before, but you jilted me."

"We've got that in common."

"I hope you're over that jock. I didn't like him."

"Why do you dislike him?"

"I didn't say I disliked him. I just said I didn't like him. I don't think there's anything there to dislike."

"You're a jock too, you know, in your way. Carrying all that furniture. You love being a mass of muscle. You're almost beefcake, you know."

I visited her the next evening, and the following afternoon and evening. We watched a little television. *Casablanca* to be exact. At some point my hand lay on hers, stole forward along her forearm, slowly, toward that embrace from which I knew I could never extricate myself, resisting it yet seeking it, and there it was at last, my lips on Columbine's.

"Marry me."

"Yes."

There is something to be said for insanity, always granting that being a secretary-treasurer is the norm. We honeymooned in North Africa, of all places, putting up first in a hotel in Casablanca. Columbine was virginal, in case you're curious, certainly a surprise these days, especially to a youth of twenty-seven even with a girl of twenty-one. We got lost on a motor jaunt to Marrakesh, when a pagan suckled in a creed outworn misdirected us somewhere along the line, and we wound up in a small town in time to witness a bank robbery. Luke was satisfied, Islip mollified, and the rest of the d'Amboises ranged from resigned to ecstatic. I think Ambrose was pleased mainly because it got me off his back, probably not the best way of putting it.

Sandy gave birth to a fine boy, who, as the months go by, looks ever more like her. So we shall never know. Never. We call the baby Doc. His actual name is Daniel. A simply beautiful, cherubic, cross-eyed child, who wears glasses to facilitate and speed the remedy for a perfectly correctable condition. The lenses of the spectacles are ground to coax the eyes slowly, steadily away from each other until the simple surgery required can be performed, if it's needed at all. Meanwhile we must keep watch on him to see that the glasses themselves don't do the job too fast and too well, and the pupils diverge to a point where Doc becomes wall-eyed. Not very likely, the way he's dandled and fussed over.

Of course the minute Columbine and I settled back in New York, Sandy and Ambrose and I all realized the triumvirate must be dissolved — as must any quadrangular liaison with the Peppermint Sisters, who began, in any case, to tour the country with some kind of industrial exhibit. I am written in and out of the script of *The Adrian Family*. Columbine continues to pose as a fashion model, in particular for some designer currently hot with what he calls the Gamin Look. Sometimes the Urchin Look. Poorboy sweaters, newsboy caps, denims stuffed into midcalf boots. All very chic. Candlestickmaker has another play going the rounds, though I already feel I've gone stale in the part without even having read the script. Naturally I sought out the Prophet when last in Pocock, and found him on Findlay Street, haranguing a group of onlookers. His screeds were still liberally larded with brand names, such as Cuisinart and Roto-Broiler and

Mercedes. They and all other things associated with self-indulgent living were an abomination unto the Lord.

"'Thy inventions are a stench in my nostrils,' saith the Lord, 'and on thy inventions and finaglings will I call a curse.' And these cunning names for shops! The Cat's Meow and the Serendipity, into which thy women mince in exquisitely tailored dungarees. Now we have a Sewtique. 'A *Sewtique*, for my sake!' saith the Lord. 'I will chop them up as the Cuisinart its foodstuffs, as the Lawn King the grass blades mow them down on that terrible day, that grass which all flesh is.' Thus doth the Lord chew you out, through the mouth of this his servant."

When he had concluded this blast and his hearers had dispersed, I accosted him. Not having bathed since the year one, he was his usual fragrant self. I tried only to exhale. "People have asked me to run for mayor of Pocock," I said. "The better element. What dost thou think?"

"I see thee in a landslide victory," he answered, and marched away.

Clairvoyant pretensions of my own enable me to fantasize the details, because I think I spotted a hot local issue in the course of my brief visit.

I run for office on a platform involving squirrel-related power outages in the area. A squirrel population explosion combined with no natural food supply for the rodents has found them foraging everywhere for sustenance, including such hitherto unusual places as power lines and utility substations. Result: blackout after blackout. In the early stages of the campaign there seems nothing for a candidate to do but go around in a sound truck advising people what to discard after a twenty-four-hour-or-more fridge blank. "My fellow Americans: Throw out dairy products and other foods that are warm to the touch, such as milk, yogurt, fresh orange juice, ice cream, sherbet and open jars of baby food. By no means retain anything smelling strangely, especially if runny

— chuck that Brie! — and closely inspect all eggs and discard those that are cracked. Now, people of Illinois, prepared foods such as tuna or chicken salad, stews, leftovers and custards are also highly susceptible to spoilage and should not be eaten. Frozen foods that were only slightly defrosted can be refrozen, but those completely defrosted should be used immediately or thrown out. Thank you, my fellow Pocockians, and do not lose heart! We shall find a solution yet! We shall conquer this thing!"

But how? A stop at the railroad station for a speech to homecoming commuters is in vain. No listeners arrive. The power is off clear to Chicago — another squirrel-related power outage. Then at last the vision comes to me. Of course. What is a natural enemy of the squirrel? The owl. I suggest that styrofoam decoy hoot owls be perched everywhere along power lines and in substations. This is done and, presto — no more squirrel-related power outages.

Now for the landslide victory.

Getting to the polls to vote is difficult, in some cases impossible. Torrential rains for what seem forty days and forty nights have reduced the state of Illinois to crankcase sludge. An election day on which eighty people turn out, forty-seven of them for me, including a cripple who makes it to the polls on stilts, breaking my heart. Then waiting for the returns in our party office as a hillside breaks in two and comes slowly down like a colossal gray pachyderm, to bulldoze our storefront headquarters off its foundation, across the street, and onto a vacant lot, where it stands to this day. That's the landslide. It was not for me.

Still, I often wish I'd made the race. That was the road not taken. Whenever I have premonitions of impending tepidity, fears that I will wind up a secretary-treasurer in a situation fraught with safety, I wonder if staying in politics mightn't have kept me more adventurous, more risk-willing. A race for senator in the cards, perhaps, who knew? A run for the governorship on the Surrealist ticket? But this is all right, a good living in the soaps for a talent not sufficiently appreciated, here in New York, with Doc now two and a half and hardly cross-eyed any more (though looking a bit owlish himself in those glasses) and Columbine expectant. The day will come when she'll fling her arms aloft and swear she's going to recover her figure by starving herself back into her wedding suit. Then it will be lettuce leaves and stalks of celery, and all of us, as the fellow said, snow-blind from cottage cheese. But then that's nothing new, and in any case another story, one for which I must be quite braced. Every new woman is a change of venue for a man perpetually on trial, but mine is a gentle judge, and I wish the same for you, and for your partner too, of course.

My father is currently troubled with insomnia, which must be hell for a hibernator. He lies staring at the ceiling through the wee months, or daydreaming (sic) of Mrs. Jessie Tankous — the eight rooms coming from the other end of town, remember, with whom he took up — or, perhaps, sits propped up in bed rereading his comics, caressively lingering over those that have made him a connoisseur. There has been another Sunday-supplement story about him in that respect, with photographs of him holding up the particular treasures of his collection, heavily insured against fire and theft. God damn — no, God bless dear old Barney Peachum, who has status at last.

You the unknown reader I salute in farewell. You are silly like me (and Yeats, to throw in a parting echo of Auden), praying for the wisdom to survive your follies. You steam the stamps off of return envelopes enclosed with charity appeals before throwing them away, because you're not going to mail checks to those causes anyway, but to others for which it would be wasteful not to use the stamps. Don't be ashamed. We all do it. Still furtively sofa-crevice poking, when not suggestively folding the upholstery tassels during

the Humperdinck? Not the end of your oddities. You clip
your ball-point pens to the *outside* of your breast pocket, a
quirk for which Viennese explanation can be offered by any
schoolchild. I'm not calling you a sneaker fetishist just because you have eight pairs for your tennis which you keep
spotless by spin-washing and tumble-drying them in the
machine. You have a slowly diminishing bottle of rare pre-
Expulsion chartreuse costing a hundred and some dollars,
which you feed selected guests from an eye- or, possibly,
nose-dropper. Yes you do. I've heard about it, I've been told.
You stretch them out on the couch after dinner, your guests,
and drip a drop or two of the precious liqueur into their open
mouths. Well, get you. And you don't even know what Expulsion the stuff is pre, or who was expelled from where, or
why. Huguenots? Some monks? I know but don't intend to tell
you. Well, all right, I will. It was the Carthusian monks, who
were expelled from France in 1903 and fled with their secret
formula to Spain, where they continued to make their exquisite elixir. You mustn't take anything I say amiss. I *like*
you. Always have. *Mon semblable, mon frère.*

Et moi? Ah, well. Leap forward in time, and imagine with
me a scene when the hour strikes, and I must, you know,
cross over into campground.

There is the doctor with skin like old mortar obscuring my
view of the nurse with gelatinous breasts, which I long to
reach out from the covers and fondle yet a moment in farewell. A fingernail paring of moon gleams beyond the window,
recalling explanations to Candlestickmaker, light years ago,
that lambent means having a gentle glow. Beyond it, brain-
boggling, stretch the terrifying savannas of infinity. Draw
the mind back indoors. We shall never get the universe down
to room temperature. On the far wall hangs the obligatory
Utrillo print. How many I have removed from over a hotel-
room headboard before slipping between the sheets with a
girl smelling like meadow clover. There is after all nothing

as fine as wallowing on a double bed. Name something. But now the smoking candle-inch that was Ted Peachum all but gutters out with some murmured pleasantry to the nurse, so faint as to be lost amid the sibilance of her uniform as she enacts some ministration at the foot-end of the bed. She stoops to crank it, starting my motor for the flight upward into Nowhere. Such is the fancy that takes me. A hovering disciple asks me something. Would I sum myself up in a word. "How would you characterize yourself?" he says, bending low to catch my last utterance, for there is a rattle in my throat like the noise at the end of an ice cream soda when you go on sipping with no more left — sometimes known as the Scotch national anthem.

"Think jilted Narcissus, O.K.?" I say, in dear, dear Columbine's tradition.

"You mean — ?"

"Yes. Not returning this crush I have on myself. Or put another way, I'm a . . ."

"A what?" the disciple prompts as my voice falters.

"A suh — suh — "

I must die with a paradox on my lips or it will kill me.

"Yes?"

"A self-disparaging egomaniac."

"Ah."

I nod. "Yes. I guess that about wraps it up," I whisper. And so . . . . *Abstract me, silent ships.*